STARSHIP ALEXANDER

THE HIVE INVASION – BOOK 1

JAKE ELWOOD

This is a work of fiction. A novel. Totally made up. Any similarity to actual persons, places, interstellar invasions or dilapidated starships is purely coincidental.

Copyright © 2016 Jake Elwood

All rights reserved.

ISBN: 1535312408
ISBN-13: 978-1535312400

CHAPTER 1 – HAMMETT

Captain Richard Hammett needed a drink.

He tucked the bulky box that contained his ceremonial sword under his arm, took a deep breath, and stepped into the drop tube. He hated the damned things. Thirty years in space gave him reflexes that tried to kick in every time the pull of gravity changed. Drop tubes, perfectly ordinary things to the planetside population, frayed his nerves every single time. He fell forty stories in a few seconds, stepping out of the tube at the bottom with a fine sheen of sweat on his forehead.

The ground floor of Spacecom headquarters was a majestic vault of a room, and he peered around, taking it in as he crossed the wide floor. Once this view had been ordinary. Once, long ago, he'd been a student here, back when this was the

Naval Academy. He'd been full of himself in those days, barely noticing the magnificent room as he'd hurried through on his first day.

Now, thirty-five years later, he felt like an old man. Spacecom was deteriorating along with him. The entire organization now fit into one building that had once been just a school. He shook his head as he crossed the echoing marble floor. If someone had told him, back when he was a young cadet, that it could ever come to this …

He plodded outside, feeling weary and heartsick. The sword under his arm was supposed to be a great honor, a symbol of three decades of loyal service. It felt like a mockery, though. A bauble, given to an old man just before they decommissioned his ship, even as they dismantled the organization around him.

"Poor baby," he muttered, and chuckled. He'd never had any patience for self-pity in others, and he wasn't going to start indulging in it himself. "Sounds like somebody needs a beer."

The Rusty Cutlass still stood at the corner of Constitution and Fleet. Hammett stood across the street from the pub, smiling as he took it in. Things changed, it was the way of the universe, but perhaps a few things remained the same. The sign above the door looked like carved wood, but as it hadn't changed in a quarter of a century, it was probably polymer. The sign showed a bearded old sea captain with a cutlass in one fist and a beer stein in the other, leering out at passers-by.

Hammett shifted the sword to his other arm and hurried across the street. His pleasant cloud of nostalgia lasted until he pushed open the front door. Instead of dark wood and exposed ceiling beams, the pub was filled with white light and gleaming chrome. He stood in the doorway, muttering a curse, then headed for a booth near the front window. The place didn't even have live servers anymore. He scowled at the table console, then pressed his thumb to the scanner and ordered a pint of stout.

At least the beer tasted like he remembered. He sat back with his eyes half closed, sipping the drink and superimposing his memories over the bones of the room. He'd frittered away some of the best days of his youth in this pub. He let the faces scroll past in his mind's eye, all the friends he'd studied with, served with, fought alongside. Some had died. Most had retired. The war took some of them much too early, robbing him of decades of friendship. He thought of the war and felt the familiar cold fury rising within him. Why the hell had it all been necessary? Why did so many bright young people have to be fed into the maw of a meat grinder?

Someone jostled him, and he looked up. For a moment he thought he recognized the brawny young man who stood over him. Hammett started to smile, the name on the tip of his tongue, but this was not Rick Olson. Olson, if he lived, would be in his fifties. And Olson had never had the predatory gleam that Hammett saw in the eyes of the man who put a large hand on his shoulder and leaned in close with a sneer.

"Sorry, Gramps. Didn't see you there. Say, you sure you have the right bar?"

Hammett reached up, took a good grip on the man's smallest finger, and twisted, not too far. The man yelped, and Hammett lifted his hand several centimeters. "Hands off, kid. Don't touch me with anything you want to keep."

They locked eyes, Hammett half hoping the man – he was just a kid, really – would push it. Brawling with some punk would be stupid, but it would be a chance to prove he wasn't so old. Whatever the man saw in Hammett's eyes, though, he didn't like it.

The man wasn't the problem, though. The problem was his friends, two more punks right behind him, snickering at his humiliation. He couldn't just walk away. Not with an audience. There was something close to desperation in the man's eyes. He was in over his head, but he had to do something.

"Leave me alone," said Hammett. "Please."

It was the opening the man needed, and he took it. "Sure, sure. Don't wet your pants, Gramps." He gave Hammett a sneer and walked away, his friends ribbing him as they followed. Hammett watched them go, relaxing his grip on his beer stein. He'd come close – very close – to swinging for the side of the man's jaw. It would have been stupid. It would have meant trading a perfectly good beer for a couple of hours in a police station. Still ...

"Kids," he muttered. They were young and

feeling their oats, that's all. When Hammett was that age, he'd had a war for an outlet. He'd had a way to challenge himself, to prove himself. It was the only real difference between him and the three punks. Hell, he'd had his share of stupid, pointless confrontations in bars, even with a war going on.

He took a pull on the beer. The Outer Settlements War was long over, and humanity hadn't had another war since. Hammett was one of a handful of actual veterans still in service. There were good big ships out there without a single person on board who'd seen combat.

What was the galaxy coming to?

"What we need is another ..." He stopped himself. Another war?

Tell it to the dead.

"More alarming news from the colonies. Another jump Gate has gone off-line, and Spacecom seems to have no idea why." The voice came from the next table over, and Hammett turned his head. A young couple watched a newsfeed, and he tapped at his table controls until he found the same feed.

A bland-faced announcer stared out from a screen projected in the air in front of Hammett. "It's the third Gate malfunction in three weeks, and it could mean economic disaster for the affected systems. Here's Earth Central's Michael Noburo with more on this developing story."

The screen switched to another announcer. The man kept his face suitably solemn as he talked about the economic repercussions of a

Gate closure. The Aries system was more than three weeks away by ship, instead of the two days or so that it took to go from Earth to Aries through three jump Gates. "Don't forget," he said gravely, leaning forward to peer into the camera. "Most ships don't even have the ability to make faster-than-light jumps."

Hammett rolled his eyes. What kind of idiot didn't know that? Ships with jump drives could cross a light-year in a day or so, but they seldom bothered. The overwhelming majority of ship traffic was through the jump Gates that linked Earth to her fourteen colonies and outposts.

Now, three Gates were down. That meant four outposts were cut off from Earth. No doubt Spacecom had sent jump ships to investigate. If the Gates couldn't be repaired *in situ*, it would take days or weeks for those same jump ships to come back with a report.

Hammett poked a finger through the screen, interrupting the reporter in mid-sentence. He rummaged through the data stream until he found a link to background details.

Gate Eleven was the latest Gate to fail. Hammett frowned. Gate Fifteen had failed first. It was the most distant gate in a long chain, connecting Tanos System to the far-flung colony of Calypso. Gate Thirteen had failed next. Gate Thirteen connected Aries to Tanos.

Gate failures happened occasionally. They were delicate technology, after all, and loaded with safety features to make sure a ship was never lost in the wormholes between gates. For two consecutive gates to fail was unusual, but not wildly unlikely.

Now, though, the Gate to the Aries system was down.

"Whatever's going on," Hammett murmured, "it's only two Gates from Earth now."

Well, it wasn't his problem. Spacecom would investigate, but it was a dead certainty they wouldn't send him. His beer was close to empty, and he was thoroughly sick of the Rusty Cutlass. He drained the glass and headed outside in a sour mood.

A dry desert wind stirred the litter on the sidewalk. The air was unpleasantly hot, particularly to a man who'd spent most of the last thirty years in climate-controlled ships. It was late afternoon, though, and the deepening shadows held the promise of coolness. He walked the streets of a city that hadn't existed before the twenty-second century. The first spaceports had needed plenty of open ground, and the politicians of the day had worried about crashes. So the ports were built in open countryside far from any major settlement. As the decades passed and no crashes occurred, cities had sprung up around the major ports.

Hawking stood in the center of the Baja Peninsula, close to the north end. Spaceports needed much less real estate now. Every city had one. Hawking had reinvented itself, becoming the headquarters of Spacecom and the Naval Academy. In its heyday the streets had bustled with sailors. Hammett remembered it as a raucous and vibrant place, but it was the domain of Spacecom bureaucrats now.

His mood was so foul that it was almost a relief when he realized he was being followed.

He didn't look back. The quiet scuff of feet behind him and a distorted reflection in a store window told him all he needed to know. One person, staying directly behind him where they were hardest to see. The punk from the bar? Either that or a mugger, he decided. Or some random pedestrian on his way home from work.

It was time to find out.

A narrow alley opened to Hammett's right, and he turned in. He found a recessed doorway and pressed himself into it. He set down the sword and waited.

Footsteps made a soft rustling sound, right at the edge of his hearing. The sound grew faint, and then stopped. Either the pedestrian had moved on, or ...

The footsteps started up again. The sound was different, though, louder on the rough surface of the alley.

Hammett smiled to himself. *Gotcha*.

When he saw the first flicker of movement he lunged. He had a quick impression of a startled figure, arms coming up defensively. Then he crashed into the man, driving him across the alley. The two of them slammed together into the back wall of another building, and he got a forearm under the guy's chin. His other hand caught hold of a wrist.

Quite a slender wrist. Hammett looked at the

face a few centimeters in front of his own. Wide brown eyes stared into his. The eyes were set in a delicate, distinctly feminine face.

"Who the hell are you?" he said.

She tried to speak, then swallowed. "I'm Janice Ling."

He looked her over. She wore a skirted business suit and the sort of ridiculous shoes that only a civilian woman would own. She couldn't have run a dozen steps if her life depended on it, not in those heels.

Not a mugger, then.

He released her and stepped back, embarrassment warring with irritation inside him. "Who the hell are you, Janice Ling, and why are you following strange men into alleys?"

She stared up at him, clearly flustered. She stood barely taller than his chin, and she couldn't have been much more than half his weight. *And you threw her against a wall? What's the matter with you?* "I'm sorry," he said. "I shouldn't have been so rough."

That brought a ghost of a smile to her lips. She straightened her clothes, took a deep breath, and said, "I should have known better than to sneak up on a veteran."

Well, she had a point.

"I'm a reporter with United Sky Services." She was visibly throwing off the shock of the ambush. He could see an aura of professionalism settling on her, and he was impressed in spite of himself. She reminded him of the very best Naval personnel, men and women who could set aside overwhelming stress and do their jobs well in the middle of a crisis. She may have been a tiny woman in ridiculous shoes, but she would have done all right in the Navy.

"And why is a reporter from USS following me around?" He realized as he asked the question that he probably knew the answer, and he gritted his teeth.

A delicate flush spread across Janice Ling's cheeks. "You, ah, have a certain reputation for being ... outspoken."

"You mean, I speak without thinking, and you thought I'd be good for a controversial sound bite."

Her blush deepened.

"Well, you told me the truth straight out and you didn't blow smoke up my ass." He surprised himself by grinning. "I can respect that. My ... certain reputation, as you so delicately put it, is nobody else's fault but my own. I guess I can't blame you."

She returned his grin. "Do you have any comment about the recent unexplained failure of three jump Gates?"

Hammett shook his head.

"How about rumors that Spacecom might decommission the *Alexander*?"

That took the grin right off his face. "No. No comment." He turned away, not wanting her to see how much the question upset him. He retrieved his parcel, tucked it under his arm, then took a deep breath before turning to face her.

"I'm sorry," she said. "No more nosy questions,

okay?"

He made himself give her a thin smile. "All right."

She handed him a business card. "Call me if you decide there's something you want to get off your chest. It can even be off the record, if you like." Her grin returned, just for an instant. "I'd rather it was on the record, though."

He pocketed the card without comment.

"Thank you for your time, Captain. I won't bother you any further." She turned and left the alley, and he watched her calves as they swished back and forth under the hem of that businesslike skirt. Those shoes were ridiculous, but he liked what they did for her legs.

He followed her to the end of the alley, leaning against the corner of an office building as he watched her stride up Fleet Avenue. The adrenalin in his blood stream stirred up old ghosts. When he closed his eyes he saw narrow corridors jammed with men who fought and screamed and bled and died. His hands trembled, and he exhaled, focusing on Janice Ling. Those legs of hers made an excellent distraction. In a few moments his ghosts were all back in their lockers. He leaned out to keep Janice in view until she disappeared around a curve in the street.

"Good job, Richard," he muttered to himself. "You finally meet a pretty girl, and what do you do? First you throw her against a wall, and then you get all stiff and offended." He smiled at his own foolishness. Pretty girl? She was young enough to be his daughter.

Still ...

"There's no fool like an old fool." He tucked the sword more firmly under his arm and continued on his way, leaving Fleet Avenue and moving onto a side street. He indulged himself in an unlikely fantasy where she was really determined to get a sound bite from him, and they went back to her hotel room ...

The daydream faded as he saw his destination on the far side of the street. Amazing Armaments, the sign read. A pair of holographic knights stood on either side of the doorway, stern figures in full suits of armor. One knight lifted a visor to peer at him as he approached. The other put a hand on the hilt of a vast broadsword. Hammett ignored them both and entered the shop.

A long counter ran the width of the room inside. The walls were hung with medieval weapons of every description, and Hammett paused to admire a couple of halberds.

"Can I help you?"

Hammett turned. The man behind the counter was tall and broad-shouldered, with long black hair that brushed the straps of a heavy apron. By the look of his arms he still did metal work by hand. He was in his thirties, with a polite expression that was tinged with impatience. He looked like a man who did specialized work for existing customers and didn't have much use for curious street traffic.

Hammett set his parcel on the counter. "I'm hoping you can help me with this." He unsealed the box and flipped the lid back.

"Oh, very nice." The man looked at the jewelled sword nestled in black velvet. "May I?"

Hammett nodded.

The man lifted the sword from the box. It was a cutlass with a straight blade, the hilt decorated with a thick violet gemstone. The man held the sword up to the light, examined the blade minutely, then replaced it in the box. "What can I help you with?"

"They gave me this today," Hammett said. "Thirty years of service as an officer. I'm supposed to wear it on ceremonial occasions."

The man nodded.

"The problem is, it's about as dangerous as a barstool. I'm a professional soldier. I'm not going to carry around a toy."

The man nodded.

"Can you sharpen it for me?"

"That's a good question." The man stuck out a strong, calloused hand. "I'm Constantine."

"Richard." Hammett shook his hand.

"Pleased to meet you, Richard. You have a sword and you want it to be something more than a prop. You're my kind of man."

Hammett smiled.

"Now, then. I could do an analysis of the blade, but I don't think it's particularly good steel. It's shiny, and it won't rust, but I don't know if it will hold much of an edge. And then there's the balance."

Hammett lifted an eyebrow.

Constantine lifted the sword and made a couple of practice cuts in the air. "Here. You try."

He set the sword on the counter, hilt toward Hammett.

Hammett mimicked him, slicing up the air. "It seems fine to me."

"No." Constantine shook his head decisively. "It's dreadful." He reached under the counter and brought out a basket-hilt rapier. It was a plain weapon, made of unadorned steel, but it was superficially similar to Hammett's cutlass. "Try this."

Hammett lifted the rapier and smiled. The difference was unmistakable, though he would have had trouble explaining it. The rapier had roughly the same mass as the cutlass, but it seemed weightless in his hand, like a lethal extension of his arm. He tried a few practice cuts, marvelling at the sense of precision and control that it gave him. "You're right. My sword's dreadful."

"So," said Constantine, rubbing his hands together. "Options. I could sharpen your sword. It won't take long, and if you can't shave with it, at least it will be sharper than it is now."

"I've suddenly lost enthusiasm for that option. What else can you do?"

Constantine took the rapier from him. "If you want this kind of balance, I'll have to make you a new sword." He put the rapier away under the counter. "You've got two options. Machine-made, or hand-made. Some people want a blade that's been made by a man swinging a hammer at a forge. They want authenticity."

"Is the blade any better?"

"Nope," said Constantine cheerfully. "Just more authentic. It costs more and it takes longer, and you wouldn't believe how often that's a selling point."

Hammett chuckled. "I'll pass."

"Good. I'm a busy man." Constantine fingered the gemstone in the hilt. "I can replicate a stone that's pretty close to this one. Or I can take this one out and use it in the copy. How much do you care about getting the original sword back?"

Hammett thought of the solemn ceremony where they had presented him with a ridiculous oversized letter opener. "I don't care in the slightest. I barely need one sword. What would I do with two of them?"

"Good point. I need about fifteen minutes to program the machine, and maybe half an hour tonight to take the gemstone out, and another half an hour tomorrow to put it into the new sword. I could have it done by about nine tomorrow morning."

"That sounds fine," said Hammett. "Will it be a perfect match?"

"The shape of the blade will be slightly different. The hilt will be a just about identical, though. If you were to put the two swords side by side, you would see minor differences, but I can pretty much promise you no one will notice."

"Excellent. I'm going to need that delivered."

Constantine nodded, his fingers curling as he prepared to type into a mid-air keyboard visible through his implants.

"Send it to the captain's cabin, *SS Alexander*."

CHAPTER 2 – VELASCO

"The *Alexander*? What the hell?" Anna Velasco bounced out of her chair, fighting to contain the knot of frustration in her stomach. The middle-aged man sitting behind the desk in front of her was her cousin, but he was also an admiral in Spacecom. She could push him, but only so far. "Dammit, Alvarez, that ship is a joke."

"That's Admiral Castille to you," he admonished. "You've just been promoted. We talked about this. You need some time on ships."

She caught herself touching the commander's bars on her chest, and she lowered her hand. The promotion was barely two weeks old, and it still didn't feel quite real. "Time on real ships," she said. "Not relics from the war."

"It's the biggest ship left in the entire fleet," he said. "Someday you'll be the only officer around with time put in on a real cruiser. You can serve on a corvette any time. Everybody does that. How many people can say they've served on a cruiser? And the window of opportunity to get that experience is about to close."

"Exactly! The ship's getting mothballed. And I'll be her executive officer. It's embarrassing!"

"It's a temporary assignment," Castille said. "That's what you wanted, isn't it? A few months on a ship so no one can say you're just a desk sailor."

Velasco slashed at the air in a gesture of frustration. "I wanted to serve on a ship I could be proud of!"

"The ship has a proud history," Castille said mildly, "but that's not the point. The point is that she'll be decommissioned in three or four months. You'll be back in your office by winter. Do you know what a senior officer's term of service is on a corvette?"

"I ..." She let her voice trail off as she realized she had no idea.

"It's usually a year at a minimum. Six months, if the officer is a really bad fit."

Velasco let that sink in. A year traipsing around the dusty corners of the alliance? You didn't rise through the ranks by wandering around millions of kilometers from the Admiralty. *I didn't join the Navy to ride around on ships.*

"Trust me," Castille said. "I have your best interests at heart. Now, your first voyage is going to be a good networking opportunity for you." He held up a warning finger. "It won't seem that way at first. It's a training mission, and the ship will be full of cadets. But these will be the enlisted personnel and officers serving under you for the rest of your career."

He gestured at the chair beside her, and she sank back down. Maybe this wouldn't be so bad. She would be counting down the days, however, until the *Alexander* finally hit the scrapyard.

CHAPTER 3 – KASIM

Kasim al Faisal tilted the shuttle *Albatross* a couple of degrees to port so he could watch the Earth fall away beneath him. The Baja Peninsula was a long brown finger stretching into the cool blue Pacific. The city of Hawking glittered like a jewelled ring at the base of the peninsula. It was a nice city, but he was deeply grateful to be heading back into space. He felt reduced when he was planetside, like some gravity-bound slug dragging himself along the surface. Beyond the cloying reach of the atmosphere, at the controls of a small ship, he felt free.

He felt like a god.

The bulk of a supply ship loomed ahead of him, and beyond it the long, dark shape of the *Alexander*, with bright corvettes hovering around her like attendants. The proper thing to do – the sensible thing to do, if he wanted to avoid yet another disciplinary notice – was to trudge along behind the wallowing metal hippo in front of him and wait his turn to dock with the cruiser. He queued up behind the supply ship and behaved himself for forty-five interminable seconds.

"Oh, to hell with this." He leaned over in his seat and glanced into the passenger bay. The shuttle was filled with cadets, just like on the last trip and the trip before. They would be anywhere from 18 to 21 years old, and they'd be almost as bored as he was with this sedate bus ride. Why, it was practically his duty to show them there was still such a thing as real flying in the galaxy.

He turned on his microphone. "Attention, passengers. This is your captain speaking. In the interests of rounding out your woefully inadequate educations, I will be providing you with a demonstration of tactical evasive and pursuit maneuvers. If you're not already buckled into your seats, right now would be a very good time to strap in."

Then, grinning in anticipation, he overrode the shuttle's AI and wrapped a hand around the control stick. He accelerated, surging straight at the back end of the supply ship, and a couple of cadets in the front row cried out. Kasim chuckled, then twisted the stick and sent the shuttle corkscrewing sideways. They cleared the stern of the supply ship with a good meter to spare, maybe even a meter and a half.

No one could call Kasim reckless.

The shuttle blasted past the supply ship, and Kasim maintained the corkscrewing motion.

Centrifugal force pushed him against his shoulder straps, and he heard a babble of excited voices from aft. The sky spun around him as he zipped past the nose of the larger ship. He jerked the *Albatross* down until she was directly ahead of the supply ship, then accelerated hard. The *Alexander* swelled as he rushed toward her, and an alarm blared. The *Albatross* was being targeted by weapons systems on the *Alexander* and the surrounding corvettes.

"Oops." He fired the nose thrusters, decelerating hard.

"Shuttle *Albatross*. What the hell are you playing at?"

"Just demonstrating some maneuvers for the cadets." He winced, waiting for a reply.

"Kindly explain to the cadets that approaching a warship at ramming speed falls somewhere between stupid and suicidal on the official list of things you shouldn't do," said the clipped, starchy voice over the radio.

"Roger," he said. "Thanks for helping me, ah, impart such a valuable lesson."

"Let's not repeat the lesson, *Albatross*. *Alexander* out."

Somewhere behind him a cadet snickered. Several more cadets gave him a mocking round of applause.

"Thank you. You're too kind. Hang on for just a moment longer; we'll be docking with the *Alexander* shortly. A good ten minutes sooner than if you'd had any other pilot, I might add."

That brought fresh applause, and he smiled.

With just a little bit of luck, none of the weapons crews upstairs would bother mentioning him in a report. No cadets had puked. Kasim figured he had a better-than-even chance of getting away with his stunt.

He brought the shuttle up under the belly of the cruiser, marvelling he always did at the sheer bulk of the warship. The sleek corvettes that surrounded her seemed inconsequential, like a flock of sparrows around an eagle. They were shinier, prettier, quicker and more manoeuvrable. Their hulls were smooth and flawless, not marred by patches and seams from refits. They were better suited to the duties of the modern Navy, patrolling the vast borders of the scattered republic, intercepting smugglers, and doing customs inspections.

The *Alexander*, though, was built for war.

She was five decks high, but narrow, no more than forty meters across. She was long, almost two hundred meters from her steel prow to the massive engines in the stern. A missile bay decorated her port side, and a shuttle bay jutted from the bottom of her hull.

He tried to imagine the old days as he brought the *Albatross* in close to the shuttle bay and let the *Alexander*'s tractor beams take control. Before Kasim was born, when his father was still a child, Earth's colonies had rebelled. They'd gone to war with Earth and each other. The Navy had been a very different organization in those days. Instead of customs and police work, fast warships had slugged it out in the depths of space.

Very little remained from the days of war. A handful of officers and enlisted men. One ship.

The *Alexander*.

A gentle thump echoed through the *Albatross* as they set down on the deck of the shuttle bay. Kasim rose and stretched, nodding to the cadets as they shuffled past him and into the larger ship. Most of them smiled as they nodded back. One young woman gave him a thumbs-up and said, "Great flight." No one looked upset or annoyed, and Kasim smiled. It was going to be all right.

Then a flash of colour caught his eye, and the smile froze on his face. A man and a woman stood at the back of the lineup. Instead of the drab green jumpsuits of cadets, they wore officers' uniforms. The man was poker-faced, but the woman transfixed Kasim with a glare of pure outrage.

Kasim kept smiling, but his stomach sank as if the ship's gravity had failed. He nodded to the last of the cadets, hiding his dismay, with only one thought in his head.

I'm screwed.

CHAPTER 4 – HAMMETT

Hammett leaned his shoulder against a bulkhead and waited for the fireworks to begin. He hadn't been enjoying the uncomfortable silence he'd been sharing before the pilot had interrupted it with his wild demonstration. Commander Velasco had alternated between indignant sputtering and silent terror as the shuttle had whipped around in tight corkscrews. Now she almost seemed to swell in front of him. He didn't want to hear the dressing-down she was about to unleash, but she was blocking the corridor. He resigned himself to waiting.

"What the hell did you think you were doing?"

The pilot had a sickly smile glued to his face, and he shrugged. "Demonstrating proper combat flying?"

"You were demonstrating grossly unsafe stunt

flying!" Velasco's face was getting red. "What's your name and service number?"

A bit of the smile still persisted, and Hammett found himself admiring the kid's sangfroid. "Lieutenant Kasim al Faisal. 51983. Ma'am."

"Well, I hope you've enjoyed being a lieutenant, Faisal, because you won't be one for much longer." She didn't have the power to reduce him in rank, though it might happen. *She makes hollow threats. Not a good sign.*

"That's al Faisal, Ma'am."

"What?" Velasco looked about ready to burst a blood vessel from sheer outrage.

"My last name. It's not Faisal, Ma'am. It's al Faisal."

"I don't give a good damn what your name is! When I'm done with you, your parents will be disowning you anyway! You're a disgrace to your uniform, al Faisal. You're finished in the Navy. I'm going to make it happen." She glared at him for a time, then seemed to realize she had nothing more to say. She whirled and stomped off into the landing bay.

Hammett ducked through the shuttle's hatch, then paused to look back at the pilot. Al Faisal wore a pained grimace that contained just a ghost of his former grin. "Nice flying," Hammett said. "Keep up the good work." He grinned at the startled expression on the man's face, turned away, and clumped down the steps into the landing bay.

All the petty frustrations of his trip Earthside seemed to fall away. He was back on the

Alexander. He was home. The deck beneath his feet had chipped paint and oil stains and gouges from clumsy landings, but he loved it anyway. Every imperfection told a story. Even knowing she was headed for the scrapyard couldn't stop the smile that spread across his face. After too many days of bureaucrats and offices he was finally back on a proper ship.

Velasco waited for him on the far side of the landing bay, visibly fidgeting. He headed toward her, keeping to a slow saunter just to annoy her. *You may be the Admiralty's rising star, but I'm still the captain of this ship. I won't he hurried along by a desk pilot half my age. No doubt you'll be promoted above me soon enough. In the meantime, you can show me the respect due my rank.*

"It was courteous of you to wait for me, Commander," he said when he reached her. Her lips tightened in obvious annoyance. She was waiting because she had no idea how to find the bridge, or anything else. She'd be lost on a corvette, if the stories were true, and Hammett sighed to himself. His First Officer had never served on a ship. It was ridiculous, and it underlined how the Navy saw the *Alexander*. She was an unimportant relic, not one of the shiny corvettes that did actual work.

"You'll want to stow your bag," he said, indicating the duffel slung over her shoulder. "After that, I'm sure you're keen to learn your way around the ship."

A cadet came across the shuttle bay toward them, then hesitated, clearly unsure how to deal with two senior officers blocking a hatchway. Velasco gestured him forward. "You, there. Take this." She thrust her duffel at him, and he took it, looking uncertain. "Put it in my quarters. I'm Commander Velasco."

"Um, yes, Ma'am. Uh, where are your quarters?"

"How should I know? Show some initiative. Find it." She stepped out of the hatchway, clearing a path, and the cadet gave her a hesitant salute before hurrying deeper into the ship. She ignored him. It was a rough way to treat a youngster on his first day aboard ship, and Hammett frowned. He was beginning to dislike his new First Officer.

"No offence, Captain," she said, "but I don't plan to be aboard this hulk for long. What I need is a data lounge where I can catch up on paperwork. I haven't had good network access in almost two hours." A sailor came down the corridor, clearly busy with a task of her own, and Velasco stepped into the woman's path. "You, there. Where's the nearest data lounge?"

"Well, let me see. Two decks up in green section? The stairs are-"

"Show me," Velasco ordered. She followed the sailor down the corridor, glancing back long enough to say, "I'll see you later, Captain."

Hammett stared after her, dumbstruck. There was nothing insubordinate in her behavior, not exactly. It just wasn't the least bit respectful. Nor was there any respect in the way she treated subordinates. She was going to be a real thorn in his side, and she was going to be hell on crew morale. He sure wouldn't want to take her into battle.

I suppose she's good enough for a training run on a ship that's destined for the scrapyard. The thought soured his mood. He stared after her, replaying everything she'd said, looking for grounds for an official reprimand. There was nothing, he decided reluctantly.

"Well," he muttered, "if I can't write her up, at least I can annoy her." He touched his ear, activating his com implants. A menu appeared, projected on his retina. He reached a hand out, tapping and swiping icons. To anyone else it would look like he was poking empty air, but he could see his finger touching the projected menus. He found the AI that handled Spacecom personnel.

"How can I help you, Captain Hammett?"

"I met a remarkable pilot today," he said. "But I have reason to believe he's not entirely suited to his current assignment. He's been getting reprimand notices. Or he will be. His name is Kasim al Faisal, service number, let me see … 51983, I think."

"That's right, Captain."

"I'd like to request a transfer for the young man. I'd like to have him aboard the *Alexander*." He smiled as he imagined how Velasco would react. "He's got the instincts of a combat flier. I think he's wasted as a shuttle pilot."

"I will make enquiries," the AI said. "I'll contact you when I know if a transfer will be feasible."

"Thank you," Hammett said, and broke the

connection. He grinned.
    Velasco was going to be furious.

CHAPTER 5 – JANICE

The press scrum mostly contained robots.

Janice Ling ducked as a softball-sized camera bot zipped past her head. The bloody things were notoriously aggressive, ignoring the petty safety concerns of mere organics in their quest to capture the right clip from just the right angle.

A Channel Nine bot strutted past, a silver-skinned android done up to look like a woman, complete with an archaic steno pad and fountain pen. Those were props. Her mechanical eyes and ears would take a much better record than pen and paper ever could. It wasn't the only props the android had. Those ridiculous gigantic breasts, for instance. The android was made up like some vulgar fantasy dreamed up by a teenage boy. It was ridiculously over-sexualized, and Janice rolled her eyes, wondering what kind of knuckle-dragger followed the Channel Nine feeds.

Three other human reporters jockeyed for position in the mechanical crowd. Two were junior reporters like Janice, willing to put in long hours at long odds for a shot at a story that would make a splash. She also recognized Jerry Sturgeon, a washed-up alcoholic who'd sobered up and now worked the fringes of the news trade. On her bad days she was pretty sure she'd end up like him. If she lasted that long.

"Thank you for coming." The speaker was Alvarez Castille, an admiral who reminded Janice of her father. Her father had never had such steel in his gaze, though. "We're delighted at the opportunity to open our ships for a limited time to members of the Fourth Estate. You should have received your media packages already. We're pleased to announce that nineteen members of the press have been assigned to twelve different ships on missions ranging from three days to almost three weeks."

Nineteen assignments, given to nineteen established reporters with more clout than Janice Ling. She was a freelancer without a following, which meant she was here looking for crumbs. She would take whatever the real reporters didn't want.

Castille began to speak about the fleet and the mission of the Navy. It wasn't so much a speech as a long string of clever sound bites designed to promote the Navy in twenty words or fewer. He wasn't saying much, and Janice, despite her best intentions, felt her mind starting to drift.

Sturgeon started murmuring to the cub reporter beside him. The young woman listened wide-eyed, and Janice edged closer, eavesdropping shamelessly.

"Corvettes are where it's at. They've got a spot on the *Alexander*, but don't take it if they offer. It'll be gone at least five days, maybe longer. You'll miss a hundred good leads and you won't get anything for it." He patted the pockets of his rumpled suit as if absentmindedly looking for a bottle. "There's no news on that tub. She's ancient. When I was your age, well, that's when the *Alexander* was news. You wouldn't believe the things she did in the war. Now she's a relic. Five minutes of human interest story. Not five days' worth."

Janice tuned him out, bringing up the media package on her implants. The *Alexander* was on a training mission, giving cadets one last opportunity to serve on a real ship of war. The Navy press kit made it all sound quite positive. Glorious, even. According to most of the feeds, though, it was nothing but. Why, the pundits demanded, was the Navy wasting their cadets' time learning to operate an obsolete ship in its last year of service? It was a colossal waste of time.

She was about to close the article when a line near the bottom caught her eye. She tilted her head, making the retinal display scroll up.

The *Alexander* would be leaving the Sol system through Gate Three, carrying a group of technicians who would check Gate Four, the mirror to Gate Three in the Naxos system. The technicians would inspect the Gate thoroughly in an attempt to prevent another Gate failure.

Naxos was one Gate closer to Aries, Tanos, and Calypso, the three systems that had gone silent, their Gates offline.

Janice felt her pulse quicken ever so slightly. There was a story – a real story – behind those Gate failures. She was almost certain of it. The real answers would be in Aries or Deirdre, the system between Aries and Naxos.

Still, Naxos put her one system closer.

Can I afford to be gone for five days? What will I miss? She made a face. The sad truth was, she would miss scraps. Her "career" as a freelance journalist was a joke. This month's rent would be tight, but five days of eating the Navy's food would help.

Castille wrapped up his speech with a final one-liner about how agility meant survival in the jungle and in space. The scrum broke up, and Janice worked her way through the dispersing robots, heading for the stage at the front. Castille looked up, gave her a single unsympathetic glance, and left through a doorway at the back.

She made a face at his retreating back, then smiled as she remembered Hammett ambushing her and throwing her against the wall. She supposed she should be annoyed, but she couldn't help it. She was looking forward to seeing him again.

A young lieutenant came to the edge of the stage, smiled, then hopped down so he was at her level. "Can I help you?"

"Yes." She gave him her brightest smile. "I understand you have a spot available on the *Alexander*?"

CHAPTER 6 – HAMMETT

Hammett sat at his console on the bridge of the *Alexander*, watching status reports scroll past. Final checks were taking an absurdly long time. The cadets didn't know what they were doing, and his small handful of sailors and officers were running themselves ragged.

A yellow bar in the flow of green text caught his eye. The last shuttle from Spacecom had docked. The gate technicians were on board. They would be sedate types, used to labs and offices. He hoped they hadn't had that al Faisal guy for their pilot.

The shuttle had another passenger, he noted. A reporter. He brought up her name, and groaned inwardly. Janice Ling, the woman he'd thrown against the wall.

Well, they were taking his ship away from him in a few months. What the hell did he have left to fear? She could trash him in the press if she liked.

How could she make things worse?

Sighing, he finished scrolling through the status reports. Everything showed green. Undoubtedly there was a screwup somewhere – with more than a hundred cadets on board it was a near certainty – but it would be nothing catastrophic.

Still, he wouldn't take the ship through a jump Gate right away.

He stood, and the bridge crew turned in their seats to look at him. Velasco stood along the port bulkhead. His Third in Command, a seasoned lieutenant named Carruthers, shared the helm station with a nervous-looking cadet. A mix of junior lieutenants manned the other stations.

"We'll start with a slow sweep around Luna," Hammett said. "Then we'll swing by Sawyer Station and from there to Gate Three." He headed for the bridge doors. "I'll be in Engineering. Velasco, you have the bridge."

He glanced at her as he went past, and paused. She had something close to panic on her face. *Oh, for God's sake.* Hammett stopped, raked his fingers through his hair, and said, "On second thought, Velasco, why don't you come with me? There's things we need to discuss. Carruthers, you have the bridge."

Carruthers nodded and stood. The cadet beside him gave him a frightened look, and Carruthers chuckled. "You've done this in simulations, son. You'll do fine." Carruthers strolled over to the captain's seat and sat down. He had years of bridge experience. The ship was in good hands.

Hammett jerked his head curtly at Velasco and left the bridge.

When they were alone in the corridor he said, "You'll have to learn how to run a bridge."

"Yes, Sir."

He strode along, and she hurried to keep up. "In fact, you need to learn the entire ship."

She frowned.

"Stow it, Commander. You're on a ship now. I don't care if it's what you want. You're here. You've got a job to do, and I expect you to be ready to do it." He shook his head, exasperated that he had to have this conversation with a senior officer. "We're going to visit Engineering, and then we're going to visit the missile bay. After that you'll go back to the bridge and tell Carruthers that he's not relieved. You'll stand there and watch what he does."

"I'm busy," she protested. "I've got a mountain of paperwork to-"

"Paperwork?" He stopped and faced her. "You're my First Officer. You have whatever paperwork I assign to you, and that's it."

Velasco scowled. "This isn't my first day in the Navy! You can't just order me to-"

He leaned in close to her, and she stepped back. Her nose almost touched the bars on his chest, and he tapped them. "What do you think these mean, Commander?"

The clatter of feet and the murmur of voices in the distance saved her from having to answer. Hammett straightened up and resumed walking,

Velasco behind him. They met a sailor and a cadet coming the other way, the sailor giving a running commentary about the cables and conduits that flowed along the ceiling above them. There was a brief pause for the exchange of salutes, and then both groups continued on their way.

"Let me put it this way," Hammett said when they were alone again. "In about twelve hours you're going to take us through Gate Three. I strongly suggest you be ready."

The corridor widened as they came to an intersection, and he stopped. "Now. Pay attention. See these stripes?" He gestured at several colored bars of paint on the bulkhead. "Red is Engineering. The only red bar is on this side, so we know Engineering is this way. See this one?" He tapped a white bar with a red outline. "That's Medical. Notice it's lower than any of the others. That tells you Medical is at least one deck down. The stripe is off to the right, so the nearest ladder is that way. I expect you to learn what the rest of the stripes mean on your own."

He led her aft. The corridor curved, straightened, then ended at a broad pair of doors, painted bright red. "Engineering," he said.

The doors slid open. Engineering was busier than usual, mostly with crew explaining things to cadets. *I'm captain of a floating classroom. It's supposed to be a bloody warship.* Hammett suppressed his irritation. Forty years from now, some of these cadets would still be in uniform. At least someone in the service would remember what a real ship was like.

He and Velasco skirted around the bulk of the hydrogen fusion plant that gave the ship its power. Beyond the plant stood a vast steel globe, the tank that contained the ship's supply of liquid hydrogen. Pipes ran aft from the tank to the *Alexander's* three engines.

"It's a simple process," a voice said to Hammett's left. He turned to see Susan Rani, his Engineering Officer, lecturing a cluster of bored-looking cadets. "The engines operate on a principle of thermal rocketry. We heat liquid hydrogen to fantastic temperatures and blow it out the back."

The cadets would have learned that in their first week, if they actually made it into Basic without knowing something so elementary. There was no discouraging Rani as she warmed to her favorite subject, though.

She broke off her lecture when she spotted Hammett. "Is there something you need, Sir?"

"No, no. Just taking a look around."

"Everything's ship-shape," she assured him. "In a couple of days these kids will be able to run things without me."

Hammett smiled. "I don't doubt it. Carry on, Lieutenant."

She nodded and resumed her lecture, and Hammett continued his tour of the engine room, Velasco at his heels. "You need to be familiar with this place," he told her. "You need to be able to walk in here and tell at a glance if there's a problem." He read impatience in the narrowing of her eyes, but he ignored it. "I can tell already that everything's fine," he continued. "Come with me. We're visiting the missile bay next."

A sailor with a sidearm stood guard outside a locked hatch. The Marine Corps had disbanded a decade after the war ended. Now sailors trained in boarding procedures and intra-ship combat. It was more than adequate for the seizures and customs searches that were the role of the modern Navy. The sentry saluted and stepped aside, and Hammett led Velasco inside.

The long, shadowy bay contained no personnel. The missiles themselves were hidden by panels that would slide open in the event of combat. The missile bay could have been a cargo hold for all a casual visitor could see. Hammett looked at Velasco. "What do you know about the ship's weapons?"

She gave him an irritated glance. "There are lasers?" When he scowled she added, "Oh, and rail guns. And more than one kind of ammunition."

"We have twelve laser batteries," he said, not trying too hard to hide his irritation. "Three on the top hull forward. Three aft. Six more on the bottom hull. Computer-targeted, but they can be used manually if necessary."

Velasco shrugged.

"We have two rail guns firing forward," he added, "and one firing aft. And we have a variety of ammunition. Also just over two hundred drone fighters, able to fight autonomously or by remote control." He walked over to the nearest wall and pressed his hand against a scanner. "All the corvettes have the same weapons, on a smaller scale. Here's what makes the *Alexander* unique, though."

A panel a meter high and two meters long slid up with a hum, revealing a squat cylindrical shape on a long shelf. Hammett reached up and patted the side of the cylinder. "This is a missile," he said. "It uses a chemical rocket for propulsion, and it has a warhead of high explosives surrounded by shrapnel. It can detonate on impact, or it can explode in the middle of a fleet and spread damage with shrapnel." He closed the panel and strolled down the missile bay. He tapped another panel. "This shelf contains a nuke. I can't open it. Only the weapons officer can, and then only if it's unlocked from the bridge." He smiled, proud of his lethal arsenal. "We have six of them."

"Nuclear missiles?" she said. "What in space are you going to do with those?"

His smile thinned. "Actually, I'm going to fire them for practice." The thought soured his stomach. "It'll be a training exercise for the cadets." Not that the cadets would ever use it.

Velasco shook her head. "You're just going to ... fire them at nothing?"

"We'll blow up some rocks," he said. "These birds are almost thirty years old, and the Navy has no plans to refurbish them. They don't much like the idea of storing them, either. So we're going to get rid of them on this trip. It'll be historic, I guess. It'll be the last time a warship ever fires a nuclear missile."

"The last time?" She pursed her lips. "Has a warship ever fired a nuclear missile before?"

He nodded. "During the war. The *Custer* fired half a dozen nukes at the Battle of Helfcene Station."

Velasco's eyebrows rose. "What happened?"

Do you know nothing of military history? He said, "How can you-" then stopped himself. To him it was high drama. He'd watched it in the feeds, breathless, with his fellow officers around him. To her, though, it was history. She'd been an infant, and how much did he really know about military history before his own lifetime?

"None of the missiles hit," he said. "The RNA fleet cut them up with lasers before they even got close." He gestured around the bay. "It's why the new ships don't have missile bays." He wanted to tell her to savor the experience. He wanted to tell her she was standing in a little piece of history. But history to her meant dust and irrelevance. He frowned and headed for the hatch. "Let's go. I've got work to do, and you need to get to the bridge. You've got a lot to learn."

CHAPTER 7 – VELASCO

Anna Velasco lowered herself gingerly into the captain's chair and looked around. She was pretty sure at least one lieutenant was watching her from the corner of his eye, but most of the bridge crew seemed focused on their own stations. She balled her hands into fists to keep herself from fidgeting, took a deep breath, and searched for calm. *How bad can it be? I'm not the one doing the actual flying. If I do something really stupid, one of these lieutenants will speak up.*

Won't they?

That would be humiliating. Crashing the ship into the edge of the Gate would be much, much worse. She imagined half the ship warping through to pop out the other side while the other half remained behind. Could that happen?

I'm an administrator, not a bloody physicist! I'm not a ship's captain, either. She thought of the reports and proposals accumulating in her data stream. *I've got things to do. Important things. I'm helping direct the course of Spacecom itself. I'll be an admiral someday. What the hell am I doing out in space?*

It didn't help that she was utterly exhausted from a combination of stress and trying to catch up on projects back at Spacecom. She suppressed a yawn and gathered her wandering thoughts, checking the screens arrayed around her chair. The biggest screen, mounted just above her knee, showed the view from the forward camera. The Gate loomed there, a vast steel ring almost edge-on. *We need to move the ship over. That's not the terminology, though. What am I supposed to say?*

The helmsman, a young cadet who looked almost as frightened as Velasco felt, turned in his chair and glanced back at her. *I'm taking too long. You can't just sit here. I have to at least pretend I know what I'm doing.* "Helm." Her voice wasn't perfectly steady, but it would do. "Bring us around."

The cadet nodded, hesitated, then said, "Heading, Ma'am?"

For a long frozen second she stared at him, terror constricting her throat. *I don't know what heading! That's your job. Haven't you done this a thousand times in simulations?*

He had, of course. She couldn't talk him through it step by step, but she didn't need to. "You know where we're going." She gestured forward, where the Gate lay. "Line us up with the Gate."

"Aye aye, Ma'am." He turned to his console, and she felt the faintest of tremors as the *Alexander's* maneuvering thrusters fired. The Gate seemed to turn in place on her screen as the ship drifted sideways. She supposed it might be faster to turn the ship and fly around in a big arc using the main engines. There was no rush, though. The slow approach would work nicely.

When the Gate formed a perfect circle on her screen she felt another tremor. That would be the maneuvering thrusters on the other side, firing to bring them to a stop. The cadet seems to expect her to say something, so she said, "Well done." He beamed as if she'd promoted him to lieutenant. Strangely, it deepened her unease. *I don't want this kind of power. I'm not ready for it.*

The bridge went silent, and she stared at the Gate. *This is it. It should be perfectly simple, right? We just fly right through.* She touched her tongue to her lips, wondering why her mouth was so dry. *Am I forgetting something? If I am, someone will speak up. Right?*

The helmsman turned again to glance at her.

"Take us through," she said, then added, "Slow and steady."

The cadet didn't speak, just nodded. She could see his tension in the set of his shoulders. She felt the same tension in her own shoulders and neck. She took a quick, furtive glance at the three lieutenants managing bridge stations. None of them looked nervous. *Maybe that means I'm doing fine.*

The Gate grew larger and larger on the screen

until it disappeared completely. All she saw was the black of a starless expanse. There was a way to show distance to the Gate, but she didn't know the controls well enough to-

"One hundred meters," said a lieutenant to the right. "Fifty meters. Ten meters."

Velasco held her breath.

Her screen shimmered, and she saw a matching shimmer on screens all around the bridge. Then the stars appeared, cold and bright.

They were through.

Velasco exhaled, careful to do it quietly. "Very good, Cadet." *I'll have to learn his name.* "Take us around behind the Gate." That would take the *Alexander* out of the path of any ships coming through. "Stop us at a range of, oh, a kilometer." She stood. "Someone tell our Gate technicians we've arrived."

The bridge doors slid open. Hammett came in, nodded gravely, and said, "You are relieved."

"Thank you, Sir." Was that a hint of a twinkle in his eye? It couldn't be coincidence that he showed up right after they came through the Gate. Had he been monitoring her?

If he had any sense, he was. She supposed she should have felt relieved, but she felt unsettled. Hammett took his seat and she walked out of the bridge, heading for her quarters. She had more to do than she could possibly accomplish, but the thought of office politics and procedure papers left her strangely hollow.

I thought it was me. I thought he was trusting me to get us through the Gate. I thought the whole ship was counting on me ...

In a way they were, she decided. After all, she could have found some way to screw it up, even with Hammett monitoring her. The pressure had been sickening at the time, but now that it was over, she felt ... different.

She'd had a glimpse, she realized, of why so many officers wanted to serve on ships when it took them so far away from the Admiralty and the fast track to promotion. The sense of responsibility she'd felt was terrifying, but it was addictive, too. It wasn't just commanders who felt it, either. That cadet at the helm. He'd felt it. Every officer on the bridge would have felt it, to a lesser degree.

Velasco reached her quarters, glanced at her data station, and instead stretched out on her bunk. She was suddenly drained. *For pity's sake, Anna, you didn't even do anything. You just told a cadet to fly us through a Gate. It's not as if you ...*

She fell asleep before she could complete the thought.

CHAPTER 8 – HAMMETT

Hammett and Carruthers walked down a broad, empty corridor along the spine of the ship. The *Alexander* was losing the air of quiet efficiency he'd seen during his earlier walk with Velasco. He sighed. "Give me the bottom line, Jim."

"We can still generate a wormhole," Carruthers said, giving him a sympathetic smile. "It'll still have decent range, too. Over ninety percent." He didn't add that they weren't going to generate any wormholes on this trip. Carruthers knew perfectly well that it wasn't the point.

"Well, if that's all that goes wrong, we'll be lucky." He told himself that he shouldn't grumble, then gave in. "She's a good ship, and she deserves better."

Carruthers nodded. He loved the *Alexander* too, probably almost as much as Hammett did.

"We're last in line for every kind of service." Hammett made a frustrated gesture. "Susan reported the generator problem, what? Six months ago? Back then, it was a maintenance issue, not a repair. Now the wormhole generator's borked, and instead of a day in drydock we'll need over a week."

"Not that we'll get it," Carruthers said gloomily.

He was right, of course. Spacecom wasn't going to pay for nonessential repairs to a ship that was due for decommissioning. Hammett balled up a fist, thought about punching a bulkhead, and decided against it.

Carruthers gave him a cautious look. "You ready for more bad news, Chief?"

Hammett nodded. "Sure. Hit me."

"The rest is just little stuff," Carruthers said. "It's in the category of hardware troubles, but really, it's personnel issues. Tony ordered the guns stripped and cleaned." Lieutenant Tony DiMarco was the ship's weapons officer. "They didn't need it, but he wanted the cadets to get the experience." Carruthers shook his head. "Some young genius loaded explosive rounds in the belly gun without the steel casings."

The ship carried ballistic rounds, essentially steel canisters with a lead slug in the center to give them mass, and explosive rounds, much more delicate and expensive, with a detonator and a payload of chemical explosive. Each explosive round had to be loaded into a steel container sized for the barrel of the rail gun.

"How bad?" Hammett asked.

"Well, there were no explosions," Carruthers said. "Still, it was bad enough. The magazine jammed, and the kid decided he wasn't pushing hard enough. He just kept ramming in more rounds." He shook his head. "I haven't seen a mess like that since I did the exact same thing, twenty years ago on the *Atlas*."

Hammett looked at him, startled, then laughed. "I never did that," he said. "I did once load a magazine with empty canisters, though." He chuckled, remembering. "I had this fire-eating gunnery sergeant taking a bunch of us through a drill. She had a couple of second lieutenants firing on a derelict hull." Hammett felt a belly laugh start to build. "The rounds kept hitting, dead on target, but they bounced off the hull like so much popcorn." He gave in to the laugh, hearing it echo down the corridor. "You should have seen the look on her face! I tell you, Jim, if I'd known what it was going to do to her, I'd have done it on purpose!"

They continued on their way, inspecting the dorsal rail gun (which hadn't jammed) and then descending several decks to examine the equipment that would generate a wormhole if the ship needed to make a faster-than-light jump without the use of a Gate. Neither man had the advanced engineering degrees they would need to actually understand a wormhole generator, but they had years of experience on the *Alexander*. Hammett could tell by the background hum, by the hint of vibration he felt through the deck plates, by the very feel of the air, whether his ship was running properly.

They finished their tour in the missile bay. "Apparently there's a comet wandering through the system," Carruthers said. "It's coming within a couple of million kilometers."

"Practically scratching distance," Hammett said, wondering what he was getting at.

"Might make some good target practice," Carruthers said. "We could lob the nukes at it."

"No." The refusal came without thought, and Carruthers looked at him, raising an eyebrow. Hammett felt himself flush. "They're the last six nuclear missiles in the entire fleet," he said, feeling irritable and embarrassed. "I know we're supposed to blow the damned things up." He spread his hands, unable to articulate what his instincts were telling him. "Not yet," he said at last. "Not on a bloody comet."

Carruthers nodded without remark.

A chime sounded in Hammett's ear. He tilted his head to bring up a menu, accepted the incoming message, and watched text scroll through the air in front of him. The Gate technicians were done their inspection and back aboard the ship.

He called the bridge, reached a lieutenant named Chen, and told her to set a course for Gate Five. The Naxos system had two Gates, Four, which led to Earth, and Five, which led to Deirdre. The Gate technicians would inspect Gate Five, after which they would expect Hammett to take them back to Earth.

The sensible thing to do was to go home. Even

better, fire half a dozen nukes at an orbiting snowball, give a bunch of cadets some experience they would never be able to apply, and *then* go home. His orders were vague – aside from inspecting Gates Four and Five, he was to give the cadets training opportunities – but those orders certainly didn't include travelling through another Gate.

Still, what was Spacecom going to do? Take away his command? Put him out to pasture?

Toss his ship on the scrapyard?

"Come with me to the bridge," he said. "You can watch me trash my career."

Carruthers gave him a quizzical look, then followed him toward the bridge. "What's up?"

"I'm going to take a very broad interpretation of my orders," Hammett said. "I'm taking us through Gate Five." He watched as the lieutenant's eyebrows climbed his forehead. "That way more cadets get to fly through Gates."

Carruthers said, "Okay ..."

"Spacecom thinks everything will be fine on the other side. I want you on the bridge when we go through, though, in case Spacecom is wrong."

Carruthers stopped. "What's going on, Richard?"

"That's a good question," Hammett said. "Three Gates have failed, one after another. Each new failure is closer to Earth than the one before. And we're supposed to believe that it's just mechanical malfunctions."

Carruthers shrugged. "What else could it be?"

Hammett hesitated. It sounded absurd when

he put it into words, but he was damned if he was going to be afraid to speak. "It could be an attack."

Carruthers's eyebrows went higher. "An attack? By who?"

The word "aliens" hung in the air between them. Instead, Hammett said, "It's a big galaxy, and we've explored, what? A tenth of one percent of it?"

"Less than that," Carruthers said. "Spacecom must be sending someone to take a look."

"I'm sure they are," Hammett said. "They'll send a corvette, when they can spare it from all those terribly important customs duties." He scowled. "What if it's an invasion, Jim? That's a job for a warship, and we're the only warship left."

We're a broken-down warship that hasn't had proper maintenance in a decade, armed with a lot of decaying missiles, and crewed by cadets. He didn't put the thought into words. He just looked at Carruthers, who said, "It's probably just mechanical failures, Captain."

"Probably," Hammett agreed.

"Well, if it isn't," Carruthers said, "I guess we'll have an interesting flight."

CHAPTER 9 – KASIM

When the *Alexander* was ten minutes from Gate Five, Kasim climbed into a shuttle and turned on the cockpit controls. He wanted to know the exact moment they popped through the wormhole. He didn't believe the rumors that were floating around about rogue colonies rising up, or aliens sweeping in from the deep dark. It was absurd.

Still, if something strange *was* going on, he didn't want to miss it.

The shuttle itself was blind while sitting in the landing bay, but it connected automatically to the *Alexander's* scanners. He watched the Gate loom larger and larger, then braced himself when the screens flickered. A moment later he saw the Deirdre system, majestic, serene, and utterly boring, splashed across the shuttle's displays.

An icon glowed green in the corner of his

screen, and he touched it. It was a transponder signal from Freedom Station. There were no flags, no alerts. All was normal in the Deirdre system.

"I suppose I shouldn't feel disappointed," he murmured. Still …

Feet clomped on the entrance ramp. "Lieutenant? Are you on board?"

"I'm here, Doc." He looked back over his shoulder as a trio of technicians filed into the shuttle.

Roberts, a sour-faced old geezer who looked as if he wanted to be home telling kids to get off his lawn, dropped into a seat and said, "Let's get this over with. We're supposed to be headed back to Earth already."

Behind him Sally MacKinnon met Kasim's gaze, rolled her eyes, and grinned. He grinned back. He liked Sally. She stayed cheerful no matter what got thrown at her.

The third technician, a young man named Sanchez, was already buckling himself in, eyes squeezed shut. Sanchez was a very poor flyer. Everything about space travel seemed to terrify him. Kasim was perpetually torn between the urge to fly as gently as possible and an unkind impulse to try a few stunts, just to wind the guy up.

"Welcome aboard once again," Kasim said. It was barely twenty minutes since the trio had left the shuttle. So far every Gate inspection had turned up nothing at all. "Maybe this is the trip where you figure out what's been going on."

"Just get on with it," Roberts said.

"Thank you," Sally added. "We appreciate your help." That earned her a sour glance from Roberts, which she ignored.

The bay doors slid open and Kasim took the shuttle out, slow and gentle. He wouldn't be back behind the controls again until they got back to Earth, and he wanted to savor the experience of flying free in a new system.

He took them along the underside of the *Alexander*, the belly of the ship like a steel sky above them. Laser turrets bristled like thunderheads, and a parabolic dish gleamed like a glimpse of sunlight through clouds.

They passed the bow of the ship. A fat yellow star hung off to the right. He squinted in the direction of Freedom Station, but couldn't make it out. There was nothing else to see. Deirdre had only one planet, a cold lump of rock half a light-year from the star. Human activity in the system centered around the station, a deep-space oasis with a few hundred people on board.

He brought the shuttle around in a gentle, sweeping turn. The Gate glittered in the light of the star, a sparkling ring hundreds of meters across. He massaged the controls, bringing the little shuttle to a halt a few meters from the edge of the ring. He was always surprised by how flimsy the Gate hardware was. The ring was only a couple of meters deep, and less than a meter thick. And yet it was able to do so much.

"Here we go again," Roberts grumbled, reaching for his helmet. Kasim grabbed his own helmet and sealed it in place. When everyone was suited up he started the fans that would reclaim at least a little of the air in the shuttle. It also gave everyone plenty of time to notice an open seal on their suits as the pressure dropped.

"Everyone sealed up?" he asked, looking over his passengers. A tiny green light glowed on the point of each person's left shoulder, an easy way to tell that the suits were sealed and ready for hard vacuum. He checked all three lights, returned Sally's cheerful smile, and ignored Roberts's frown. Sanchez looked terrified, but he always did before the shuttle opened. He would be fine once he got outside and started working.

"Opening," Kasim said, and popped the hatch. The three technicians left one at a time, bracing themselves in the hatch before kicking off to float over to the ring. Kasim watched them go, then settled back in his chair to wait. He wasn't bored. He didn't mind having the stars to himself.

His console beeped, and he looked down.

Gate Eleven, a couple of thousand kilometers away, showed as a round blue icon on his screen. Half a dozen yellow triangles surrounded the blue circle.

Unidentified ships.

Kasim leaned forward, feeling his pulse quicken. He magnified the view. The shuttle's sensors were poor things, but he was still connected to the sensor grid on the *Alexander*. The image on his screen expanded, and ships appeared, clear and sharp.

Kasim sucked in his breath, his muscles going rigid with shock.

There were six ships, each of a different design and shape. He muttered, "Computer. Scale," and a grid appeared on the display. The smallest ship measured about three meters by three meters. The largest ship was perhaps ten times that size.

As he watched, though, the smallest ship, a strange craft with protrusion sticking out in four directions, drifted over to the ship beside it. The two ships seemed to latch together.

Then another medium-sized ship broke into two pieces. Each piece drifted sideways and merged with a larger craft.

Kasim shook his head, baffled, then zoomed in. He was seeing a collection of tiny ships which clumped together to form larger craft, or broke apart to form separate ships. It was like nothing he'd ever seen, nothing he'd ever even heard of. Nowhere on Earth and nowhere in the colonies was anyone flying a ship that was even remotely similar.

"Aliens," he said. Then, louder, "Aliens!" He squeezed his eyes shut, shook his head, and looked again. He was just in time to see the last few smaller craft latch themselves onto an amalgamated ship about thirty meters across. The ship expanded on the screen as the alien vessel surged forward.

Toward the *Alexander*.

Toward the Gate that led home.

Toward Kasim.

He toggled his helmet microphone and shouted, "Everybody back on board. Now!"

There was an immediate babble of voices,

which went silent a moment later. A crisp voice said, "Shuttle Five. Get your ass back into the landing bay."

"Working on it," he said, then cut the connection. "Oh my God. Oh, God. Oh my God." He squeezed his eyes shut, tried to lift his hands to his face, and had to settle for pressing his gloves against the faceplate of his helmet. *First contact. I'm witnessed to the single most significant event in human history.*

No I'm not. First contact was weeks ago, in Calypso. Then they came through the Gate to Tanos. Then Aries, then here. The three systems, and not one ship ever got away to raise the alarm.

His initial panic was starting to subside, aided by the fact that he had absolutely nothing to do until the technicians were back on board. He found himself analysing the situation, if not calmly, at least without hysteria. *I bet they were hiding on the far side of Gate Eleven. Then they saw a warship come through, and they knew they had to do something.*

We need to keep them from coming through Gate Six. We have to keep them out of Naxos. There are hundreds of thousands of people there.

His stomach constricted as realization hit him. *We have to destroy the Gate.*

He switched his microphone back to the suit network. "Hurry up! It's an emergency, and if we don't get back to the *Alexander* in time ..."

The ship will pop through the Gate and destroy it from the other side. We'll be left behind.

With the aliens.

It's war. There was no way to be certain but he knew it in his gut. Three Gates had gone silent. That wasn't something caused by diplomacy.

War. They could put me into the cockpit of a fighter. I could fly actual combat missions. A prickle of excitement washed over him, quickly followed by sour disgust. *If there are dogfights, they will be fought by drones. Maybe, if I'm really lucky, I'll fly a drone by remote control.* It was the bitter reality of modern combat. Drones were smaller, harder to hit, and could take vastly more acceleration. No pilots died when a drone was destroyed. And the reactions of a computer were infinitely faster than those of a human being.

Did those enemy vessels contain pilots? It was one vessel now, a ship just smaller than the *Alexander*, closing at high speed. Even as his heart thumped madly in his chest he wondered how it worked. Did the ship get better thrust with all those smaller ships locked together? Did it make communication faster? Maybe it let them share shielding.

Something slammed into the shuttle window right in front of him, and he flinched back, giving a low shriek. For a moment he thought the shuttle was under attack. Then he recognized Sanchez, palms splayed flat against the window, eyes wide, his face no more than a meter away. The man had panicked, thrust too hard, and slammed into the shuttle.

Kasim shook his head. If Sanchez was falling apart already, what was he going to do when he learned about the aliens?

Roberts came through the hatch and pulled himself into a seat. Kasim caught a brief glimpse of Sally's shoulder through the window. She murmured to Sanchez over the radio, her voice low and soothing. "Come on. The hatch is right here. You're doing fine."

"Shuttle Five," said another voice. "Get a move on. We have to go."

"Hurry up," Kasim told the technicians. "Get in here."

"What's the big emergency?" said Roberts.

"You don't want to know."

Sanchez came through the hatch feet-first, and Kasim smiled, relief flooding through him. Then something moved in the corner of his eye, and he turned his head.

And swore.

The *Alexander* was moving away, picking up speed as she raced to intercept the alien ship.

"Okay," said Sally. "We're on board. Kasim? Kasim, what's wrong?"

He turned to look at her, shook his head, and said, "It's too late."

CHAPTER 10 – HAMMETT

Hammett stared at the screen in front of him, distantly aware that his fingers ached from gripping the arms of his chair. The bridge was filled with an unprofessional babble of excited voices. The junior lieutenant at the communication console, a man named Singh, was piping in radio chatter from the rest of the system. It was the same mix of panicky voices that filled the bridge. Hammett closed his eyes. It sounded more like an asylum than a warship.

"Silence!" He opened his eyes. Every eye was on him, and he made himself loosen his grip on the chair. With a calmness he didn't feel he said, "Keep your mouth shut unless you have something to say."

No one spoke, but a frightened voice came over the bridge speakers. "Sweet Buddha, what is it? Can you reach Port Albuquerque? I can't raise them. I think those ships – that thing, whatever it is-"

The voice went silent, and Carruthers, with no more emotion than a man discussing the weather, said, "Her transponder just went silent. That's the *James Joyce*. Local freighter. Crew of six."

Hammett looked at Singh. "Try to raise Port Albuquerque." Albuquerque was a space station with a dozen scientists on board, doing some kind of long-term analysis of changes to the local star. "Where is Albuquerque right now?"

"About two hundred thousand kilometers on the other side of Gate Eleven," Carruthers reported.

"They're not responding," said Singh.

More panicky voices came over the speakers, someone calling out to the crew of the *James Joyce*, someone else demanding to know what was happening. "Cut that racket," Hammett said. "Let me know if you hear anything useful."

Singh nodded. After a moment he said, "There's an Administrator Carmichael demanding to speak to you. I think he just wants you to tell him what's going on."

"He can wait. What's our time to intercept?"

"Eight minutes," Carruthers said.

We could retreat. We could duck through the Gate. It's important to get word back, right?

But three Gates have gone silent, and no one has ever escaped. And there are hundreds of people on Freedom Station. I can't just leave them.

Hammett looked around the bridge. Carruthers was focused completely on his own screens. Velasco sat at the next station over, staring at Hammett. *You're not much use in a crisis, are you?* Most of the bridge crew was watching him, and he made himself lean back in his chair. "This enemy may be unfamiliar," he said. "But a ship is a ship. We are all experts in naval combat. I don't know yet what that ship out there can do. But they're up against Spacecom's mightiest warship, and they are about to see what we can do."

It sounded hokey to his ears, but it seemed to work. Some of the fear left them as they remembered what they were.

Warriors.

"Before we blow them into scrap," he said, "is there any chance that their intentions are benign, or even friendly? Are we certain that they're hostile?"

"Three Gates are down," Carruthers said. "Port Albuquerque is silent, and it looks like the *James Joyce* was destroyed."

Hammett looked around the bridge. "Anyone else?" When no one spoke he said, "I'm inclined to agree with Lieutenant Carruthers. This is a hostile force. I think we are at war. I think all of humanity is at war."

There was a moment of bleak silence.

"We are going to protect Freedom Station," Hammett said. "And the Naxos system, and Earth."

"We should destroy Gate Six," Carruthers said.

Hammett said, "If we win ..."

"If we win, we can take our time getting word

back. But if we lose?"

If we lose, they'll sail right past our shattered hull, through the Gate, and pillage Naxos. Hammett nodded. "Lieutenant Singh. Get me the pilot of Shuttle Five."

There was a pause, and then Singh turned and nodded.

"This is Captain Hammett."

A young man said, "Yes, Sir?" His voice sounded only a little unsteady.

"Lieutenant al Faisal, is that you?"

"Yes, Sir."

"Lieutenant, this is important. I need you to send those technicians back outside. I need them to destroy the Gate."

There was a moment of silence. Then the pilot said, "I understand, Sir."

"What?"

Hammett looked up. Velasco was staring at him, her eyes too large in a bloodless face. He gave her a hard look, but it didn't seem to register.

"You can't do that! We need the Gate to get home."

"We'll get home. Man your station, Commander."

"Look, you can't destroy the Gate!" She looked around wildly, as if seeking support. "You have to call them back. You have to rescind your order." She stared at Hammett for a moment, and when he didn't move, she turned to her console. Her hands chopped at the air as she worked through menus. She was going to contact the shuttle directly, Hammett realized, and he stood.

"Captain?" came a voice over the bridge speakers. It was Kasim, the pilot, sounding regretful.

"Don't destroy the gate!" Velasco cried. "You can't!"

"I'm afraid that's not an issue," Kasim said. "I've got a little mutiny on my hands. The technicians have refused to disable the gate."

"Oh, thank God," Velasco said, and slumped in her seat.

Hammett shot her an irritated glance. He would have to deal with her, but first … "Mr. al Faisal," he said. "Please take your shuttle around to the far side of the gate."

"Aye aye, Sir."

"Make sure you can't see the *Alexander*. I'll be sending a missile your way."

There was a long moment of silence. Then Kasim said, "That might not work, Sir. Hang on. I'm going to connect you to Miss MacKinnon. She was willing to disable the gate, but the other two won't let her."

Static crackled on the speakers, and then a woman spoke. Her voice quavered, but it grew steadier with every word. "I don't know if a missile would do the trick, Sir. These gates are tough. They're designed to survive an accidental collision from a ship moving at a fairly high speed. The outer casing's titanium, solidly made. It's really hard to damage a Gate without opening the casing first."

Hammett thought for a moment. "I have six nukes on board. Would one of them do the trick?"

"If you managed a direct hit, yes. That would do it."

Hammett tried to imagine what would happen if the missile was just slightly off target. It would sail through the wormhole and come out in the Deirdre system. And what would happen then?

"Get on the other side of the Gate," he said, and gestured to Singh to break the connection.

The enemy ship loomed closer and closer on his screen. He was running out of time to consider his options. "Jim," he said, and Carruthers looked up. "Nuke that gate. Don't you bloody miss."

Carruthers nodded.

"Detonation on impact only. Let's not fry the shuttle crew if you do happen to miss."

"Aye aye, Sir."

He turned to Velasco. "Commander. Pull yourself together or get off my bridge. I won't tell you again."

"Missile's away," said Carruthers.

He desperately wanted to drop back into his chair and watch the progress of the missile. Instead he made himself stroll around the bridge, hands clasped loosely behind him, the picture of unconcern.

"Impact," said Carruthers. "I can see the shuttle, so the gate must be down." After a moment he said, "I can see debris. The Gate's destroyed, all right."

"Lieutenant al Faisal says the shuttle is intact," Singh reported.

"Tell him we'll be along presently to pick him up." Hammett returned to his seat. "Now let's deal with that ship."

CHAPTER 11 – VELASCO

Velasco stared, rigid with horror, at the image of the Gate on her screen. *Maybe it will miss. The Gate is so narrow. It's a tiny ribbon of metal, and-*

The Gate vanished. She didn't see the missile, didn't see an explosion. One moment the circle of silver metal was there, glittering in the light of the star Naxos. Then it was gone. The shuttle appeared as if by magic, a blocky white shape against the darkness of space, and she heard Carruthers say, "Looks like the shuttle is all right."

They're not all right, she thought. *They're stranded here, with us. With them.* She switched her display to the forward view where the alien craft was closing with terrifying speed. *Those are hostile aliens rushing at us, and you just destroyed our only escape hatch.* She looked at Hammett, who lounged in his chair, looking incomprehensibly calm and unperturbed. *You've killed us all, you bloody maniac.*

Terror was like a gibbering specter hovering around the edges of her thoughts. She wanted to scream. In fact, she was finding it very difficult not to. *I have to do something. I have to get a message back to Spacecom. Someone has to know that this lunatic is out of control.*

Radio transmissions didn't work through wormholes, and there was no way to send a message faster than light. The only way to contact Spacecom was to fly all the way back to Earth.

Maybe we can still survive. If we flee now, if we generate a wormhole and escape through it. She looked at Hammett. *But this idiot is flying us toward the aliens. Can't he see we need to go the other way? The man is unstable. He's insane. I should relieve him from duty. I should take command and get us out of here.*

She looked at Carruthers and the other lieutenants. They were hunched over their stations, totally focused on their tasks. *Will they support me? They have to. They would be idiots not to.*

"Commander Velasco. Commander!"

She jumped and looked around. Hammett was glaring at her, and she flushed. *How long was he trying to get my attention?*

"Did you hear a word I said?"

Velasco opened and closed her mouth.

"I'm going to need you to launch drones," Hammett said with an air of strained patience. "But not until we match velocities. Get ready to launch on my command."

"Drones," she said. "Right." She looked down at her console, feeling some of her terror recede. *It's too late to run. We'll have to fight our way out of here. But we have hundreds of drones. We'll win this fight. We have to.*

The *Alexander* had changed course, she saw. The ship was moving laterally, putting itself between the enemy craft and Freedom Station. *You idiot. We could run away while they're busy with the station.* Her finely-tuned political instincts told her not to make the suggestion out loud. *It's too late to run. We'll fight. Focus on making sure we win.*

With that in mind she hit the icon for the console's main menu. Lines of text and translucent buttons appeared all around her, projected on her retinas. She found a red-outlined box labelled "Tactical Menu" and touched it.

The display around her changed. Now she saw menus for weapons, targeting, and damage reports. She had last looked at this interface in the Naval Academy ten years before, but much of it was coming back to her. She poked the "Drone" icon and the display changed again.

The ship had two hundred and eight drones, and she selected all of them, queuing them up for launch. *We're fighting for our lives. It would be stupid to hold anything back.*

A tactical map appeared to her right, with glowing circles around Freedom Station, the enemy ship, and the shuttle. She quickly labelled the station and the shuttle as friendly, and the enemy ship as hostile.

She looked again at the icon for the enemy ship, now circled in angry red. It was appallingly close. Less than two thousand kilometers. What was Hammett waiting for?

As if reading her mind, he said, "Launch missiles."

Half a dozen fresh icons appeared on the tactical map. The missiles streaked forward, moving closer and closer to the circle of red. The alien vessel was moving almost as quickly as the missiles themselves. Collision was only moments away, and she held her breath.

One by one, all six missiles sailed past the alien ship. There were no impacts, no explosions.

Hammett said, "Dammit, Jim ..."

"Still not responding, Captain," Carruthers said. "I can't explain it."

"Launch the nuke," Hammett said. "Velasco. Launch drones."

"Missile away," said Carruthers. Velasco slashed a hand through the launch icon and watched as new icons erupted onto the map.

"You launched them all?" Hammett said, sounding startled. He gave her a considering look and said, "Probably for the best."

She set the drones on full autonomous mode, and set the stance to highly aggressive. A cloud of tiny icons surged across the tactical map, making the *Alexander* look suddenly small and alone. Velasco reached out with her hand, swiping across a couple of dozen drones to select them. She switched those drones to defensive stance, and watched as they hurried back to hover around the *Alexander*. *If a hundred and ninety or so drones won't do it, the rest won't help. This way we're ready if they surprise us.*

"The nuke just stopped responding," Carruthers reported. "Eight hundred kilometers from the bogey, same as the other missiles." He checked a screen. "We'll be within that range in about a minute."

On the tactical map the enemy ship seemed to crumble, and Velasco felt a surge of hope. *The nuke must have exploded*! When she glanced around the bridge, though, she saw only grim concentration on the faces around her. *It's reconfiguring,* she realized. T*hey all bunched together to share thrust, and now they're breaking apart to make smaller targets.*

A course of beeps sounded in Velasco's ear through her implants, and she watched a wave of color change wash through the cloud of drones on the tactical map. The projected ships lost some resolution, too, becoming a bit fuzzy. She poked a finger into the cloud, selecting a drone at random, and read the status message.

"They're dead in space," she said, feeling a cold chill wash across her skin. "No transponders. I'm getting nothing back at all."

Carruthers said, "Thirty seconds until we're in range of ... whatever it is that's happening."

Hammett snapped, "Get the rest of those drones back on board." He touched a button on the arm of his chair. "All hands. Prepare for a possible immediate loss of power."

Velasco made quick, urgent gestures with her hands, herding her drones closer to the launch tubes. She stared helplessly at the menus for a moment, her mind filled with swirling panic, then pressed the heels of her hands to her temples. *Come on. You know how to do this. The button is right there, you just can't see it.*

She lowered her hands. There was the recall command, hovering in the air beside her. She poked the button and the surviving drones swarmed around the launch tubes. One after another they popped back into the ship, guided by force field beams from the *Alexander*.

Nine drones were back on board when static howled in her ears. Pain filled her skull, and she screamed, clapping her hands to the sides of her head. The deck dropped away beneath her, she squeezed her eyes shut, and the pain and noise vanished.

Velasco opened her eyes. She saw a moment of blackness, felt her stomach heave in reaction to zero gravity, and then emergency lights came on around the bridge. Gravity came next, a couple of seconds of gentle pull that let her get her feet under her, and then full gravity a moment later.

The tactical map was gone. She tried to bring it back up, but the menu didn't even appear on her implants. In fact, all her implant data was gone. She looked down and to the left, and the time didn't appear on a projected readout. She looked to the far left.

No menus.

She hadn't been without a data connection

since puberty. Velasco shook her head, unable to believe what was happening.

"Oh my God." Her implants were completely dead.

CHAPTER 12 – HAMMETT

Shock crashed over Hammett in an icy wave. Every screen on the bridge was blank. All his tactical and sensor projections were gone. He was blind, crippled, helpless.

Well, he could function without implants. His thumb pressed a button on the arm of his chair, and he said, "Susan. What's your status?"

There was no reply. Not even the usual beep of a channel opening and closing. He had communication with everyone in reach of his voice, and that was it.

That was when panic hit him. He'd been scared plenty of times, but training and experience had always given him something to focus on, something to do. Now he stood on the bridge of a crippled ship with an enemy closing in, an enemy he couldn't even see. And he could do nothing.

Nothing at all.

He froze. He sat rigid in the command chair, every muscle in his body clenched, his mind filled with a silent scream. His breath came in tiny, short pants, and he was dimly aware of pain from his arms and legs and chest and stomach as his muscles strained against each other.

A tiny corner of his mind scrabbled through thirty years of memories, looking for a solution, looking for something to try. Every day of his career, though, every crisis he'd faced and survived, he had used the same basic toolkit. A toolkit that was now gone. The ship couldn't maneuver, he had no weapons, he couldn't even see ...

Thirty years as an officer held nothing for him in this crisis. Instead, he found himself remembering his Academy days. The instructors at the Naval Academy had taken a sadistic glee in dreaming up bizarre, incomprehensible problems for the officer trainees to overcome. Those memories should have been blurry and distant, but the Academy had been an intense, life-changing experience.

He remembered an exercise in a shuttle simulator when he had lost sensors, life support, basic navigation, and lateral control. He remembered the voice of an instructor lecturing him from the cockpit speakers. He couldn't remember the woman's name, but he remembered her voice. "Never mind what you've lost! You can spend the rest of your life thinking about what you used to have. It'll be about five minutes, by the way. Think about what you've got.

What are your resources right now? What do you have? What can you use?"

He'd survived that exercise, getting his bearings from the view out the front window and bringing the shuttle in for a hard emergency landing. There was no window here, though, and nowhere to land.

I should step aside and let one of the cadets take command. They don't have thirty years of irrelevant experience in the way. They can still think outside the grid.

Well, we do have a lot of cadets on board. Dozens of them, in fact. Running around in the corridors or huddled at their duty stations, on the verge of panic and contributing nothing at all.

His muscles seemed to release him all at once, and he took his first deep breath. He could see nothing but Singh's face, puckered with worry, peering back at him. It was a classic symptom of extreme stress. A person in duress developed tunnel vision. He knew it from his training, but he'd never experienced it before.

As panic released its grip the bridge seemed to appear from a grey mist. He looked around. Nearly everyone was staring at him.

"Cadet!" The kid was probably in plain sight, but Hammett couldn't see him. "Where the hell's that cadet?"

"Right here, Sir." The voice was a frightened squeak.

Hammett looked around until he spotted the kid, a frightened-looking youngster standing rigid beside the helm station. Hammett pointed at him, and the kid's eyes went wide. "You're going to be my new communication network. The first thing we need is more bodies. Go find me more cadets. Send some to the bridge. Eight or ten." He thought furiously. "Send some to engineering. And the missile bay. Medical bay as well." When the cadet just stood and stared he barked, "Go! Move!"

The cadet fled, and Hammett stood, pacing around the bridge to burn some of his adrenalin. "Does anyone have a functioning station? Anyone's implants still working?" He already knew the answer. He just needed the crew to see him doing something. He needed to look as if he was still in charge while he took time to think.

Running footsteps thumped in the corridor outside, growing louder as someone came closer. A cadet appeared in the doorway, a young woman, badly out of breath. "Cadet Sm-"

"Find a laser battery," Hammett interrupted. "If you pass any more cadets, tell them the same thing. You're going to man the laser battery. The targeting system won't work. You'll find your targets visually, and fire manually. Shoot everything that looks alien."

The cadet gaped at him, then started to turn away. More feet thumped in the corridor outside, and she retreated into the bridge as three more cadets filled the doorway. Hammett repeated his instructions.

"But-" The speaker was a chunky young man with a red face. "We're not trained for this! We've never done it before."

"None of us are," said Hammett. "Nobody gets

trained on how to function in a ship that's lost every computer-controlled system." He made sure his voice carried to every corner of the bridge. "None of us trained for an alien invasion. None of us trained for whatever weapon it is that incapacitated us." He turned to survey the bridge. "But we're all professionals, and we'll cope." He turned back to the cadets. "You cadets have an advantage. You're fresh out of school. You're not set in your ways, like we are. You've been trained to be flexible, to think on your feet. And that's what we need right now. People who are quick. Nimble. People who don't panic."

They were nodding, straightening up, losing some of the lost, fearful look in their eyes.

"We've lost our computerized systems. We've lost our implants. But there's more to this ship than the computer, and there's more to us than our personal electronics. This ship has twelve laser batteries, which means twelve lucky cadets get to take a direct shot at the enemy. Now get moving, and kill me some enemy ships."

The doorway emptied in an instant, footsteps fading in the distance. More footsteps came closer, then stopped, and Hammett heard the chunky cadet say, "You two come with me. I'll explain on the way."

The bridge went silent, but the air of desperation was gone. They were thinking about solutions now. They were thinking about what they could do.

"I notice we're still alive," said Carruthers. "Do you think they're being careful? Creeping up on us? Wondering if we still have any teeth?"

Singh said, "Maybe they know we're helpless. Maybe they're focusing on the station."

That would buy them some time, Hammett reflected, but he hated to think what would happen to the civilians.

"Cadet Rogers reporting, Sir."

Hammett looked at the doorway. "The next time I see you, Rogers, you'd better be out of breath."

The cadet blanched.

"Run to the engine room. Tell Lieutenant Rani that I need a good engineer to meet me in the missile bay right away."

Rogers ran out, shouting, "Aye aye, Sir," over his shoulder.

"Velasco. You're in charge here. You won't have much to do except coordinate information." He looked at Carruthers. "Jim, I want you to visit every laser battery and make sure they're all manned. After that, use your own judgment. Try to make yourself useful." He looked at the others. "We can't really do much from the bridge. A couple of you stay and help Velasco. The rest of you, pick a section and go see what's going on. Keep my ship functioning. Do all the things I haven't thought of yet."

He made himself smile. "Every one of you has earned that uniform you wear. I know I can rely on you. I'll be in the missile bay, preparing a nasty surprise."

He hurried out of the bridge.

CHAPTER 13 – KASIM

There was silence in the shuttle. Kasim hadn't repressurized the interior. He wanted everyone suited up in case of an attack and a hull breach. They had the suit radios turned off, though, for fear of attracting attention. The shuttle was powered down, just another chunk of debris giving off very little in the way of light or heat.

Without instruments there was no way to tell how the battle was progressing. The *Alexander* was a tiny point of light, stripped of detail. Kasim couldn't see the enemy ship at all.

The lack of communications was a mercy. Without radios or air the technicians couldn't ask him what he was going to do. The truth was, Kasim had no idea. He was terrified to do anything. Even powering up the shuttle might bring alien craft swooping in. But they sat where the Gate had been, an obvious spot to search for any pesky stray humans. *We should move*, Kasim thought. *We should run. We should hide.*

But where will we go?

His eyes strayed to the sparkling band of the Milky Way splashed across the void to his right. Gate Eleven lay in that direction. It was the one way he could flee the system. The shuttle would pop out in Aries.

Aries, which had gone silent several days ago. Aries, where the aliens came from.

Aries, where enemy reinforcements would come from if the *Alexander* managed to hold its own.

For a long time he sat there, staring through the cockpit window, grappling with the treacherous thought that was growing in the back of his mind. He told himself that it would be safer. He would creep away from the remains of Gate Six. He would take the shuttle thousands of kilometers to a place no alien would expect.

To the only thing he could hide behind.

To Gate Eleven.

"It doesn't mean I have to do something stupid," he whispered. "I'll just fly over there. I don't have to do anything at all." After all, disabling Gates wasn't his responsibility. Maybe all the aliens were already here. Maybe it would be best to do nothing at all.

"Oh, hell," he muttered, and turned on the shuttle's main power. "You wanted to be a real pilot, didn't you? You never wanted to be a glorified bus driver."

A hand closed on his shoulder and shook him. He didn't bother looking back to see who it was. He just turned on his suit radio and said, "We're going for a little ride. You might as well strap in. You never know when things might get rough."

CHAPTER 14 – HAMMETT

When he reached the missile bay, Hammett found a young lieutenant named Yoon on one knee beside the door, her arm buried up to the shoulder in the bulkhead. A cadet stood beside her holding a wall panel that trailed several wires. Yoon gave Hammett a distracted look and said, "I'll have the hatch open in a jiffy, Sir."

"Sure, Lieutenant. Just tell me if I can help."

The hatch gave a loud click and slid open a couple of centimeters. Yoon said, "You can grab the edge of that hatch and pull like hell."

Hammett did as she said, bracing his feet against the deck plates and heaving until the tendons in his wrists creaked. Yoon worked her arm free and took the panel from the cadet. The cadet tucked trailing wires into the bulkhead, and Yoon fit the panel back into place. A moment later they both joined Hammett, heaving on the hatch.

The hatch retracted, one grudging centimeter at a time. When it was more than half open Yoon said, "That should do it, unless you need to take missiles out into the corridor."

"Nope." Hammett let go of the hatch and straightened up, opening and closing his fingers.

"That shouldn't have worked," Yoon said. "I'm going to send a memo to Spacecom. It's a potential security issue."

Hammett didn't comment, just gestured for her to precede him into the missile bay. He followed, and the cadet brought up the rear. Yoon looked around, squinting in the low emergency lighting, and said, "Now that we're here, what are we doing, Sir?"

"We're going to tinker with a nuke," Hammett said. "I need it to explode on impact, with no electronics."

She stared at him, silent, and her eyes went out of focus. Hammett, recognizing the look of an engineer lost in thought, gestured to the cadet. The two of them opened a cabinet and pulled out the long shallow drawer inside. Naturally the pneumatic system wasn't working. He and the cadet had to brace a foot against the cabinet and heave with both hands to get the drawer open.

The missile gleamed softly in the dim light. Designed to be used in vacuum, there was nothing aerodynamic about the missile's design. It was built like an antique refrigerator, squat and bulky, flat on the sides and both ends. A single thruster nozzle projected from the bottom. Aside from that, it was essentially a featureless box.

Yoon pushed her way between Hammett and the cadet. "I'm going to need my tools." She rummaged in her pockets, produced a driver, and handed it to the cadet. "Here. Start taking off the top panel." She scanned the cabinets, tapped the front of a drawer, and said, "Captain. Do you mind opening this one? Have the cadet take off the nose assembly when he finishes with the nuke." Hammett nodded and she hurried out.

He got the drawer open with some difficulty, then helped the cadet lift a panel from the side of the nuke and set it on the deck. The cadet was just starting on the nose assembly of a conventional missile when Yoon returned with a bulky toolbox in each hand.

Hammett left them to it and set off down the corridor at a jog. He found three cadets wearing vac suits, helmets clipped to their belts, clustered at the intersection of two corridors. They had firefighting equipment stacked around them. He stopped. "What are you three doing?"

"We didn't know what else to do," said a dark-skinned girl. "We thought we'd find a central spot and watch for damage. We've got fire equipment and hull patches and medical kits." She gestured up and down the four corridors around them. "We can see and hear for a long way."

"That's good thinking," Hammett said. "However, I need you for something else. I need to launch a missile, and I'll have to do it by dead reckoning. That means I need spotters, and someone to run messages." He looked around, making sure of his bearings. "There's an observation lounge that way," he said, pointing starboard. "There's another one to port, but we're going to fire a missile from a starboard tube, so that's the way we'll have to look. The missile tube is on this deck and slightly aft. I'll need you to get a message to the missile bay as quickly as possible when we have a decent target."

The three cadets looked at one another, then at him.

"The missile can't turn," he said. "It will fly straight. The target will have to be pretty much dead ahead, or we'll miss."

The three cadets nodded as one and headed down the corridor. The girl said, "I'll spot. You run. In fact, go to the missile bay now and make sure you know the route."

A blond-haired boy nodded and ran aft.

Hammett followed the other two into the lounge. The long room was deserted, tables and chairs making an obstacle course in the deep shadows. Windows ran from floor to ceiling, and he walked up to the steelglass surface with a cadet on either side.

For a moment he saw nothing but stars. Then, far aft, he saw a flicker of movement. A ship was retreating from the *Alexander*. It had a strange – alien – design, and nothing near it to give it scale. It was maddeningly difficult to tell the size and range.

Then lines of crimson fire lanced out from two different laser batteries. The angle of the shots gave Hammett an instant sense of perspective. He was looking at a craft no more than a couple of hundred meters from the hull, a ship at most of the size of a one-man fighter. It was strangely built, with lumps jutting out in four directions.

As he watched, laser fire touched the alien hull. There was a burst of white vapour, and then a spray of some dark fluid. The little ship tumbled, then raced away into the dark.

"Good," Hammett said. "We're giving them a fight." He looked at the girl on his left. "We won't waste a missile on a dinky ship like that. We'd never hit it, anyway. Sometimes they clump together and form a larger ship. That's the target we want. Something big." He considered. "Anything big enough and close enough that you're pretty sure we can hit it."

The cadet nodded, and Hammett hurried out. He met the blond boy in the corridor. The kid had a fire extinguisher in one hand. He nodded to the captain without stopping.

Hammett was a couple of steps from the missile bay when three metallic clangs echoed through the corridor. He felt his stomach tighten, and he hurried through the half-open hatch.

Yoon looked up from a half-assembled missile. "What the hell was that, Sir?"

"I don't know."

He turned at the sound of running feet in the corridor. The blond boy stuck his head in and panted, "Did you hear three clangs?"

"Yes."

The boy beamed. "Great! Five in a row means open fire." He vanished from the hatchway, then reappeared a moment later, looking flustered. "Sir." He gave a hasty salute. "I forgot, Sir."

Hammett said, "You can waste your time with that foolishness when the battle is over. Now get moving."

The cadet flashed him a grin and disappeared again.

Yoon said, "Was I ever that young?"

"What have you got, Lieutenant?"

She raked fingers through her hair, leaving a shine of grease. "I need ten more minutes. Well, maybe five more after that to get the missile in the tube." She rubbed her chin, thinking, and left another smear of grease beneath her lower lip. "Actually, Sir, I could use three or four more cadets to move this bird." She reached over and tapped the casing of the nuke.

"I'll see what I can do," Hammett said, and squeezed his way out through the hatch.

CHAPTER 15 – JANICE

Janice Ling stood in an alcove in a corridor, her back pressed against a snarl of pipes and conduits, trying to stay out of the way. From time to time a cadet would gallop past, and sometimes a crewman or officer. None of them paid the slightest attention to her.

She'd been in the engine room, listening to a lecture from Lieutenant Rani, when all hell had broken loose. She had quickly realized she was in the way. Now she stood in a corridor, wondering what was happening, wondering what she should do.

Another cadet rushed past, then paused and backtracked. It was a girl, twenty at the oldest, with brown skin and straight dark hair. She looked the way Janice felt, as if she was barely holding panic at bay. "Do you know where the laser batteries are?"

Janice thought about it. "I'm pretty sure I do. Follow me." She felt a huge sense of relief at having something to do. She headed down the corridor at a trot, then climbed a ladder to the next deck. "They gave me a tour yesterday," she said. "If I remember correctly ..." She moved down another corridor, then stopped at a bright red line on the deck plates, marked "Authorized Personnel Only".

On the other side of the line a small hatch opened like the mouth of a tunnel. Above the hatch was stenciled "Battery Five". The cadet leaned over and stuck her head and shoulders through the hatch.

A man's voice said, "Hey, Lanny."

"Is there a battery that isn't manned yet?"

"I don't think so," the man said. "They want someone on the maneuvering thrusters, though."

"Where's that?" said Lanny.

"No idea."

Lanny straightened up and turned to Janice. "I don't suppose you know where ..."

"I think so," Janice said. "Come with me."

They returned to the ladder, descended three decks, and took a lateral corridor, heading for the port-side hull. A harried-looking lieutenant came around a corner in front of them and stopped short. "Cadet. I need you on the controls for Thruster Four. Figure out the manual controls, and then wait. The thruster is that way." He pointed, and she hurried away.

The lieutenant looked at Janice. "Come with me." He hurried down the corridor, and she followed.

"Where are we going?"

"Thruster Five."

She trotted along in silence for several more steps. Finally she said, "Why?"

"Same as Lanny," he said. "I need you to man the controls."

"What?" She stopped. He didn't, so she ran to catch up. "But I'm not trained!"

He glanced back over his shoulder, giving her a wry grin. "Lady, there isn't one person on this entire ship who's been trained in manual thruster control. It isn't something we do. We have computers for that sort of thing, after all. You know just as much about it as I do."

She wanted to protest, but it was clear the lieutenant wouldn't listen. And besides, did she really want to return to her alcove in the corridor?

"Here you are," said the lieutenant. "Good luck." He stepped through a hatch and vanished.

"Wait!"

It was too late. He was gone.

Janice sighed and turned in a slow circle. She was close to the starboard hull. Two corridors stretched away, one leading to port, one leading aft. The forward bulkhead was a mix of unadorned aluminum and plastic pipes. The starboard bulkhead, though, held a number of gauges, several dials, and a large handle marked "Do Not Touch". Janice stared at it for a long moment, then sighed. "I suppose I better pull on that and see what it does."

CHAPTER 16 – WEST

Mathew West sat alone on the stage of the Stardust Ballroom, a glorified lounge on Freedom Station. According to the clock he was supposed to be in the middle of his first set, but the room stood empty. Towering stacks of chairs marked the spots where the staff, in a panic, had abandoned their duties. He still didn't know what was going on. All he'd heard was rumors, wild tales of hostile ships swooping in through one Gate or the other. None of it made any sense.

He'd ventured briefly into the corridor outside, and found it jammed with panicky people elbowing each other aside without actually knowing where they were going. So he'd retreated to the stage, the closest thing to a safe place he could find in this unfamiliar tin can floating in deep space.

Jessica rested against his knee. She was his best guitar, a hand-crafted Patricia Stratton six-string, almost forty years old but the closest thing he'd ever found to acoustic perfection. She was locked securely in her case, the one concession he'd made to the apparent crisis.

From time to time an excited voice would harp at him from the speakers set in the ceiling. Some fool was shouting into a microphone somewhere, the volume overloading the system so that all West heard was an incomprehensible burst of sound.

He hoped it wasn't anything important.

If the crisis was real, he decided, he'd write a song about it. If not, he would write something melancholy about a man left behind on an empty stage while people rushed off to do important things. He hummed a few bars to himself, trying to piece together a few lines. *Outside, storms may blow and wars may rage/I'm safe here on my empty stage.*

A man stuck head and shoulders through the doors at the far end of the room. He spotted West and said, "You have to get out of here, man! They're shooting at us. They already breached Deck Nine."

The man vanished before West could ask any questions. He swallowed, felt his ears pop, and frowned. For a long moment he sat there, weighing his options. Then he stood, lifted Jessica, and headed for the doors. He leaned his ample stomach against the door frame and leaned outside.

Instead of chaos he found the corridor eerily empty. That scared him, and he hurried down the corridor, imagining emergency pressure doors slamming shut and trapping him on the wrong side. He came to a broad staircase and paused, dithering. Voices shouted and footsteps echoed somewhere above, and he felt air moving past his face. The air was flowing down, which meant the hull breach, if there was one, was down below.

He lifted the guitar and hurried up the steps.

He found a dead man on the first landing. He stopped, staring. It was a skinny middle-aged guy, his head twisted at an impossible angle, his eyes staring blindly at the ceiling. It felt wrong to do nothing, but the man was beyond help.

West trotted up the stairs, panting.

A terrible thunderclap of sound came from somewhere far below, and the banister trembled under his fingers. The faint breeze against his face was suddenly a strong wind, and someone screamed up above. West muttered a curse and broke into a run, taking the stairs two steps at a time. He gasped for breath, wondering if it was the unaccustomed exercise or a lack of air.

He reached the top of the staircase and suddenly there were people everywhere, running from left to right. He joined the flow, his terror feeding on their terror. He wanted to ask what was going on, but he didn't have the breath.

"Evacuation," said a voice from hidden speakers. Either the acoustics were better up here or the man on the microphone had stopped shouting. "Make your way to the closest lifeboat. I repeat—" the speaker died in a burst of static, and West, with no idea where the nearest lifeboat was, continued to follow the crowd.

The corridor went dark, gravity failed, and his last step took him sailing upward. He clutched Jessica to his chest, his scream blending into the screams of everyone around him.

Gravity returned and he plunged toward the floor. He hit carpet, felt a stab of pain in his ankle, then grunted as his elbows hit the floor, followed a moment later by his forehead. Knees crashed against his ribs, and someone cried out as they tripped over him.

Lights came back on, and West heaved himself to his feet. He staggered, light-headed, wondering if it was anoxia. It was the gravity, he decided. It was on at no more than fifty percent. The pain in his ankle was fading, which was a relief.

Beside him a woman rose to her feet, crashed into his shoulder without seeing him, and fled down the corridor. He looked around, trying to get his bearings.

Flashing light caught his eye. There was a smart panel on the wall beside him, and it showed the words EMERGENCY LIFE BOAT in giant letters. An arrow flashed underneath, and he followed it into a narrow side corridor. A hatchway loomed before him, and he smiled, filled with a sudden relief. He could see "LIFEBOAT" stenciled above the opening.

He had one foot through the hatch when strong fingers closed on his shoulders from behind. Someone yanked him backward, and he turned, clutching Jessica to his chest. There were four men, burly and rough-looking, eyes wild with terror. The man in the lead, a thick-stomached man with hair the color of ketchup, tried to shove him aside, but there was simply no place to go. A fist crashed against West's forehead and he landed on his backside, halfway through the hatch. Grasping hands tore the guitar case from his fingers, and he cried out. Then fists and boots hammered into him. It was a mindless, frenzied attack, and he curled his arms around his head and drew his knees in, protecting himself as best he could.

A low buzz cut through the noise, and an electric tingle lifted the hairs on his arms. He looked up and saw one of his attackers flopping against the wall.

The buzz sounded again, then again. He recognized the sound of a stunner, less dramatic than it sounded in the vids. One man after another fell to lie twitching in the corridor. The one with the garish hair was still aiming a kick at West, oblivious to the attack, when one last stun beam caught him and he collapsed.

A man and a woman came forward, sturdy figures in blue coveralls. They filled the narrow corridor, working shoulder to shoulder as they dragged his attackers back to the corridor behind. When the last man was gone West rose to his feet.

A man stood at the junction of the two corridors, a slim, elegant figure in a business suit. He was in late middle age, with sharp, confident features. He held a stun pistol in his hand, and he said, "Mr. West. Are you all right?"

West nodded shakily.

"I couldn't let them harm you. You're a national treasure."

That was overstating things, but West said automatically, "Always nice to meet a fan."

"It was all for nothing anyway," the man said. "This lifeboat's damaged." He gestured at a red light blinking beside the hatch. "Come with me. We have to hurry."

West hurried after him, a figure in blue coveralls on either side. They had the corridor to themselves for a hundred meters or so. When they came to the next lifeboat station, they found a jostling crowd fighting for position. It looked like bedlam to West, just a hair short of a riot. He was sure that nothing short of liberal use of the stunner would bring the mob to anything resembling order.

His savior didn't raise the gun, though. He just said, "All right, that's enough." West, a professional musician for the last twenty years, knew a thing or two about projecting his voice. This man, though, could have given him lessons. His voice cut through the babble like a laser through tissue paper, and there was a moment of shocked silence.

"Form a line," the man said. "The next person who shoves someone gets left behind."

A big man turned, a belligerent challenge in his eyes, and the man in the suit looked at him. That was it. Just a look, from eyes that flashed with authority and righteous indignation. The big man had to be half again the man's weight, but he wilted like a scolded child. In moments there was an orderly line snaking back and forth, with people moving briskly down the narrow corridor that gave access to the lifeboat.

The man took West by the arm. "I want you on board that ship. You're a cultural icon. I won't have you dying here."

He took a step toward the front of the line, but West planted his feet. "I'm not jumping the queue."

The man gave him a hard look, and West almost gave in. Then the man nodded. "I can respect that. We'll wait our turn." The two of them moved to the end of the line. "I'm Dalton Hornbeck. I arranged for your visit."

West felt his eyebrows rise. Hornbeck was the administrator of Freedom Station, essentially the most powerful man in the entire star system. "Mr. Hornbeck. I've been wanting to thank you for bringing me all the way out from Earth. Now, though …"

Hornbeck laughed, then shook his head and grimaced. "I'm not sure if that's funny or not."

"Do you know what's going on?"

The administrator made a face. "Nothing good." He leaned closer and lowered his voice. "A Navy battleship came through Gate Six, and then, fifteen minutes later, we started getting emergency calls from all over. Three different ships and a research station either came under attack or just went silent. I know for certain that one ship was destroyed. Now the station is taking fire." He touched his ear. "The main data node is down, but I know at least half the station has lost air."

West shuddered. Sudden, catastrophic depressurization was every space traveller's nightmare. "Do you know who's doing it?"

"It has to be rebels from one of the colonies," Hornbeck said. "It's strange ships. Like nothing I've ever seen. Certainly hostile, though. They seem to have crippled that Navy ship."

West looked uneasily at the queue in front of him. More than a dozen people still shuffled along. He guessed he was a minute from the safety of the lifeboat. *Almost there. Looks like I'm going to make it.*

A metallic boom echoed through the corridor, and a woman screamed. There was a sudden wind, and West leaned sideways, planting his feet. One of Hornbeck's companions, the woman in the blue coveralls, staggered, and he caught her by the shoulder, steadying her until she had her balance.

He glanced at Hornbeck, and the man surprised him by grinning. "I didn't get to hear your show, but at least the evening hasn't been dull!" If the man was frightened he hid it well, and by the look of him, the idea of jumping the queue hadn't even crossed his mind. West grinned back. *We won't die screaming, trying to trample the people ahead of us. We'll die like men.* Despite a sick knot of fear in his guts he thought, *This is going to make a hell of a song.*

Step by step he shuffled forward, trying to

catalog every sensation, every sound and smell. If he lived, it was going to be the stuff of a legendary ballad.

The man in blue coveralls stooped and moved through the hatch into the lifeboat, followed a moment later by the woman. West glanced at Hornbeck, who made an "after you" gesture.

West ducked, then glanced one last time into Freedom Station. Hornbeck stood straddle-legged, the wind whipping his silver hair around his face, waiting stoically for West to get out of the way.

"So long, Jessica," West murmured. Then he stepped through the hatch and into the lifeboat.

CHAPTER 17 – HAMMETT

Hammett stood in the port-side lounge, fighting the urge to beat his fists on the steelglass in frustration. Every maneuver, every order, every communication took a maddeningly long time. His tactics were working, though. Cadet messengers had reported the destruction of half a dozen small alien craft and the damaging of several more. The little ships seemed to be pulling back now, out of the effective range of manually-aimed lasers. The actual range of the lasers was tremendous, of course. With a computer to assist in targeting, he could have carved the invading fleet into scrap.

Where the starboard lounge was laid out like a saloon, with tables and chairs and a bar along one wall, the port lounge was designed for quiet introspection. The only seating was a long couch facing the window. There was a telescope on a pedestal at one end of the room, and Hammett walked to it. He swiveled the cylinder around until it pointed at the distant gleam of Freedom Station, and pressed an eye to the eyepiece.

And swore.

A lifeboat filled his view, with little alien ships swarming around it like wolves pulling down a stag. He watched a chunk of the lifeboat's hull peel back and then tear away, felt his gorge rise as bodies erupted from the hole.

Beyond the lifeboat the station burned. There were gaps in the hull, and swirling walls of smoke where fires burned behind emergency force fields.

He tracked sideways, scanning the hull of the station. He saw a larger alien craft, perhaps half a dozen of the smallest ships joined together. It hovered a dozen meters or so above the station, playing a pillar of fire across the station hull. They seemed to get more firepower when they joined together.

A voice cried out somewhere nearby, a shout of triumph, and in the corner of his eye Hammett saw chunks of debris drifting past the window. The cadets were doing good work with the laser batteries. It seemed to catch the attention of the aliens. The amalgamated ship in the telescope broke off its attack, tilting and then surging toward the *Alexander*. Hammett felt a cold lurch in his stomach. It was worth it, though. A second lifeboat rose up behind the approaching vessel, then raced away into the darkness.

Hammett walked to the doorway of the lounge.

"Good shooting," he bellowed. "It's working! We're drawing them away from the station." A cynical corner of his mind wondered if that would inspire the cadets, or discourage them. They were good kids, though. They always were. You didn't take up the profession of arms because you wanted to keep yourself safe.

He returned to the telescope and watched the amalgamated ship loom larger and larger. More ships merged with it, until he left the telescope and found he could see it with his naked eye. It was coming up rapidly from the aft. If more ships really meant more firepower, it would be capable of fearsome damage by the time it reached the *Alexander*.

Would it be big enough for the missile crew to hit it with the nuke?

He was turning away from the window when the enemy ship fired. A column of scarlet flame stretched toward him, and he flinched back from the steelglass. Fire touched the hull somewhere below his feet, one or two decks down. Laser fire lashed out, and he saw gleaming circles of red play across the surface of the enemy ship. If the laser batteries were doing any damage, he couldn't see it.

"It's got some kind of shield," he muttered. "But only when a bunch of ships come together." Well, that was what missiles were for.

The *Alexander* shuddered, and a cloud of vapor momentarily obscured his view. When it cleared he could see wreckage, spinning and tumbling as it moved away from the *Alexander*. He saw jagged chunks of hull, a couple of chairs, and then the body of a cadet.

"Christ!" He ran to the doorway and bellowed, "Thruster control! Can you hear me?"

A woman's voice echoed down the corridor, barely audible. "I'm on thruster control."

"Fire now!" He didn't know which thruster she was at, and he didn't care. The *Alexander* needed to move.

He heard the hum of a thruster, felt the deck move beneath his feet. A glance over his shoulder showed the stars sliding past, the enemy craft falling away aft as the *Alexander* turned. It was enough to spread the damage around and save them from another hull breach. He didn't need the ship spinning out of control, so he shouted, "Cut thrust!"

The thruster hummed for several more seconds, then stopped.

Hammett could smell scorched metal and burned plastic. People screamed in the distance, and he heard running feet. The emergency force fields would not have come up, not without computer control. The automatic fire suppression system wouldn't work either.

He had a small core of experienced crew, though, and plenty of willing cadets who would pitch in to help. Someone would be patching the hole by now. Someone would be fighting the fire.

In the meantime, he had that enemy ship to worry about. Was it big enough and close enough to hit with a missile?

He was about to find out.

A metallic clang echoed through the ship, then another, and another. He imagined the blond cadet slamming that fire extinguisher against the deck plates. There was a fourth clang, and then a fifth. And then silence.

Hammett wanted to run to the starboard lounge. He wanted to watch the missile race toward its target. The ship was still turning, though, so he stayed where he was at. The stars moved past in stately majesty, and then he saw the alien ship.

Relief hit him hard enough that he staggered. Not much remained of the enemy vessel. A small alien craft, perhaps two of the smallest ones joined together, tumbled through the void less than a kilometer from the *Alexander*. There were other bits of metal, small ships ripped apart by debris from the explosion. These, he guessed, were outlying craft that had been coming in to link up with the larger ship. They had been shredded when the nuclear explosion had reduced the larger craft to so much jagged shrapnel.

Of the larger ship, nothing remained. Whatever hadn't been vaporized in the blast had been flung into the depths of space. It was simply gone.

The *Alexander* continued to spin, and the wreckage slid aft and disappeared from sight. What had the range been when they fired the missile? Five hundred meters? Eight hundred? What were the odds of hitting anything smaller than a space station by dead reckoning at that kind of range?

We were lucky, he thought. *We were very, very lucky.*

Without scanners it would be very difficult to tell how many alien ships remained. He saw nothing through the windows. Were they annihilated? He doubted it. Fleeing in disarray? Regrouping, and preparing for another attack?

Swarming Freedom Station instead?

He had done what he could for the station, Hammett decided. He'd given them time to evacuate. It was time to retreat from the battlefield and see if he could repair what was left of his ship.

"Hello?"

Hammett turned from the window and walked to the doorway of the lounge. A cadet stood at the intersection of two corridors, a familiar pile of firefighting and medical equipment near her feet. She peered in every direction and said, "I'm looking for Captain Hammett."

"Over here." He waved.

She trotted down the corridor and said, "Lieutenant Rani says to tell you she has the main engines working."

"Go tell her to fire them up. Tell her it doesn't matter which way we're pointing." There was very little to run into, and nowhere in particular to go. They simply needed to flee.

The cadet ran toward engineering. Hammett watched her go, collecting his thoughts. He would visit a couple of thrusters, and have the cadets make random course adjustments. Wherever they ended up, it would be impossible for the enemy to predict. He plodded down the corridor, deep in thought. "What we need is a destination."

A face appeared ahead of him as a woman peeked around a bend in the corridor. She was out of uniform, he was surprised to note. He didn't recognize her until she spoke. "How about Baffin?"

He said, "You're that reporter."

She nodded. "Now I'm your civilian auxiliary corps." She grinned.

"That was you firing the thruster?"

"Yup. Did I do all right?"

"You were perfect." He frowned. "What did you say before? About a puffin?"

"Baffin. It's a research and mining station on Kukulcan."

He frowned, irritated that a civilian knew more about the system than he did. "It's new, I take it?"

"They built it six or eight months ago." She closed her eyes for a moment, thinking. "There's only about a dozen people there. Most of it's automated."

It didn't sound like much of a haven, but it was all he had. "All right," Hammett said. "I'll need you to stay at the thruster controls. You're an expert now." He moved past her and headed for the nearest ladder. Navigating to Kukulcan was going to be just about impossible. Just getting the ship pointed in roughly the right direction would be a logistical nightmare that he didn't want to contemplate.

"If you see any cadets," he said to Janice, "send them to the bridge." He was going to run them ragged, but he was going to get the ship to Baffin.

CHAPTER 18 – KASIM

The shuttle drifted through the silent void of space, and Gate Eleven slowly grew before them. Kasim was using a passive visual scan only. Radar, he was sure, would be suicidal. The Gate was still too far away to see with the naked eye, but it glittered on the screen before him.

The cabin was pressurized now, and the four of them wore their helmets with the faceplates retracted. They would breathe the shuttle's air, and save what remained in their suits for an emergency.

A greater emergency, Kasim thought. Every second was an emergency now.

Sally sat beside him in the co-pilot's seat. He glanced at her, and she gave him a reassuring smile. He was deeply grateful for her presence. She helped keep him calm, and if she couldn't keep the other two from being frightened, at least they were too embarrassed to voice their fears in front of her. Kasim's meagre supply of courage needed all the help it could get. It wouldn't take much fretting from his passengers to push him over the edge into panic.

"When we reach the Gate, you'll have to get out there and disable it, and no screwing around." Sally nodded. Behind him, he heard Roberts mutter, "Yeah, I understand." Sanchez was silent, which Kasim took as agreement.

"How much longer, do you think?" Sally said.

Kasim was starting to shrug when Sanchez said, "Can't we use the engines? I just want it to be over."

"He can't use the engine," Roberts said irritably. "Those other ships might see it. And the faster we go, the more we'll have to use the engine to brake at the other end."

"Ballistic, and slow," Kasim agreed. "That's the safest way."

"The safest way to do something suicidal," Roberts grumbled.

Kasim said, "We have to-"

"I know, I know," Roberts interrupted. "You're right. We have to close the Gate before more of those things come through."

"It must be rebel colonists," Sanchez said. "I mean, it stands to reason, right? No one's ever found alien life."

Kasim was pretty much certain it was aliens, but he said, "Sure. Stands to reason."

His console beeped, and he looked down. Sally

gasped, and Kasim felt a cold rush like ice water through his veins.

"What is it?" said Sanchez.

"We get another chance to figure out if they're aliens," Kasim told him. "There's a ship coming this way."

He zoomed in, careful to use optical cameras only. It didn't look like it would matter, though. An alien ship, one of the littlest ones, was racing in on an intercept course.

"Has he seen us?" Sally's voice was a breathless whisper. Kasim started to say "Of course," then stopped himself. The little ship could be on a standard patrol, or on its way to pick up donuts for all he knew. His fingers ached with the need to grab the controls, fire up the engine, and race away, but he made himself wait.

Without engines, radar, or radio, the little shuttle had to be tremendously difficult to see. Without radar he couldn't be sure how far away the alien ship was, but he guessed the range to be in the hundreds of kilometers. That was practically collision distance in astronomical terms, but what if the other ship was simply patrolling around the Gate? The alien might have no idea the shuttle was even there.

Unless Kasim did something stupid, like starting the engine.

Sally whispered, "What will they do if they see us?"

With hard vacuum separating them from the alien, there was no reason at all to whisper. Nevertheless, he found himself murmuring softly as he replied. "The *Alexander* went silent, but it wasn't destroyed. Its transponder and radar stopped at the same instant. I bet they used some kind of EMP weapon. Fried all the electronics."

Sally looked at him, wide-eyed.

"I guess that's the first thing they'll do." He squinted at his screen. "I bet we're already in range. So it's too late to run. If I start the engines they'll fry us." He tried to look confident. "Don't worry. I don't think they see us."

The console beeped again.

"What's that beep?" Roberts demanded.

"They made a course correction."

"Does it mean they saw us?"

Kasim gestured at him to be quiet. *It's not a patrol. It knows we're here. It's coming for a closer look.*

But it doesn't know. If it knew we were a ship, it would have fried us already.

Wouldn't it?

He had maddeningly little information, he realized. Guesswork and supposition, mostly. But one thing he knew for sure.

The enemy ship was coming closer.

So what can I do about it? If the shuttle had guns, I could put up a fight. Well, for a second or two, until he fried all my electronics. Or just blew up the ship, or whatever they do.

He's almost on top of us. What can I do?

The alien was directly below them, or he would have tried to spot it through the window. It had to be a good ten kilometers away, still too far to see without the shuttle's sophisticated cameras, but it was closing rapidly. When would it recognize the shuttle? How long would it take for the alien to react and fire its weapon?

Can I take it by surprise?

He reached for the controls, not actually sure what he was going to do, but trusting his instincts. With one quick motion he started the engines, brought the nose of the ship sweeping down, and accelerated hard. He activated radar, kept a thumb on the little red switch on the control column that would override the shuttle's safety protocols, and aimed for the approaching alien ship.

Acceleration shoved him back against his seat. The combined velocities of the two ships meant that he closed the distance in something less than two seconds. He didn't even have time to hold his breath before the little alien craft loomed suddenly huge in front of him.

He felt the collision as a tremor through the deck plates, the seat, and the control column. It was over in an instant, and the shuttle tumbled through space. Stars whipped past the window, and he lifted his hands from the control column, letting the shuttle's computer stabilize them.

"What did you do?" Sally's voice, shrill with fear, came through the speakers in his helmet. His faceplate was down. He looked at the dash controls.

Half the display screen was dark. On the other half he read a damage report. *Collision. Hull damage. Atmospheric integrity lost.*

"We seem to have bumped into the alien,"

Kasim said. "Sorry, the hostile colony ship. We have an air leak, but we're not badly damaged." He had a giddy urge to laugh, but if he started, he wasn't sure he could stop.

"What happened to them?" Roberts said.

Kasim checked his console. The alien ship was about a hundred meters to starboard, slowly drifting away. He zoomed in on the ship, and whistled. It was a crumpled mess, like a drink container someone had stomped on. "They aren't really built for collisions," he said.

He shut down the radar, then gave the engines a little squirt. If the alien had a transponder or an emergency beacon, he wanted to be a long way away when help arrived. He shut down the engine, then brought up a sensor log.

Quite a bit of information had come in during that brief few seconds when he'd used radar. He could see the circular shape of Gate Eleven, and half a dozen fuzzy blobs spread in an arc around it. He muttered a curse.

Sally touched his arm. "What is it?"

"They aren't as stupid as we hoped. They're keeping an eye on the remaining Gate."

She leaned over to look at his screen. "What do we do?"

"We can't keep ramming them," he said. "We'll have to avoid them." There was a bitter taste of disappointment on the back of his tongue, but also a treacherous spike of relief. *I took out an alien ship. I made a contribution. I proved my courage. We can't take out the Gate, but damn it, I did something.*

He checked the shuttle's trajectory. The collision had knocked them off course. Their new vector would take them past the Gate at a range of several thousand kilometers. With the least bit of luck they would sail past undetected. After that ... Well, after that he had no idea what he would do. Park somewhere behind the Gate, patch the hull, and wait for Earth to send reinforcements, he supposed.

He sighed, stretched to release some of the tension in his muscles, and resigned himself to a long, tense wait.

CHAPTER 19 – WYATT

Bennelong Wyatt, known as "Benny" to his friends, tightened his grip on the cricket bat and squinted down the pitch at the bowler. The harsh Australian sun blazed from a cloudless sky, and he felt a trickle of sweat between his shoulder blades. He knew none of it was real, not his dream team of the ten greatest Aboriginal cricket players of the last two hundred years, not the visiting team from London, not even the bat in his hands. But the illusion was perfect. He could have sworn he was back on Earth, standing on a field under exactly one gravity, in the middle of a close-fought cricket match in front of hundreds of breathless spectators.

The bowler took a couple of steps back, his arm went back for the windup, Wyatt felt a tingle of anticipation, and the bowler started to move.

And the entire world flickered.

Wyatt swore and let go of the bat, which vanished before it hit the ground. Everything went dark as he struggled with the transition between controlling his virtual eyes and his real eyes. Then he blinked and looked up at the ceiling of the immersion pod.

Another face looked down at him, a red-haired woman with her forehead wrinkled in concern. "Sorry, Benny. There's something really strange going on."

He nodded and sat up, feeling his head swim as it always did in the first few moments after he left the illusion of Earth-normal gravity. Kukulcan's gravity was just over 60 percent, and he needed a few seconds to adjust.

"We got an emergency message from Freedom Station. There was another call from the *James Joyce*. Now everyone's off the air."

Wyatt stood, keeping a hand on the side of the pod until he was sure his dizziness had passed. "What do you mean, everyone?"

"We can't raise Freedom Station, or the *James Joyce*, or Albuquerque." She looked pale and frightened in the subdued lighting of the game room. "It's not our com systems, either. Joey went out and sat in the runabout. It's the same thing. Everybody's silent."

Wyatt stared at her, baffled. What kind of calamity could shut down all the radio traffic in an entire star system? It made no sense. "All right," he said, heading for the door. "Let's see what's going on."

As he walked to the command center he found

himself wishing, not for the first time, that he wasn't the man in charge. As the manager of Baffin Station he was the man with full responsibility in every crisis and disaster. Sometimes he deeply envied his subordinates, who could throw their hands up in despair and hand things over to him.

The little command center buzzed with activity. Jarvis, his second in command, stood leaning over a technician's shoulder. Jarvis met Wyatt's eyes and sagged with relief. He made a beckoning gesture. "You need to see this, Chief."

Wyatt stood beside him and watched as the technician tapped at the empty air in front of her. An image appeared on her screen, blurred and shaking with distance. Wyatt saw the familiar outline of Freedom Station.

"This is a recording from the main telescope," Jarvis said. "It's from less than five minutes ago." It took about twenty minutes for light from the station to reach Kukulcan. The events on the screen would be just under half an hour old, then.

He watched as strange ships swarmed around the station. When a lifeboat launched, it was little more than a bright point of light that rose from the station, then veered wildly to escape as hostile ships pursued. A minute later he could still see the shape of the lifeboat, but the attacking craft were moving away, leaving it alone.

"We got a distress call from the lifeboat," Jarvis said softly. "It went silent. I think they're dead in space."

A plume of vapour erupted from the station.

They were losing air. Wyatt could see the technician's shoulders shaking softly as she cried. The recording ended and the screen went dark.

Wyatt looked at Jarvis.

"It's an attack," Jarvis said. "Either they don't know we're here, or they haven't got around to us yet."

Wyatt stared at him, trying to shake an overwhelming sense of unreality. He wanted to tell himself it was a hoax, an elaborate practical joke his staff was playing on him. The look on Jarvis's face robbed him of that sad hope.

"I want radio silence," Wyatt said. "Turn off the nav beacon. Don't send any transmissions. We can't achieve a single bloody thing by calling anyone on the radio." He raked his fingers through the curly tangle of his hair. "Bring in all the staff. I want all personnel inside the building. And load the runabout with extra water and air." They could use the little ship to evacuate perhaps half the staff. Where they would go he didn't know, but he meant to be ready for anything.

There was a brief flurry of activity. Finally Jarvis turned to Wyatt and said, "What now?"

Wyatt shrugged helplessly. "Now we wait."

CHAPTER 20 – HAMMETT

The *Alexander* rode its braking thrusters and fell endlessly toward the planet Kukulcan. Hammett was back on the bridge. Every bridge station was still dead, but the bridge was in the heart of the ship, which made it an ideal communication hub. Every few minutes another breathless cadet would appear with a fresh sighting on the planet. Carruthers would do a quick calculation, then send another cadet to one of the maneuvering thrusters to make a correction.

It was an exhausting way to travel, veering constantly back and forth as they tried to keep the ship on target. For eight long hours they had careened through the void, but the long journey was nearly over.

"It's a good thing the station isn't armed," Carruthers said. "They must be trying to raise us on the radio by now."

Hammett nodded. There was simply no way for the *Alexander* to identify itself. They had no communications at all.

Lieutenant Yoon paced along one wall of the bridge. She had done rocket racing in her youth, which meant she had priceless experience with navigating a ship by visual data and dead reckoning. She was probably the only person on the *Alexander* who had ever put a ship into orbit without computer assistance.

"I can't promise a proper synchronous orbit," she said, not for the first time.

"Just do your best." Hammett glanced at the doorway to the bridge as another cadet appeared. It was a girl, short and solidly built, slumping with weariness. Her hair stood up in clumps, and a mix of dirt and smoke coated her face. At some point she had wiped her eyes, leaving streaks of white skin that stood out vividly against the soot. She gave him a sketchy salute and said, "I've got the final roster."

For a moment Hammett didn't know what she meant. Then he remembered. An hour or two before he'd sent her to get a casualty count. That meant making the rounds of the entire ship and counting who was left.

"Forty-seven dead or missing," she said. Her chin started to tremble. "I guess the missing ones aren't going to turn up, are they?" She looked at him with haunted eyes and said, "That's forty-seven dead. Thirty-two cadets, thirteen regular crew, and two officers." She held up a rumpled strip of paper towel, marked up in grease pencil. "I have all the names if you want, Sir."

She looked down at the list and her whole body started to shake. She looked up again, and two lines of tears made tracks through the dirt on her face. "I'm s-sorry, I-"

"Cadet," Hammett said.

The corners of her mouth drooped and she lifted a hand toward her cheek, then lowered it. She looked exhausted, traumatized, and deeply embarrassed. "I'm sorry, Captain, I-"

"Cadet," he said again. She finally met his gaze. "You did a hero's work today," he said. "I can tell by looking at you. You fell into a situation that was far beyond anything you trained for. You rose to the occasion, and you did what you had to do." He stood and moved toward her. "Every cadet on board was magnificent today. Together you saved the ship."

She put a hand to her mouth. She looked on the verge of collapse.

"And now the crisis is over for the moment," Hammett said gently. "You've held it together until now. Now, it's okay to let go."

She looked down at the deck plates, and he saw tears splashed the tops of her boots.

"Keep that list," he said. "Keep it safe. They were your friends, and my shipmates. They died giving the rest of us a fighting chance. You keep that list, and when the time comes to honor them, I'll find you."

She nodded without looking up.

"Now go wash your face and find a place where

you can be alone. Take some time for yourself. Report back to the bridge when you're ready. But I don't want to see you for at least an hour. Preferably two. Understand?"

The cadet didn't look up, didn't answer. She folded the paper towel with trembling fingers and tucked it into a thigh pocket. Then she wiped her face with her sleeve, turned, and hurried out of the bridge.

Hammett returned to his seat, feeling a hundred years old.

Velasco came onto the bridge. She had washed and put on a fresh uniform, and Hammett frowned, wondering how he himself looked. "Report," he said. He had sent her on a tour of the ship to get status updates from every department.

"Still no rail guns," she said. "Lieutenant DiMarco has a couple of people working on it. He says he needs several more hours before you'll have manual control. The automatic loaders won't work, though. He says he'll need half a dozen people on hand just loading magazines."

Hammett nodded.

"The engines are good. The manual controls are actually really simple, so no problems there. We lost two of the port maneuvering thrusters. I don't know if they can be repaired. No one has even looked at them yet."

That was hardly surprising. The repair crews had far more serious priorities.

"We lost two laser batteries," she continued. "I had a look at both of them. Portside dorsal forward was completely destroyed. The gun is gone, and most of the hull plates around it. Central dorsal forward is in much better shape. We can't repair it, but we can pillage it for spare parts if we need to."

"The other batteries are good?"

She nodded. "Both missile tubes are intact as well. We still have four nukes and most of the conventional missiles." She paused, thinking. "Let me see. Every bay in Medical is full. Doctor Havisham is unpacking some spare diagnostic and monitoring equipment. She's hoping it might not be fried because none of it was turned on when … whatever it was … happened. She doesn't know yet, though."

"All right. Anything else?"

"Well, I visited the galley. No one was there. People are just going in and helping themselves to meal replacement bars. There's no hot water, but there's plenty of drinking water."

"I guess that will do for now." For the thousandth time he stared in mute frustration at the blank screens all around the bridge. How the hell was he supposed to fly blind? Yoon was a marvel, telling cadets how to estimate the distance to Kukulcan by the degrees of arc it took up in the sky. The faint vibration of the main engine died away as they stopped braking. Yoon sent cadets running to three different maneuvering thrusters as she tried to get the ship into a stable orbit.

"That's brilliant work, Lieutenant," he told her, and she gave him a tired smile. "Now we need to figure out how to get down to the surface." The

Alexander had two more shuttles, but they were not designed for manual flying. He scratched his jaw, noting that his stubble was starting to come in. "Do we actually know that the shuttles are fried?" He looked around the bridge. When no one spoke he said, "I assume they are, but we should make sure." Five tired-looking cadets stood in a line near the bridge entrance. "Anyone have experience with Delta-level craft?"

All five cadets raised their hands.

"Okay, whoever's next, run down to the shuttle bay and see if either shuttle will start." As the cadet on the end started to move he said, "Actually, don't run. It's not urgent. Save your legs for the next crisis."

"Aye aye, Sir." The cadet plodded out.

Hammett sagged in his seat, exhaustion tugging at his limbs. "We should get some food sent in here." He thought about it. "No, what we should do is rotate some staff out. We could all use a break." He looked around. "Yoon?"

"I'm not sure if our orbit is stable yet, Sir."

"All right." He looked at Carruthers. "Jim? Ready for a break?"

"That I am. But why don't you go first, Sir?"

Hammett considered it. "You know, that's not a bad idea. I knew there was a reason they made you an officer." He stood and started for the bridge doorway.

A cadet came running in and stopped in front of Hammett, drawing himself to attention. It was the young man he'd sent to check on the shuttles. Hammett said, "I thought I said you didn't have to run."

"There's a ship, Sir. From the surface. It's landing in the shuttle bay."

CHAPTER 21 – JANICE

The shuttle bay was a long, barn-like room with a high ceiling and one wall that was open to space. Janice wasn't sure why the force field at the end of the bay still functioned while every other complex system on the *Alexander* was dead. When she considered how many people might be killed if the field ever failed, she decided it probably had solid components and a lot of redundancy. Whatever the reason, it still worked. The little runabout from the surface had been able to sail right through and touch down on the deck.

A pilot had come up with two passengers, middle-aged men who looked almost as frazzled as the crew of the *Alexander*. One man wore reinforced coveralls with reflective stripes. The other man wore a pinstripe shirt, the equivalent of a business suit for an outpost is isolated as this one.

She watched as the two visitors filed back onto the runabout, followed by Hammett and Commander Velasco. She had no idea what sort of meeting would take place down on the surface, but it was certain to be interesting. Newsworthy, in fact. And she was going to miss it. There hadn't been any opportunity to ask permission to tag along.

Which meant, of course, that no one had told her she had to stay behind.

She stood for a moment, frozen with indecision. She hated to be pushy. Oh, she didn't mind annoying a politician or two, but she felt a sense of camaraderie with Hammett. She felt like part of the team, and she liked the feeling.

The hatch of the runabout started to close. Janice muttered, "Oh, hell," and started to run. She got a shoulder in the hatchway and the hatch beeped, then slid back open. The other passengers looked up, surprise or annoyance on their faces, as she clambered aboard.

There were only five passenger seats, and all of them were taken. Janice stood frozen for a moment, feeling a flush climb up her throat and spread across her face. Then she stepped over Velasco's feet, squeezed through a narrow opening that led to the cockpit, and wormed her way into the empty co-pilot's seat.

The hatch clicked shut behind her, and the runabout lifted off.

Kukulcan was a red-brown orb that filled the sky. She caught a brief glimpse of the hull of the

Alexander, and winced as she saw scorched and bubbled hull plates. Fresh patches showed in a breach the size of a small boardroom table, and a burned line trailed aft and down. Her stomach twisted. The damage was bad – really bad – but it had nearly been much, much worse.

The nose of the runabout tilted down and the planet filled her view. It had the crater-pocked look of a world with little to no atmosphere. The surface was a pale brown near the equator, fading to dark rust at the pole. She could see no sign of human activity.

Down and down they went, until the large craters showed a texture of many smaller craters. There had to be some atmosphere, because she could make out the striation of honey-coloured dunes beside the sharp, un-weathered peaks of a mountain range. The pilot brought the runabout in low over the surface, and for a time all she could see was the distant horizon and a black, starry sky above it.

Then the nose of the craft swung to the right and she saw a vast black dome looming before her. Five smaller domes surrounded it, all of them connected by a complex network of girders and enclosed tunnels. Rectangular buildings littered the plain all around, and she saw a robotic truck rolling along, following a pair of ruts as it headed out across the sand.

The runabout set down on the roof of a long, low building close to the ring of domes. There was a moment of silence as the engines shut down, then a metallic clatter as automatic systems latched a retractable tunnel to the side of the little ship. A green light appeared on the dash in front of Janice's seat, and the pilot said, "That's it. Welcome to Kukulcan."

The hatch slid open and Janice waited as the other passengers climbed out, one at a time. When the passenger area was clear, the pilot gestured to her. She extricated herself from the co-pilot's seat, clambered into the back, and stepped through into an accordion-style walkway.

She followed the others through a hatch and down a staircase. She caught a glimpse of enormous ore-processing machines off to one side before walking through a connecting tunnel into one of the smaller domes. The little group wound its way through a maze of cubicles and into a boardroom where several more people waited.

"All right. Welcome to Baffin. I think our first order of business is to figure out what the hell is going on." The speaker was the man with the collared shirt. He had very dark skin, and spoke with a distinct Australian twang. "I'm Benny Wyatt. I'm the station manager here. This is Peter Breckenridge. He's my chief of operations."

The man in the reflective coveralls nodded.

Another man stood. He was white, slim and middle-aged, wearing a very nice suit. "I'm Dalton Hornbeck. I'm the station administrator for Freedom Station." He grimaced. "At least, I was. Eighty-five of us fled the station in a lifeboat. If any other lifeboats escaped, they haven't turned up. I think we're the only survivors." He sat back down.

"I'm Captain Richard Hammett of the battlecruiser *Alexander*. This is my First Officer, Commander Velasco." He looked at Janice, and a hint of a grin touched his features. "And this is Janice Ling. She, ah, represents the civilian population aboard the ship."

Janice nodded to the group and lowered herself into a chair. It was entirely too soft. After so many long hours of stress she was going to have trouble staying awake.

When everyone was seated, Wyatt spoke again. "Mr. Hornbeck and his people arrived about an hour ago. I've already heard his story. Why don't you tell us what you've seen? What happened to you?"

Hammett gave a brief summary of the trip through the Gate, the appearance of the aliens, the destruction of Gate Six, and the crippling of the *Alexander*. He described the battle, the nuclear strike on the alien craft, and what he had seen of Freedom Station as the *Alexander* retreated.

"It's not completely outside the realm of possibility that we are facing human attackers," he told them. "However, it's preposterous to think so. There is no human technology that even distantly resembles what we saw today. We are under alien attack."

The others looked at one another and comfortably. No one argued, though.

Hornbeck said, "Why in the name of all that's holy did you destroy the Gate? You've robbed us of our only escape."

Velasco shifted in her chair. She didn't say anything, and her expression was blank, but Janice was suddenly sure that she agreed with Hornbeck.

"The Naxos system will be no haven for us if the aliens get there first," Hammett said flatly. "We can still get home. The *Alexander* has a wormhole generator."

"That will take weeks!" Hornbeck protested. "With the Gates we could be back on Earth already."

"That's enough," said Wyatt. "The Gate is gone. Let's focus on what to do next."

"You'll have to evacuate this facility," Hammett said. "We'll take you on the *Alexander*." He turned to Hornbeck. "We'll take your people as well. I'm afraid you'll have to leave the lifeboat behind. The *Alexander* can't take other ships with it through wormholes."

Hornbeck nodded unhappily.

"Where will we go?" Breckenridge said. "Straight for Earth?" He frowned, thinking. "I guess Naxos is closer?"

Janice said, "New Avalon." The words were out before she could stop them. Every eye in the room turned to her, and she swallowed. "New Avalon is the closest system to us as the crow flies. Or as the crow jumps through wormholes." New Avalon connected to Earth via Gates Seven and Eight. It was only fifteen or sixteen light years from Deirdre. There was very little at New Avalon – just some abandoned mining facilities, she thought –

so no one had set up a Gate to link it directly to Deirdre. New Avalon would put them only two Gates from Earth. They would be home in a few hours, once they reached the system.

No one believed her, of course, until they opened up star charts and checked for themselves. "Sixteen light years," said Hornbeck, and looked at Hammett. "How long will it take to go that far?"

"Eleven days, under ideal circumstances," Hammett answered. "The ship is damaged, though, and we've been having some trouble with the wormhole generator. Navigation won't be an issue. We can see the star and travel directly toward it." He scratched his head. "I would say, two weeks minimum. We should be ready for it to take three weeks."

The others looked at one another. Finally Wyatt said, "I guess that's the plan, then. We should leave immediately."

"Not so fast," said Hammett. "The *Alexander* is in rough shape. We need to do some repairs. And we need to rig some kind of internal communications." He described how they had used cadets running with messages to try to maneuver.

That set off a long technical conversation as Wyatt, Breckenridge, and the two officers talked about non-electronic communication systems. None of it made much sense to Janice, and she settled deeper into her seat, yawning. The low gravity on Kukulcan was really quite restful.

"Copper wire and telephone handsets," Wyatt

said. "It's really simple technology. An EMP pulse, or whatever it was that hit you, won't affect it for more than a moment. It'll give you immediate communication throughout the ship, and it's totally reliable."

"That sounds great," Hammett said, "but where are we going to get telephone handsets? That's, what? Nineteenth century technology? Where would we even get copper wire?"

"We'll manufacture it here," said Wyatt. "We have a Level III replicator, and a couple of million template files. Handsets and wire will be child's play."

"Really?" Hammett sat up a bit straighter. "That changes things."

That set off a fresh discussion about all the things they could manufacture that they might need for the journey home. In the middle of it Breckenridge called someone and gave instructions to get started on the manufacture of three dozen telephone handsets and two thousand meters of copper line.

"I need non-electronic detonators of some kind," Hammett said. "Some kind of fuse. I've got a lot of perfectly good missiles that are so much scrap metal now, because the electronics are fried. If I can make them explode at a set distance from the *Alexander* ..."

Janice found herself gesturing at the empty air, trying to activate the note-taking feature in her implants. Her implants were still dead, but the habit of years was hard to break. If only she had something as quaint as a pen and notebook! She thought of the cadets, running through the corridors, trying to recite reports or instructions from memory when they arrived. What if the telephones didn't work, or the wires were cut?

"Pens and paper," she blurted. "Or pencils, if that's easier to manufacture." Hammett gave her a baffled look, and she said, "It's a great replacement for half the things our implants used to do." She shrugged. "Well, an adequate replacement."

He nodded, and Wyatt said, "I'll add it to the list."

They considered everything from hand weapons to telescopes before deciding to stick with the essentials. Every extra minute they spent at Baffin increased their danger.

The meeting was breaking up when Hammett's stomach growled. He looked down, a startled expression on his face, and said, "What about food?"

Wyatt said, "I could call for a plate of sandwiches."

"No, I mean what about food for the next three weeks?" He looked at Velasco. "How much food do we have on board?"

She gave him a blank look.

"This wasn't supposed to be a long trip," he said. "We have about a week of rations. We lost a lot of people today." A momentary shadow crossed his features. "But we're taking on nineteen people from Baffin?"

Wyatt nodded.

"And eighty-five from Freedom Station?"

"Yes," said Hornbeck.

"We have about three weeks of supplies on hand here," Wyatt said. He looked at Breckenridge. "Does that sound about right, Peter?"

"Bit less than that," Breckenridge said.

"We didn't bring anything but the clothes on our backs," said Hornbeck. His fingers swiped the air as he accessed his implants, and Janice felt a pang of jealousy. Life without implants was driving her crazy.

"We could make it," Hornbeck said. "We'd be on about one-third rations." He patted his stomach. "We'll all be a bit thinner, but we'll survive."

"If all our supplies survived the hull breach," Velasco said gloomily.

"And if nothing goes wrong," said Hammett. "The wormhole generator operates on transduction coils. We have twelve of them. Each time one of them burns out, our distance per jump drops by eight or nine percent. And we're badly behind on our maintenance."

There was a long, gloomy silence. Wyatt said, "It's a problem, but I don't see what we can do about it. Where can we go to get food?"

Hornbeck looked from one face to another. Then, his voice slow with reluctance, he said, "We could go to Freedom Station."

Janice stared at him, shocked. *Freedom Station? Where the aliens are?*

"The station wasn't completely destroyed," he said. "Captain Hammett and his crew have done a lot of damage to these invaders. Until they get reinforcements, until they regroup, maybe they'll leave the station alone."

"Surely it's too risky," said Wyatt.

"The idea on its own merits has a risk-to-reward ratio that's unacceptably high," Hornbeck conceded. "However, food is not the only factor." He sighed. "There is a possibility – statistically not negligible – that the station contains other survivors."

That set off a babble of voices, everyone talking over each other.

"I assumed they would destroy the station behind us," Hornbeck said. He gestured at Hammett. "From what the good captain says, however, I must revise my estimate. It seems the hostile force broke off its attack almost immediately after the launch of the lifeboat, in order to prosecute an assault on the *Alexander*. Some of my people may not have made it to lifeboats. They may still be alive."

Breckenridge said, "Can we risk everyone trying to save some people who may not even be there?"

"There are other factors," said Hammett. "Other reasons to go back." The rest of the group fell silent, looking at him. "I lost a pilot and three technicians," he said. "And when I say lost, I mean that literally. I don't know where they are. I hoped they would see us leaving the scene of battle and follow, but they haven't turned up yet. They may be dead, of course." He shrugged. "In addition to four lives, they were in a shuttle with intact electronics. That could be quite useful."

Breckenridge said, "I don't know if-"

"There's one more thing," said Hammett. "Gate Eleven is still intact. If we can destroy it, we could delay pursuit from the aliens by several weeks. We could give Earth and the rest of our colonies crucial extra time to prepare."

That set off a fresh storm of debate. Breckenridge pointed out that, for all anyone knew, the aliens didn't even need Gates. Velasco declared that the *Alexander* had a duty to all of humanity to bring back word of the attack. It would be grossly irresponsible to risk the ship. They had to flee. Hornbeck talked about his duty to his people and reminded everyone that any delay in their journey to New Avalon would put them at real risk of death from starvation.

Janice didn't participate in the debate. She listened, and she watched Hammett. He sat with his eyes half-closed clearly deep in thought. Finally he lifted a hand, and the others went silent. "We're going back," he said.

A babble of voices rose up, and Hammett snapped, "Enough!" Janice wasn't sure how he managed to put so much force into one little word, but she jumped in her chair, and the others instantly went silent. "This isn't a debate," he said. "I'm happy to listen to your opinions, and I want you to always feel free to speak up if you have advice or useful information. However, the *Alexander* is a warship, and I am her commanding officer. The decision is mine. We're going back."

CHAPTER 22 – HAMMETT

Hammett stood on the transformed bridge of the *Alexander*, telling himself he wasn't horrified.

Communication stations lined the starboard bulkhead. Each station consisted of a mouthpiece and earpiece, each about half the size of a clenched fist, each attached to a copper wire taped to the bulkhead. The wire, coated in plastic insulation, snake across bulkheads and ceilings and in some places deck plates. Several cadets were busy taping down wires that posed a trip hazard.

"It'll get better," Breckenridge said cheerfully as he installed another station. "We'll drill holes, we'll put up brackets. It won't be such a mess by the time we get to New Avalon." Now that the decision was made to return to Freedom Station, he'd thrown himself into the task of refitting the

Alexander with real enthusiasm.

Each telephone station had the name of the other terminal painted on the bulkhead above it. No one had used stencils. The words were a messy scrawl, but Hammett could read them. He went to the station labelled "Engine Room", picked up the mouthpiece and earpiece, and stared at them for a moment, trying to figure out which was which. Finally he held one piece to his mouth, one to his ear, and said, "Bridge to engine room."

"This is Cadet Burke." The voice was tinny, with a low hum of static in the background, but Hammett could understand the words.

"This is Captain Hammett. What's your status?"

"We're standing by," the cadet announced.

"Great," said Hammett. "Bridge out." There was no way to close the connection. It was, in effect, always open. A little metal bracket held the wires to the wall, and Hammett lowered the two components until they dangled from their wires. He shook his head, marvelling at the primitive simplicity of it all.

A cadet came bustling up. He thought it might have been the girl who had gathered the casualty list. She was transformed now, looking scrubbed and rested and ready for anything. "All laser batteries are manned, Sir," she announced.

"Thank you, Cadet." He didn't add that, if all went well, they would cross off four names from that grim list. He didn't want her thinking about the dead.

"Ms. Cartwright," he said.

A woman of forty or so looked up from what had once been the weapons station. She wore a sailor's uniform, and she looked frightened. She was his new helmsman. Yoon could have done the job better, but he wanted her in the missile bay, installing fuses.

"Bring us around and point us at Freedom Station," Hammett said.

Cartwright gulped and nodded. She had two telephone terminals at her station. One terminal linked her to all of the navigational thrusters. The other terminal linked her to spotters at four different windows. She picked up a mouthpiece and said, "Thruster One, three-second burn. Thruster Five, four-second burn."

Hammett felt the ship begin to move, and he nodded his approval before turning away. She would work more effectively without him watching her.

Once the ship was oriented he would give the order to start the main engines. Then there would be nothing but a long, tense three-hour wait as they flew back into the crucible.

CHAPTER 23 – KASIM

The air in the shuttle was getting foul. Kasim had changed the filter in the CO_2 scrubber, but it didn't put oxygen back into the air. He floated in the middle of the cabin, looking at the rack of spare oxygen tanks for the suits. He could open a tank. It would improve things, but he wanted to hold the suit tanks in reserve. He was panting, but not yet anoxic. He decided he would wait a little longer.

"Something's happening," said Sanchez. He'd insisted on watching the cockpit displays. It gave the boy an outlet for his nerves, so Kasim allowed it. Now, perhaps it was paying off.

Kasim pulled his way into the cockpit and went to the co-pilot's seat. Blurry shapes moved on the console. The alien ships that hovered around Gate Eleven were moving, heading toward Freedom Station and the place where Gate Six had been.

Sanchez looked at him. "What you think it means?"

Kasim shrugged. "There's no way to tell." He gestured at the passenger area. "Scram. I want my seat back."

Sanchez didn't move. "What are you going to do?"

"I'm going to wait until those ships disappear from the screen. I'm hoping that if we can't see them, they can't see us."

"Okay." Sanchez gave him a suspicious look. "Then what?"

"Then I'm going to move us closer to the Gate." Sanchez looked alarmed. "I'm going to put us right behind it," Kasim said. "It's the only place I know we can't be seen." He didn't add that he was going to have them destroy that Gate if he had to shove Sanchez bodily through the hatch. One battle at a time. Just having the ship move was all the stress Sanchez could handle at the moment.

Sanchez reluctantly moved into the back, and Kasim switched seats. The enemy ships grew ever more indistinct on the screen, and finally faded completely. Kasim made himself wait another minute, then two. Finally he couldn't control his impatience. For all he knew, reinforcements were about to come through the Gate. He needed to get on with things.

"I'm powering up," he called, and heard a rustle as everyone got their feet close to the floor. He turned on main power, and felt artificial gravity settle onto him. He heard a thump and a grunt from the back as someone was caught off-balance.

He headed for the Gate, moving quickly.

When the ship had a good velocity he cut the engine, then checked the screen. Not a single blip showed.

"Looks like we're free and clear," he said, and turned in his chair. Flying was the easy part. The difficult part was about to begin. "We'll reach the Gate in about five minutes."

"Forget it," said Roberts.

"I haven't even said anything!"

"You want us to disable the Gate."

"It'll keep the aliens away," Kasim said.

"The aliens are already here," said Roberts. "Enough of them to destroy Freedom Station and send the *Alexander* running for its life. If we mess with the Gate, they'll know we're here."

Kasim looked to Sally for support. "I don't know," she said.

"I think he's right," said Sanchez. That was hardly surprising – until Kasim looked at him. Sanchez was speaking to Roberts. "It's our duty," he said. "These aliens, whatever they are, they are attacking all of humanity. And we can slow them down."

Kasim stared at Sanchez. So did the other technicians. All of them were speechless.

"I don't know," said Sally again. "What if it draws them in? What will they do to us?"

"We don't even know that there *are* any more aliens," Roberts said. "Maybe this is all of them. Maybe destroying the Gate will stop them from retreating."

Kasim let the three of them bicker, turning his

attention back to the controls. The Gate loomed before him, and he brought the ship around in a beautiful, sweeping arc that not one of his clueless passengers appreciated.

"We're a small, unarmed ship," said Roberts. "We need to avoid their attention."

"I think it's too late for that," said Sanchez. Something in his voice sent a chill across the back of Kasim's neck. He glanced back. Sanchez was staring past him, looking through the cockpit windows with wide, frightened eyes.

Kasim turned.

A single enemy ship sat directly behind the Gate. It was no bigger than the shuttle, but it was clearly a ship of war. Kasim's hands froze on the controls as the little alien ship spun around. He found himself staring at what had been the underside of the ship. There was a black circle on the hull of the little craft, ominous as the muzzle of a rifle. The black circle began to glow an angry red. Then a line of flame shot toward the shuttle, and Kasim heard himself scream.

CHAPTER 24 – HAMMETT

"Range to Freedom Station approximately eight thousand kilometers."

Hammett said, "Thank you, Cadet." Range estimate was accurate to within no more than fifty percent, he knew.

"The forward telescope reports that the station looks largely intact."

Hammett nodded, not sure if he was relieved or disappointed. He was deeply rattled by the ease with which the aliens had crippled the *Alexander*, and by the luck that had been needed to allow them to escape. He itched with the need to flee the system and begin the long journey home.

"Do we have a line to the shuttle bay yet?"

"No, Sir," said a cadet. He was going to have to start learning their names. They were all in vac suits, helmets clipped to their chests, which didn't make it any easier to tell them apart. He wasn't going to lose any more people to a hull breach, though.

"I need a runner." A cadet stepped forward, and Hammett said, "Go to the shuttle bay. Tell the runabout pilot he can leave as soon as he's ready." The runabout would head for Gate Eleven, where a sailor would strap a couple of bundles of high explosives to the ring. In the meantime, Hammett would dock with Freedom Station. Hornbeck would take a team onboard to gather survivors and food.

"Captain!"

Hammett looked at the row of telephone stations along the starboard bulkhead. A cadet stood at every station. One young man held an earpiece to his ear in a white-knuckled grip. "Port lounge reports enemy activity near Gate Eleven." He listened, then said, "How big?" He lowered the mouthpiece and said, "One ship. Very large. 'Bloody big' is the official size estimate, Sir."

Hammett swallowed a curse. "Runner!" A girl stepped forward and he said, "Go after that last runner. Stop him. Don't let the runabout launch." She fled, and he stood, pacing back and forth.

Cartwright said, "What heading, Sir?"

"No change," he said. "We can fight them here, or we can fight them beside the station. It makes no difference."

He wanted to ask if there was any sign of Kasim and the missing shuttle. There was no point, though. If there was word, someone would have told him. The shuttle remained lost.

"What's the status of my rail guns?" he said. He knew the answer; he just wanted to remind the bridge crew that the ship was much more prepared than they'd been for the previous battle.

"Lieutenant DiMarco reports all three guns ready to fire, with crews standing by to reload."

"Excellent," said Hammett. "It sounds like we're ready for this fight." His job was as much about maintaining morale as running the ship.

"The enemy ship is closing," a cadet announced. "I don't have a range estimate. Close and getting closer. That's as specific as anyone will be."

A squeal of static came from every speaker on the bridge, and a couple of cadets jerked earpieces away from their ears. There was a moment without light or gravity, and then light and weight returned. "I think we can forget about using the runabout," Carruthers said to no one in particular. "It's a big expensive brick now."

A cadet said, "Test. Missile bay, can you hear me?" He lowered the mouthpiece and said, "The phones still work."

"Excellent," said Hammett. "They should think we're helpless. It's time to give them an unpleasant surprise." He turned to Cartwright. "Bring us around. Point us right at those bastards." The gun crews knew to open fire as soon as they saw the enemy, or got word from a spotter.

It was a bizarre way to run a battle, Hammett thought. It reminded him of exercises he'd done at the Academy. Hundreds of cadets had gone charging through the desert of the Baja Peninsula, firing low-power lasers at one another. In theory there had been a larger strategy for the war game, but in reality is it been dozens of little battles fought on a very small scale by whoever was there. In this battle, each gunner was an army of one.

"Rail guns firing," reported a cadet, earpiece pressed tight to her ear. "We're hitting them. No visible damage so far. Now there's damage. Several ship components have been destroyed on the enemy."

"Missiles are away," said a second cadet.

"The enemy ship is breaking apart," someone announced. "Not a missile strike. It's separating into smaller ships."

"Missile crews are holding fire," said the second cadet. "They have no decent targets."

Someone screamed, the sound faint and tinny. It came from one of the telephones, Hammett realized, and he watched as a young woman pressed an earpiece to her ear. Then she smiled. "One of them shot at Janie through the steelglass. She's all right, though."

"All three rail guns are firing," said a cadet. "Mostly they're missing, but when they hit one of those little ships they destroy it completely."

"Taking fire and evading," said Cartwright. The observers in the two lounges and the small number of other compartments with windows each had a direct line to a maneuvering thruster. The standing order was to get the ship moving to keep the aliens from doing concentrated damage.

"One missile hit. One enemy craft destroyed, some others damaged by shrapnel. Damn. It looks like most of the barrage missed."

"Negligible damage to our hull so far, Sir," said a cadet. "Laser batteries have damaged several ships." He paused to listen, then said, "They seem to be breaking off the attack."

"Tell the missile crews to stand by," Hammett said. "They could be gathering into one big ship again."

Several tense minutes passed. Then a man appeared at the entrance to the bridge. He was short, but his erect posture made him seemed taller. He had a weathered face and gray hair cropped close to his skull. He wore civilian clothes, but Hammett took one look at him and knew he was ex-military.

"John Crabtree reporting, Sir." He addressed himself to Hammett. "I was with your cadets in the starboard lounge. We agreed that someone should come report to you directly, and save a lot of back and forth on your intercom system."

Hammett nodded. "What can you tell me, Mr. Crabtree?"

"The attack has broken off for the time being. The youngsters – pardon me, the cadets – tell me it's not as many of the bastards as attacked last time. I would estimate their numbers between twenty and thirty-five of the smallest ships, though some of them were in groups of up to four or five. I personally saw three ships destroyed and four more damaged. Now they've retreated to a range of several kilometers. The ships haven't clumped back together yet."

"Thank you," said Hammett. "Are you from Freedom Station?"

Crabtree nodded. "Yes, Sir."

"See to it that you join the party that goes into the station for supplies. You know the layout, and you keep your head during a crisis."

Crabtree didn't quite smile, but he looked thoroughly pleased. "Aye aye, Sir."

"It seems we have a respite," Hammett said. "I'm tempted to fly straight at them and continue the fight, but the truth is they're more manoeuvrable than we are." He looked at Crabtree. "Is that your evaluation as well, Mr. Crabtree?"

The man nodded. "We're like a bear up against a swarm of bees. We could chase them, but we won't achieve much."

"Very well," said Hammett. "We'll take advantage of the break they're giving us. Ms. Cartwright. Take us to Freedom Station at your best speed, please."

She nodded and murmured instructions into the telephone.

"Someone show Mr. Crabtree to the docking ring on Deck Two. And make sure the boarding party is ready to go." The plan was to send in Dalton Hornbeck and a dozen cadets. Half of them would carry food stores to the *Alexander* while the others made a quick search of the station.

"Remind them not to dawdle," Hammett called to the departing cadet. "We don't know when our friends outside might come back for another round."

"We came through that scrap okay," said Carruthers. "They're learning from us, though. They didn't give us any good missile targets this time."

Hammett nodded. The alien ships weren't fleeing in disorder like they had after the detonation of the nuke. They were waiting for something, and whatever it was, he knew he wouldn't like it. His only hope was to be gone before the hammer fell.

CHAPTER 25 – CRABTREE

Metallic clatters echoed through the corridor in front of the aft docking ring, and John Crabtree smiled. He was leading men into a hostile environment full of unknown danger, something he hadn't done in a very long time. He was surprised to realize how much he'd missed it. He'd been a Sergeant of Marines until the corps had been disbanded twenty years back. By that time he'd been well and truly addicted to adrenalin.

Now he was back in action, and it felt good.

All of them wore vac suits and helmets with the faceplates retracted. They would be able to move through depressurized parts of the station, or areas filled with smoke. The suits would also offer some protection if they were attacked, or if there was an accident.

A light over the hatch turned green, and he

turned to the crowd of cadets. He had no authority over them, but it felt natural to take command. "This is it. We're going to go in and move quickly. No one goes anywhere alone. If you're on a search team, you keep an eye on your companion. This should be quite straightforward, but we could encounter anything from hostile aliens to panicking civilians, so keep your eyes open."

He looked each cadet in the eyes. "We don't have any time to waste rescuing one of you, so keep yourselves safe. If you get hurt, I'm not carrying you back to the *Alexander*. I'm kicking your ass every step of the way. Is that clear?"

A couple of cadets nodded.

"The suit radios are fried. Once we hit vacuum it's all hand signals and charades. So keep your eyes open." The hatch slid open and Crabtree said, "Follow me." He headed into the station at a trot.

He was three steps past the hatch when he felt his helmet bump the ceiling. The station gravity was down. He glanced back, and saw to his annoyance that the cadets were handling zero gravity better than he was. He hadn't experienced null gee since about the time most of them were born, but the basics came back to him quickly. He got an elbow against the ceiling and spun along the axis of his torso. Once his hands were against the ceiling it was easy. He pulled himself along, ricocheting down the corridor, bouncing from walls and ceiling and floor as he went.

They came to a hatch, a red light on the panel showing vacuum on the opposite side. He pried the panel from the bulkhead, found the emergency handle by touch, and took a firm grip. "Venting atmosphere," he announced, and closed his faceplate. "Everyone check the person beside you." He waited a couple of seconds, and then pulled the handle.

The hatch popped open a hand span, and a sudden wind pulled him forward. The air in the corridor was gone in a moment. He peered through the gap, saw darkness beyond, and heaved the hatch open.

He moved through to the Sunset Deck, a broad enclosed plaza with restaurants and a promenade lined with actual living trees. They were dead now, he supposed. The glow of a dozen helmet lights didn't do much to push back the darkness, but he was able to make out a jagged tear in the ceiling. Stars gleamed in the darkness beyond.

"This way," he said. "Don't get lost." No one reacted, of course, and he chuckled as he realized he'd forgotten the dead radios. He launched himself forward, sailing along a couple of meters above the deck. He slid neatly between the stretching branches of a couple of trees, pleased at the accuracy of his jump. On and on he went, until the opposite bulkhead loomed before him. He brought his legs up, curled his body, turned, and bent his legs to absorb the energy of impact as he hit the wall. He got it just about perfect, coming to a halt beside the bulkhead.

Cadets sailed in around him. Most of them landed flawlessly, but one cadet hit the wall head-first. Another cadet landed feet-first, but bounced away and had to use a squirt from a compressed-air maneuvering jet to get back to the bulkhead.

Hornbeck was the only real civilian in the group. His borrowed vac suit was the same design as that worn by Crabtree and the cadets, but Crabtree had no trouble picking him out. The man had only the most rudimentary zero-gee skills. He clung to the branches of a tree halfway across the concourse. As Crabtree watched, the administrator braced his feet against the trunk and kicked off. He bounced from a patch of grass and floated helplessly toward the ceiling. He managed to stop himself at the junction of floor and ceiling, then worked his way cautiously down to rejoin the group.

Crabtree led them to a narrow service corridor between restaurants. He sent the others ahead, then paused to examine the mouth of the corridor. There was an emergency pressure door, he saw. It should have closed automatically when the Sunset Deck lost pressure. It had failed, like every other computer-controlled system on the station.

There was a manual override, of course. He found a small plastic dial on the corridor wall, marked "Emergency Use Only". He pulled out a metal pin that kept the dial from being turned by accident, then gave the plastic circle a good hard twist. Somewhere behind the wall a canister of compressed air opened, and the pressure door slid shut.

He followed the cadets down the corridor, watching helmet lights play across the walls. A cadet reached a closed pressure door at the opposite end, then tapped a panel beside the door where a green light glowed. There was air on the other side.

"Open it up," said Crabtree, then lifted his hands above his head where they'd be visible to the cadets at the other end of the corridor. He mimed a door opening, and got a wave in reply. There was nothing to hold onto, so he braced his feet against one wall and his shoulders against the other.

A bar of light appeared as the hatch slid open several centimeters. Air rushed in, a gale that sent cadets tumbling and bouncing. A couple of people banged against Crabtree, not quite knocking him loose. No one could hear him, so he went ahead and cursed.

A couple of cadets pulled themselves from the tangle and heaved the hatch open. They swarmed into the room beyond, and Crabtree pulled himself along behind him. While he was trying to think of a safe way to test the air he saw a cadet retract her faceplate. She didn't die, so he copied her.

He was in some kind of storage bay for the restaurants. Tables and chairs loomed around him in precarious stacks, and he saw bins of napkins and table linen. This was a part of the station he had never explored. He said, "Mr. Hornbeck?"

"I can guide you from here," the administrator said. "If your assignment is to purvey foodstuffs, come this way." He headed for the far end of the room, and six cadets trailed after him.

"Search teams, come with me," said Crabtree.

He headed for a closed door in one corner. It was a proper hinged door, not a hatch, and he twisted the handle, hearing the lock click open. Then the door slammed against him and he tumbled back, spinning through the air. A figure came at him, a burly man in a dirty jumpsuit with hair as red as tomato sauce. The man's face was twisted in a rictus of fury, and he hurled himself at Crabtree.

"We're taking your ship!" A wave of fetid breath washed over Crabtree's face. The two of them were still flying through the air, the man gripping Crabtree's upper arm with one hand, clawing for his throat with the other.

Crabtree hadn't been in zero-gee combat for a very long time, but his muscles hadn't forgotten a thing. He twisted his body without conscious thought, pressing his knees to the other man's stomach. He cupped a hand around the back of the man's head and pulled, and by the time they collided with a stack of crates the two of them had turned completely around. The man's back collided with the crates, and then Crabtree piled into his stomach, knees first. A fresh wave of stink hit his face as the air left the man's lungs.

By the time the man had his breath back, Crabtree had him in an arm lock with his wrist up high between his shoulder blades. Several more men loomed in the doorway, looking wide-eyed from Crabtree to the cadets and back again.

"Let's try this again, shall we?" Crabtree said. "You want to take my ship?" The man struggled, Crabtree lifted his wrist another centimeter, and the man yelped. "I'm thinking about breaking your arm," Crabtree told him. "Do you think it'll be necessary?"

"Sorry, mate," the man said hoarsely. "We was scared, that's all. You can't leave us here. You gotta rescue us."

"Oh, shut up," Crabtree said, let go, and gave him a little shove. He pushed the man up and out, which drove Crabtree against the crates but sent the man tumbling helplessly into the center of the room. He spun, arms and legs waving, every surface out of reach.

"You lot are drafted," Crabtree announced. "You're going to help Mr. Hornbeck and some nice cadets carry food out to the *Alexander*. If you work hard and behave yourselves, we *may* lend you vacuum suits and let you come on board. Now, how does that sound?"

"Great," said the man in the doorway. "We'll help." The man beside him nodded vigorously.

"How about you?" Crabtree said to the scarlet-haired man. He was drifting slowly closer to the ceiling. In fifteen or twenty seconds he would be able to kick off and get back in control of himself.

"Brilliant," said the man. "We'll carry your groceries for you."

"See that you do," Crabtree said, "or we'll revisit the question of breaking arms." He kicked off from the stack of crates and sailed over to the door. "Now, is there anyone else alive on board?"

The men in the doorway exchanged furtive looks. "I don't know."

"I take that to mean 'Yes, but we've been terrorizing them'." Crabtree shook his head.

"You've got me to answer to now. You act up again and I'll slap you down." He moved back from the doorway. "Now go make yourselves useful."

They found three families and a handful of station staff huddled in a laundry room, swathed in layers of sheets and blankets. Crabtree, covered by a vac suit, hadn't noticed the cold, but the survivors shivered as they emerged from their cocoons of fabric. "You're going to need those blankets," he told them as he played his helmet light across their faces. "That's something nobody thought of. Take it all with you, as much as you can carry, and follow me."

By the time he reached the restaurant storage room all the search teams had returned and the inner pressure door had been re-sealed. There was no food in sight. The five would-be bullies floated near the ceiling. "Your other people are taking supplies over to your ship," the red-haired man said. "Say they'll be back with vac suits for us." By the look on his face he doubted it.

Crabtree looked at his gaggle of refugees. There were seventeen of them, including a handful of children too small for any suit on the *Alexander*. Someone would have to bring over some emergency vac sacks. In the meantime, he couldn't even signal the others until they closed the far pressure door and opened this door from the outside.

How much food had they collected? How long would it take to ferry it all through the Sunset Deck to the ship? "Too bloody long," he muttered.

"We better hope nothing goes wrong."

CHAPTER 26 – HAMMETT

A tense silence filled the bridge of the *Alexander*. Every head turned when a tinny voice came from a telephone set along the wall. A cadet said, "Please repeat," listened intently, then looked at Hammett. "Something's coming through Gate Eleven."

More people pressed earpieces to their ears as other spotters called in. "The first batch is still hovering there," a cadet reported.

"It looks like five small ships have come through. Uh-oh. Five more."

"Get word to the boarding party," Hammett snapped. "Tell them to get back on board now. I want someone standing by to open the docking clamps."

"They'll come through slowly, until they're sure it's safe," Carruthers predicted. "Then we'll get a huge storm."

It was one possibility. There was no way to know what the aliens' strategy was. That they had a strategy, Hammett didn't doubt. I *need to disrupt it. I can't just sit here and react to them. I need to force their hand.*

"We have six cadets on board," the cadet announced. "They found survivors. They have to go back with suits."

"Forget it," Hammett said. "We're uncoupling now."

"Captain!" He wasn't sure who'd spoken, but more than one shocked face was pointed in his direction.

"We'll come back," Hammett said. "First we need to clean up the neighborhood."

Carruthers said, "We can pick 'em up faster if they're all suited up."

It was a valid point. Hammett said, "Send the cadets back with enough suits for the survivors. Then open the docking clamps."

"Aye aye, Sir." Thirty long seconds passed while Hammett tried not to fidget. Then a cadet looked up and said, "We're clear."

"Bring us about," snapped Hammett. "We're heading for the Gate."

Cartwright spoke into her mouthpiece, and Hammett felt the ship move. A faint hum and a hint of vibration through the deck plates told him the main engine had just engaged.

"Group One is coming toward us," said a cadet. "That's what they're calling the first bunch, the ones we already fought with."

Hammett nodded. There were no orders to

give. Shooting would commence as soon as his gun crews had a target.

He heard a distant sound, like fingertips tapping on a tight drumhead, and he knew one of the rail guns was firing. A moment later a cadet said, "Aft rail gun firing. Group One is dead astern." A moment later he said, "They're dispersing. Still pursuing, though."

The rail gun was a powerful weapon, but it couldn't be aimed. Well, with luck they'd hit one or two of the bastards with that last barrage. For the thousandth time he wished for decent sensors. Oh, to be able to see what was going on!

"About thirty ships have come through the Gate," said a cadet. "It looks like all of them are coming to meet us."

Good. They're reacting, which means we're messing up their plan. Whatever that is. Maybe we can keep fighting them piecemeal, not let them gang up.

"Group One is closing in!"

At almost the same instant another cadet said, "Group Two is at ten kilometers and closing fast."

"Five more ships have come through the Gate," someone said. "And five more."

After that it was like listening to an announcer describing a vector ball match. Alien ships swept in, moving quickly to avoid laser fire, and scorched the hull of the *Alexander*. When that did no significant damage, they gathered together into clumps of five or six. Hammett had Cartwright make random small adjustments with the maneuvering thrusters, so the *Alexander* was never a stationary target.

"Firing missiles," said a cadet. "Eighteen missiles fired."

Hammett winced. That was almost half their inventory.

"Wow," said the cadet, holding the earpiece back from her ear. "Lieutenant DiMarco sounds really mad." Hammett could hear a faint string of profanities coming from the telephone. That would be the last panicky missile salvo, he guessed.

"Direct hit to a cluster of five ships," someone said. "Another cluster was damaged by a shrapnel warhead."

A girl said, "I just lost the engine room."

The cadet beside her said, "My line is dead too."

"We've got a hull breach on Deck Two."

"Lieutenant DiMarco reports a fire in the missile bay," a cadet reported. He shook the earpiece, pressed it to his ear, and said, "My line is dead."

Hammett made himself lean back in his seat, hiding his dismay. The ship was in real trouble. They might still fight their way free, though. It was a close match, but the *Alexander* was putting up a good fight. There was still hope ...

"Oh my God." Hammett looked at a white-faced cadet in the line of telephone stations. She said, "Forward telescope reports more aliens coming through the Gate. Hundreds of them."

CHAPTER 27 – KASIM

The shuttle burned.

Kasim floated, completely disoriented, watching smoke swirl against his face plate. His whole body hurt. He had a vague, distant sense of urgency, but he couldn't remember what he had to do. Well, he was wearing a suit, and suits had radios. He cleared his throat, then said, "Can anybody hear me?"

There was no response. Not only that, but he didn't hear the usual hum of static from the voice-activated mic. *Wait. Didn't we turn our radios off? Because of the aliens ...* He started to reach for the radio switch, and hesitated. *The aliens might hear.*

Something bumped his arm, and he put out a hand. He felt a lumpy shape and explored it absently with his fingers. It felt almost like a person. There was only one arm, though. One entire shoulder and part of the chest was missing.

When the full horror of it penetrated his consciousness he flinched and shoved the body away. That sent him floating backward until his head hit a bulkhead. Waves of pain lashed through his skull, and he moaned. He couldn't see a thing through the smoke. There was no way to clear the smoke, though. If he vented the atmosphere ...

He would lose nothing but air that was too polluted to breathe. If any of the technicians still lived, they had their suits sealed. Otherwise they would have asphyxiated by now.

He took his time, examining the thought from every angle. He didn't want to kill anyone by accident. Concentration was difficult through the pain and a strange mental fogginess, but he finally decided he was right.

He needed to pop the hatch.

The endless swirling smoke distracted him, so he squeezed his eyes shut and worked by touch. The familiar interior of the shuttle was impossibly strange in the darkness, and it took him an endless time to orient himself. At last he found the outline of the hatch. His questing fingertips found the control panel, and he pressed a thumb against the safety override. That allowed him to grab the release handle, twist, and push.

He felt a brief tug as smoke-laden air rushed past him. He opened his eyes and turned to survey the remains of the shuttle.

A corpse floated past him, the faceplate obscured by blood. He watched, frozen in horror, as the body drifted through the open hatch and out into space. A gibbering voice in his head told him he should secure the body, but he couldn't make himself move.

A hand appeared in the corner of his eye, and he flinched away. Then he took a closer look, and his stomach convulsed. He swallowed hard, fighting an overpowering urge to vomit.

A glove floated in the void beside him. A vac suit glove, with a wrist and several centimeters of arm attached.

With a convulsive motion he reached out, batted at the glove, and sent it tumbling out of the shuttle.

He looked through the rest of the ship. Roberts sat in a passenger seat, staring straight ahead. Kasim touched his shoulder, and the technician floated sideways, his body limp. Kasim leaned in close and peered through the man's face plate.

Roberts was dead. His eyes were wide open, staring blindly straight ahead. Kasim watched the bottom edge of his face plate, waiting for a telltale mist to appear as the man breathed. After thirty long seconds he gave up.

There was no one else in the passenger compartment.

Kasim stuck his head and shoulders into the cockpit. Most of the steelglass window was gone, the edges melted and twisted. The co-pilot's seat was a charred mess. He could see the faint shimmer of an emergency force field where the window had been.

Ahead of the shuttle the Gate loomed at a range of several hundred meters. Just beyond the rim of the Gate he saw a metallic flash, rapidly receding, as an alien ship came through, racing away in the direction of Freedom Station. It was one of the littlest ships, which reassured him until he saw another flash, and then another.

I need to do something. The thought crept quietly into the back of his mind, like an unwanted guest. He tried to shy away from the thought, but it persisted, and it grew. Another ship came through, and he knew there had to be more that he couldn't see, hidden by the Gate. Just one ship had been enough to destroy the shuttle and kill the technicians. This was a swarm, and it terrified him.

"Come on, Kasim," he whispered. "You think it's bad now? How much worse is it going to be after you've floated here dithering for ten minutes?"

He pulled his head out of the cockpit and moved to Roberts's corpse. He told himself that he hadn't made his decision yet as he unbuckled the toolbelt from around the man's waist. *I'm just looking around. Hell, it's probably safer out there than in here. A man in the suit is a much smaller target.*

He braced himself in the hatchway, fingers gripping the edge, legs bent, feet planted against the hull of the shuttle. This was it, his last chance to turn back. He was going forward into real danger now. If he missed the Gate he would sail past it and into the path of the next alien ship to come through. It was a huge risk, an unacceptable risk. He crouched there, dry-mouthed, and knew that he didn't have the courage to go on.

He was already outside the shuttle, though. Already in position. He would feel pretty stupid just giving up and getting back into the shuttle. And what would he do inside that floating coffin with the corpse of Roberts?

Oh, hell," he muttered, and kicked off.

He missed the ring.

His trajectory took him inside the circumference of the Gate. He expected to sail on through, but he collided with an invisible surface that was hard as steel. He rebounded, started to drift away, and used his navigation jet to steer himself to the ring.

When he was clinging to the back side of the Gate, he reached around with his left hand to explore the inside of the ring. His fingers met a barrier he couldn't see. He shrugged to himself. The physics of Gates were well beyond him.

He started examining the titanium surface that he clung to, looking for bolts or screws that he could remove. He was pretty sure the technicians had removed some sort of cover plate as they did their inspections. He just had to find one.

Nothing showed but a blank, smooth expanse of metal, and he worked his way along, feeling a mixture of frustration and relief. He felt like a fly clinging to a doorway as a war raged around him. He was invisible, unnoticed, and the closest thing he could be to safe. So long as he didn't start to buzz around, and attract a fatal slap in passing ...

He pulled himself along, swept the surface of the ring with his helmet light, and moved along further. A quick visual sweep, he advanced again – and he froze. He backed up and re-examined the surface of the ring.

Had he seen a tiny dark circle? He couldn't see it now. He twisted his head from side to side, changing the angle of the light, and muttered a curse when the tiny circle of shadow reappeared, close to the outside perimeter of the ring.

The imperfection in the titanium case was a circle no more than a millimeter wide. Kasim couldn't make out a bolt head or an inset shaped for a tool, so he rummaged through the contents of the belt and pulled out a force driver. He set the miniature force field generator to "Rotate – Counter-clockwise", pressed the end against the depression in the ring, and hit the power button.

The head of a bolt appeared like the stalk of a magical plant emerging from fertile soil. The bolt spun and spun, growing longer and longer. It was impossibly thin, and as long as his index finger. At last the bolt came free, and he let it go drifting off into the void.

If there was a seam in the metal it was so perfectly machined he couldn't see it. He searched instead for another bolt, and found it a finger width from the inner edge of the ring. He drew that bolt out as well.

He set the force driver to "Pull", pressed the end against the titanium, and pulled hard. The cover didn't budge. There were more bolts, then. He went hunting, focusing his attention on the inner perimeter of the ring.

He was a dozen meters along before he found

the next bolt. He drew it out, then removed the corresponding bolt from the outer perimeter. Then he adjusted the driver and pulled on the case.

A crack appeared, and a long sheet of titanium lifted several millimeters. When he stopped pulling, the titanium cover sank back into place and the crack disappeared.

Kasim stared at the ring for a long moment, then pressed the driver to the titanium and used it as a handle as he swung his body around. He planted his feet on the other side of the gap he had seen, and then he heaved.

For ten long seconds nothing happened. He let go, then took a good big power wrench from the toolbelt. He pulled on the driver with his left hand, and used his right hand to bash the sheet of titanium with the wrench. It seemed strange to hear nothing as he slammed the steel wrench against the metal cover with all of his strength. He couldn't see the vibration he was causing, but he knew it had to be there. Again and again he hit the panel, and then he put the wrench away and grabbed the driver with both hands.

With shocking suddenness the titanium cover popped free.

He flew backward, tumbling, letting out a shout of surprise. He lost his grip on the mass driver, and the titanium panel went spinning away into the darkness. He straightened his body and spread his arms and legs to slow his spin. It was maddeningly difficult, but at last he stopped tumbling and oriented himself, helmet toward the

Gate.

The ring slowly shrank with increasing distance. He swore and gave a squirt with the little maneuvering jet on his belt. He wasn't quite lined up, and he had to make several more squirts to adjust his course. Finally he was sailing directly toward the Gate, but he was going much faster than he liked. He twisted his body around, pointed his toes at the Gate, and turned on the little jet.

Air jetted out, and he felt the belt push against him. Then the thrust stopped.

"What the hell?" Kasim looked down, checked that his thumb was on the button, and moaned. The little jet was empty. If he missed the Gate, he would spend the rest of his life sailing along in a perfectly straight line as he watched his air run out.

The metal ring loomed closer and closer, he knew he wasn't going to make it, and he contorted his body, twisting sideways. He couldn't move his center of gravity, but he could make his body turn. He got his hands pointed toward the Gate and stretched just as hard as he could.

The fingertips of his left hand touched the ring. He felt the impact, and his body started to turn. His fingers slipped free, but most of his momentum was gone. He scrabbled frantically at the ring, felt metal slide against his gloves, and then his legs swung around until his knees touched the inside of the ring. He stopped moving.

Allah preserve me, are my feet in the wormhole? Can some alien on the other side see my feet kicking? He was pretty sure that wasn't how it worked, but he was filled with horror nonetheless. *I can feel my toes. That means my legs are still attached, right?*

He moved one hand down and gripped the inner edge of the ring with his fingertips. Then he straightened his legs, taking a quick glance to be sure they were unharmed. With infinite care he worked his way around until he once again clung to the back side of the Gate.

It was the same position he'd been in when he removed the panel, but knowing that his maneuvering jet was empty made it all seem infinitely more perilous. He had trouble getting himself to straighten his arms, pushing his head far enough back from the ring to take a look around. He could see where the panel had come loose. A dark opening showed, perhaps a dozen meters away. He took a deep breath, reminded himself that he'd done this before, and started pulling himself along the ring.

There was nothing inside the metal circle that he recognized. The exposed inner workings of the Gate were a lot of incomprehensible dark shapes moulded from metal and plastic. Kasim stared, frustrated, and worked his way along, looking for something vulnerable.

A blue glow caught his attention. Deep inside the metal case, mostly obscured by lumpy plastic protrusions, he saw a long tube that glowed a bright, eerie blue. He didn't know what it was, but it gave the impression of great power. He imagined sticking a wrench into that stream of cerulean fire and being instantly electrocuted.

"I need to think of something else." He lifted his head, looking out at the stars, seeking inspiration.

Instead, he saw ships.

Three or four of the little ships, and then something from a nightmare. It was a mass of metal, growing bigger and bigger as it emerged from the portal. All around that steel behemoth he saw smaller craft, swarming like flies. They spread out, forming a protective cloud around the larger craft, moving out in every direction.

They'll see me. They'll come around behind the Gate. But I'm small. If I hold very still, if I don't do anything, they might not-

He screamed, a primitive howl to drive back the terror that filled him, and then he pawed at the toolbelt, grabbed a tool at random, and drove it with all his strength into the shining blue line in the depths of the Gate.

And the galaxy vanished in a terrible flash of blue-white light.

CHAPTER 28 – HAMMETT

"We still can't get through."

The cadet looked frazzled and weary, but Hammett didn't care. "Well, keep trying!" He looked at Cartwright. "What's your status?"

She threw her hands up, then banged a frustrated fist against the console in front of her. "I can't reach any of the forward thrusters. I just lost another aft thruster, too. I can move the tail up, or I can move it to starboard. That's it."

Even if the cadets found a way through the obstacle course of depressurized compartments and fires that separated the bridge from the forward end of the ship, it would take a hopelessly long time to run messages back and forth. A few lucky shots had cut more than half the copper wires that connected the bridge to the rest of the ship.

Never mind what you've lost. Focus on what you have. Focus on what you can do. "Fire that port thruster. Bring us around." The ship would have to swing through almost 250 degrees before the tail would be pointing toward the Gate. Now he just needed to get word to Lieutenant Rani to fire the engines at the right moment to send them fleeing for deep space.

The people on Freedom Station would have to look out for themselves. Hell, they'd probably outlive Hammett and everyone aboard the *Alexander*.

By a few hours, at least.

A man backed his way into the bridge, a fat coil of wire over each shoulder. Two long wires trailed out behind him. He was a civilian, a stranger, and he clearly didn't care much about military protocol. He stopped in the middle of the bridge, looked around, then headed for the line of telephones along the starboard bulkhead. He dropped one coil, shifted the other coil to his left hand, and said, "Which sets are dead?"

A cadet with an earpiece in one hand and a mouthpiece in the other said, "My station is the only one that's live."

The man nodded, dropped the second coil of wire, and pulled a pair of pliers from his hip pocket. He spent several seconds cutting wire, stripping back insulation, and twisting wire ends together. Then he grabbed a mouthpiece and spoke into it. "Can you hear me?" He listened. "Engine room," he said, and grabbed the second spool of wire. "This one goes to the starboard lounge." He got to work with his pliers.

A couple of cadets hurried over to man the phones, and Hammett barked, "Tell the engine room to get ready. We'll need full speed in just a moment."

He heard a cadet repeat the order into a handset. Then the cadet beside her said, "Are you sure?" She looked at Hammett, her eyes shining with hope, and said, "The Gate just closed, Sir."

Her eyes went out of focus as she listened, and then she said, "There was a great huge ship coming through. Then it just got … cut in half." She shuddered. "The Gate failed when they were part way through."

Hammett started to speak, and she held up a finger, silencing him. He watched as she listened. Then her eyes met his, and she seemed to realize what she'd done. Her face turned bright red, and she said, "Sorry, Sir."

"Never mind that. What's happening?"

"The big ship, the one that was cut in half, it's breaking apart. Little ships going in every direction. Some of them are crashing into each other. And the ships close to us are pulling back."

This is our chance. We can break free while they're in disorder. We can run for it. We can- He smothered the rising wave of exultation and terror, crushed it, drove it ruthlessly into a shadowy corner of his mind. Then he closed his eyes and took a deep breath. *This isn't your first scrap. Don't get excited. Don't let adrenalin do your thinking for you.*

He opened his eyes. "Cadet."

The girl who had been speaking to the starboard lounge said, "Yes, Sir?"

"Tell me when we're facing directly away from the Gate." He pinched the bridge of his nose, trying to separate terror and battle lust from rational thought. "Belay that. Tell me when we're facing directly *toward* the Gate." He pointed to the cadet beside her. "Don't tell me. Tell her. I want Lieutenant Rani to give us full thrust toward the Gate. We're going after the swarm that just came through."

The words were barely out of his mouth when the cadet said, "Now!"

Instantly the cadet beside her said "Engines, now," into her telephone. Hammett felt his body sway ever so slightly as the ship accelerated.

A bustle at the bridge entrance drew his attention. Hammett hadn't seen the civilian leave, but he was back, with a civilian woman beside him. They carried a metal bar between them, with a dozen coils of wire hanging from it, unspooling as they walked. "We found a pipe that runs all the way to the tail," he said. "Once you get one wire through, you just use it to pull the others. Now, somebody give me a hand making splices." He pulled several pairs of pliers out of his pockets.

Cartwright was able to reach the engine room and almost every navigational thruster by the time the *Alexander* reached the thick of the enemy fleet. She made the ship spin and dance, and the forward rail guns tore up three different clusters of enemy ships as fast as they formed, before they could move in to tear up the *Alexander's* hull.

Finally the alien ships fled in every direction. Dozens of them survived, more than enough, Hammett suspected, to overwhelm and destroy the *Alexander*. It seemed they couldn't recover quickly from a devastating blow. The enemy could do terrible damage, but they cracked under pressure.

It was a heartening sign, but, as Carruthers had pointed out, the aliens were learning. And they kept gaining reinforcements, while the *Alexander* picked up damage and refugees. Speaking of which ...

"Bring us about," he said to Cartwright. "Let's get back to Freedom Station and pick up the rest of our people."

"Aye aye, Sir."

"That's odd," said a cadet.

Hammett looked at her. "What's that, Cadet?"

She frowned. "The starboard lounge says the Gate is flashing."

Hammett blinked. "Flashing? What do you mean?"

She shrugged. "They say there's a red light on the edge of the ring, and it keeps flashing on and off. They say it's some kind of pattern."

Hammett said, "Well, we know the gate is malfunctioning, so it probably-" He frowned. Why, exactly, had the gate failed at such a perfect time? "Pattern?" he said. "What pattern, exactly?"

The cadet said, "Flash, flash, flash, flash-flash-flash, flash, flash, flash. Then it repeats."

"It's Kasim," said Hammett, and he smiled. "He knows his Navy history. Him or one of the technicians." When the cadet gave him a blank look he said, "It's an SOS." He laughed. "I wonder if anyone has used Morse code in the last hundred years." He looked around the bridge. "Does anyone have a working line to the shuttle bay?"

Carruthers said, "I don't think we had one even before the battle."

"Never mind," Hammett said. "The runabout is probably fried." He turned to Cartwright. "Take us to the Gate, but gently. Our people are out there."

Thirty long minutes passed before a tired-looking cadet arrived from the shuttle bay. "We retrieved two survivors, Sir. That's all there is."

"Get us to Freedom Station," Hammett told Cartwright. He turned back to the cadet. "What else can you tell me?"

"Lieutenant al Faisal is in pretty bad shape. He's unconscious. They took him to Medical."

"He's unconscious?" Hammett said. "Then who was signalling us?"

"It was one of the technicians, Sir. I don't know his name. The young man with the big nose. He says he was floating behind the Gate when he saw a big spark. Mr. al Faisal went floating past, leaking air from his glove. The technician got him patched up. There was some kind of electrical fire inside the ring, and he used an emergency suit patch as a mirror, reflecting the light toward us."

Hammett shook his head in disbelief. *Fire and mirrors? This is what we've been reduced to?*

Well, it worked, didn't it?

"Were coming up on Freedom Station," Cartwright announced.

"Good," he said. "Let's get our people and go."

CHAPTER 29 – WEST

The long, wide expanse of the shuttle bay looked like a garbage dump. Mathew West looked around him and sighed. It was chaos, and he'd volunteered to clean it up.

It was all that Asian woman's fault, he decided grumpily. She'd smiled so brightly as she strolled through the dining hall asking for volunteers that he'd bounced right up out of his seat and stuck a hand in the air. Anything to make her direct that stunning smile at him.

He still remembered the petty stab of disappointment he'd felt when she held up a notebook and asked for his name. She hadn't reacted when he told her, either.

Not a blues fan, then.

Decades of songwriting had given him a deeply entrenched habit of self-awareness, and he chuckled at his own immaturity. The truth was, he'd been feeling pretty useless. It didn't look as if he would be giving a concert any time soon, and he wasn't good for much without a guitar. Another day of loafing in his room or hanging around the dining hall would have driven him mad. This was infinitely better.

Several blocky, inelegant ships filled one end of the bay. The rest of the bay was given over to heaps of junk. He wandered through stacks of detritus, getting his bearings. There was an order of sorts, he saw. Not much of one, but something. What he'd taken for a single pile of trash was in fact several dozen separate heaps that bled into each other. Each heap was just one thing, much of it incomprehensible.

There were metal ingots, each the size of his fist, cylindrical and flat on both ends. Those at least stacked properly. There was a mountain of bedding, all different sizes and fabrics, and beside it a mountain of gray cloth that seemed to be one impossibly long bolt.

A pile of notebooks caught his eye. They were palm-sized, little booklets with maybe a hundred pages each. He picked one up and flipped through it, mystified. He recognized them, of course. He'd seen such things in old movies. He'd just never seen one in person. They would be useless without some sort of stylus, though.

A little box caught his eye. It was big enough to hold a good-sized pair of boots, and it was completely full of pencils. He picked up a pencil, examined it, and touched the sharp point. Then he tested it on the cover of a notebook.

And smiled. "I'm back in the songwriting business," he said, and pocketed pencil and notebook.

Not knowing where else to start, he knelt and began re-stacking notebooks that had spilled across the floor. *Deck*, he corrected himself. It was a ship, which meant everything had to have a stupid new name. Stairs were ladders, doors were hatches, and walls were bulkheads. At least there weren't a lot of ropes around, which he supposed he would have to refer to as lines.

Sailors. Who understands them?

As if summoned by the thought, a man in a blue uniform came striding through the piles of goods toward him. He looked about thirty, with a weary face looking out from under a blue uniform cap. He stopped in front of West, frowning. West considered the effort involved in getting himself back upright and decided to stay on one knee.

"What are you doing? Passengers shouldn't really be in the shuttle bay."

West sighed. *This is what I get for over-reacting to a pretty smile.* "Miss Ling sent me. She's putting together civilian volunteers to help out with ..." He gestured around him at the entire ship. "Everything. She said I was to come here and help organize things."

The man frowned down at him. Then the frown vanished, replaced by a tired smile. "Really?" He took the silly blue cap from his head and raked fingers through an untidy forest of short dark hair. "I asked for help, but really, I was just going through the motions. I never actually thought I'd get any help." He stuck out a hand. "I'm Raleigh Neal."

West reached up to shake his hand. "Matt West. Pleased to meet you. Are you a cadet?"

A look of annoyance flashed across Raleigh's face, then disappeared. "Sailor," he said. "I haven't been a cadet for ten years."

"No offense."

Raleigh waved that away. "I'm just grumpy because I've been on duty for, oh, nineteen hours straight." He did the same thing West kept doing, glancing sideways and down to activate his implants before remembering they no longer worked. "No reason you should know all our uniforms and ranks." He grinned. "Actually, I'm so happy to have some help, you can call me whatever you like. I'll answer to Chief Numbskull if it means I get to take a break."

West chuckled, liking him. "Any instructions for me, Raleigh?"

The sailor scratched his head. "You know what would be really grand? I'd love it if you would just run things here for a few hours." He yawned. "For a bunch of hours, actually. Be quartermaster while I grab some rack time." He gestured around the bay. "Familiarize yourself with what's where, so you know where to find it, or if it exists, if someone asks for something. Give 'em whatever they want. Just make a list of who took what." He gestured at the stack of notebooks. "Grab yourself a notebook and pencil. We've got lots."

West put a hand on the pocket containing his notebook and tried to look innocent.

"Other than that, if you get bored, you can do some tidying up. Like you were already doing." He gestured at the vast pile of gray cloth. "You could cut that into bedsheets if you really wanted. I wouldn't worry about the size. Just make 'em plenty big. Don't use all the cloth, though. The lieutenant says we might have to make clothing if we're out here too long. Some of the passengers only made it out of Freedom with the clothes on their backs."

Like me, West thought. It was four days since the fall of Freedom Station and he was sick of washing his underwear at night, then putting it on still clammy in the morning.

"I'm sure there's more you could do, but I'm too tired to think straight. Thanks, Matt. I really appreciate it." He started to turn away, then paused and looked back. "Did you say your name was Matt West?"

"Er, yes."

Raleigh peered closer at him. "As in Mathew West? *The* Mathew West? The blues singer?"

West grinned and nodded.

"Oh, my god! I saw you live at the Blue Cat in Hawking. You were amazing." The weariness was gone now. "We have to arrange a concert!"

West shook his head. "I lost Jessica. She didn't make it off Freedom Station."

The sailor's face fell. "Oh, I'm sorry." He gave West a sympathetic look. "She was ... someone close to you?"

West frowned, embarrassed. People had lost family and friends when the station fell. It made his own loss trivial.

Still, it was Jessica.

"She was my guitar," he said. "I'm no good without her."

A silent moment passed while Raleigh processed this. At last he said, "You could sing a cappella?"

West shook his head.

"Oh. Well, all right. That's too bad." He put his uniform cap back on his head. "I'll see you in five or six hours, okay?"

"Don't be late," West told him. "I have a lot of important appointments, you know." When Raleigh just stared at him he said, "That's a joke. I have exactly nothing else to do. Take your time. Get a good night's sleep."

"All right." Raleigh grinned, "See you in the morning."

West explored, wandering among the stacks and telling himself that it wasn't so bad. Then he discovered that things were only going to get worse. A large object that he'd taken for a shuttle turned out to be a fabricator salvaged from Baffin. A bored young woman operated the machine, turning out hollow plastic handsets. It was a task that didn't require much attention, and she seemed happy to chat with him.

"With the big replicator back at the station we could have made handsets with the speaker and microphone parts already built-in. Someone's going to have to assemble these by hand." She pushed blonde bangs out of her eyes. "I'm almost done this run. Any requests for what I make next?"

He wanted to say, how about underwear with a fifty-inch waist? If she hadn't been a pretty young woman he might have. Instead he looked around the bay and said, "I could really use some boxes."

The girl leaned to look past him. "I see what you mean." She thought for a moment. "I can make flat panels easily enough, but you'd have to seal the edges yourself." She frowned. "I know. I can make glue. Let me see. I need a container to put it in, but I need the glue to make a container …"

West left her to it and continued strolling around the bay. He was debating the merits of taking a nap in the giant pile of fabric when a woman in a Navy uniform walked in. He looked at her uniform, not wanting to repeat his gaffe of calling a sailor a cadet. Her outfit looked pretty formal, he decided, with rigid epaulet boards and lines of white piping that ran from her shoulder to the top button on her blouse. Did that make her an officer? He was pretty sure there were lots of lieutenants on board. The Captain was a man. He knew that much. She was most likely a lieutenant.

She marched over to him. There was no other word for the way she walked. She stopped a little bit closer than he liked and looked him up and down. By the look on her face, she wasn't too impressed with what she saw.

Not a blues fan, then.

"I'm looking for the quartermaster." Her voice was crisp and peremptory. *And I don't expect to be kept waiting* was the unmistakable subtext.

"That would be me, I guess. I'm Acting Quartermaster West." He almost saluted her, but restrained himself. "How can I help you, ah, Lieutenant?"

She scowled. "That's Commander. Commander Velasco."

They're so touchy about their ranks. I'm sure glad I didn't say cadet. He didn't speak, just lifted his eyebrows and waited.

Velasco sighed and took out a familiar-looking notebook. "I'm here to take inventory. Specifically I need to check on the rail gun ammunition."

West spread his hands in a shrug. "I don't know what everything is, but I haven't seen anything that looks like bullets."

She gave him an irritated look, then stepped past him. "Here they are." She gestured to him. "Come on. You'd better take a look. If someone needs these in a hurry, you should know what they look like." She surprised him by smiling. It made her look almost human. "Besides, you can help me count them."

She led him to the ingots, the fist-sized metal lumps that stacked so nicely. Apparently they could be fired from guns. He plopped himself down on the floor and counted the height, width, and depth of the stack. He counted the loose ingots in the top layer while she did some quick multiplication.

The stack didn't seem large, but apparently it contained almost two thousand rounds. West whistled.

"That's great," Velasco said, "until we need

them in a hurry. I can't have cadets running back and forth with one round in each hand." She chuckled. "Actually, I suppose I could. I wouldn't be too popular with the cadets, though."

"Or with the civilians," West told her. "Some of us have volunteered to help out."

She looked at him as if seeing him for the first time. "That's good of you. Thank you." She frowned. "Now, how to move large numbers of rounds in a hurry ..." She looked to the vast bolt of fabric. "I wonder if we could make sacks."

"Actually," West said, "I have someone working on a better solution." He jerked a thumb over his shoulder. "The lady with the fabricator is going to make me some boxes."

Velasco smiled. "Excellent! You're a resourceful man." She looked around at the surrounding mess. "I realize you've got a lot going on here, but if we end up needing that ammunition, we're going to need it in a hurry. I hope you can make boxing the ammunition something of a priority." She looked around again. "It's a pity, though. It's just about the tidiest thing in here."

West found himself smiling back at her. She was very good at charming people when she worked at it. He was pretty sure she held him in contempt, but it didn't make her current persona any easier to resist. He would box the ammunition first, before he started on anything else.

"Thank you, Mr. West. I'm going to get out of the way and let you get back to work now. It was nice meeting you." She shook his hand.

I'll bet, he thought, but when she smiled at him he smiled back. She marched out and he watched her go, shaking his head. He was torn between wanting to like her and wanting to wash his hand where she'd touched him. Aloud he said, "Am I just being cynical?"

"Nope."

He turned around. It was the young woman from the fabricator, standing a couple of paces away. She wore plain brown coveralls with some sort of company logo above the breast pocket. She was a civilian like him, then. She seemed to know Velasco, though.

"The crew doesn't like her," she said. "They say she's not a real sailor."

West shrugged, not really knowing what that meant.

"She's second in command," the girl said. "But she's never served on a ship before." She rolled her eyes. "It's like ..." She cocked her head. "What line of business are you in?"

"I sing and play the guitar."

"It's like going on stage with your road manager doing backup vocals. Or maybe your agent. Someone who's never been on the road before, much less played an instrument. It's ridiculous."

He nodded. "I see what you mean." He didn't care, but she was attractive and he didn't want to argue with her.

"All I can say is, if something happens to the captain, we are all in a shit-load of trouble."

That made him chuckle. "Let's hope he takes

care of himself."

She nodded. "That's why she's down here checking inventory, you know. Because she doesn't know how to run the ship. The captain doesn't want her anywhere near the bridge, so he's giving her logistical stuff to keep her busy and out of his hair." She shrugged and gave him a self-deprecating grin. "At least, that's what the crew is saying."

With a little jump she boosted herself onto the stack of rail gun rounds and sat there, drumming her heels against the metal cylinders. West watched, cringing. They weren't dangerous, were they? "Um, should you do that?"

She looked down. "What?"

He reddened, feeling foolish. "Are they ... I don't know, dangerous? Do they explode?"

She laughed. "Actually, it's a good question. There are some that explode, and they look just like these ones." She drummed her heels harder. "Don't worry. These ones are solid."

"Are you sure?"

"I made them." She gave one last hard kick and then sat still, much to West's relief.

She said, "I suppose it's the captain I should be annoyed with. He's the one who sicced her on me."

"Um, Velasco?"

She nodded. "He told her he wanted one of the shuttles converted to manual controls. If that works, he wants to add guns." She rolled her eyes. "That's the military for you." A hint of a mischievous grin touched her features. "Actually, that would be kind of cool."

West nodded uncertainly.

"Anyway, that Velasco woman came in and told me she needed me to drop everything and get to work on, and I quote, manual ship control parts. And that was the sum total of her instructions. As if some kind of standard template exists for technology that's been obsolete since before wormholes." She made a rude noise. "And she just kept badgering me. Told me she wanted solutions, not excuses. Told me to, and I quote again, requisition manpower as needed."

"Takes herself a bit seriously, does she?" West said.

"You have no idea! I finally told her I wasn't in her stupid Navy. Told her that meant two things. One, the "manpower" I was supposed to "requisition" was going to laugh in my face if I started ordering them around. Second, I said, you can go suck vacuum because I'm not in your stupid Navy." She smiled at the memory.

"I bet the sailors and cadets love you," West said. "You're living their dream." She giggled, and he said, "It sounds like a folk ballad. It could be the best song ever."

She leaned toward him, her eyes merry. "Do you think so? Will you write it? Do you write songs, or just sing them?" She giggled. "I've never been in a song before."

You will be if I survive this trip, he thought.

She turned, looking toward the exit door. "What's this?"

West turned around. Raleigh came in, his left

hand cradling a large bowl against his chest, his right hand gripping the handle of a battered guitar case. He walked up, heaved the case onto the pile of ingots, and set the bowl beside it. He said, "Hi, Dulcie."

"Hey, Raleigh. What's in the bowl?"

Raleigh lifted away a covering cloth and said, "I brought fruit. It's almost the last of the fresh food, and I suggest you enjoy it. You're not going to like what we'll be eating tomorrow."

There was more chatter, and the sound of Dulcie biting into an apple, but it was all just background noise to West. He stared at the guitar case. Finally Raleigh noticed the direction of his gaze and cleared his throat. "So, um. Matt." He looked embarrassed. "There's this guy in the room next to mine. Plays the guitar, once every month or two. He's not very good at it. So I talked to him, and I told him you were here. And I told him about Jessica."

West looked at him, trying to sort out a churning stew of emotions.

"Anyway, it's probably not as good a guitar as yours. But if you want to borrow it, he says it's yours for as long as you like."

West didn't say anything, just stared at the guitar for a time. Then he moved past Raleigh and rested a hand on the case. It was cheap plastic, scuffed and battered. It didn't bode well for the guitar inside.

Oh, well. It wasn't as if he had a lot of guitars to choose from. He pressed his thumb to the little panel on the top of the case.

Nothing happened.

"He couldn't open it either," Raleigh said. "He said you should just go ahead and pry it open if you like. If you don't, he'll have to, sooner or later. The lock is toast."

Before West could answer, Dulcie set down a half-eaten an apple and said, "I've got just the thing." She trotted across the bay, disappeared behind a shuttle, and came back holding a pry bar. West wasn't sure he was ready to force open someone else's guitar case, but Dulcie had no such qualms. She jammed the end of the bar against the first seal, thumped the other end with the heel of her hand, and twisted. The seal popped open. She got the other seal open and stepped back.

West stared down at the guitar case. *Well, I guess it would be stupid not to open it now.* He flipped open the lid.

The guitar was nothing special, some generic brand with a faux-wood finish and six strings. He ran a thumb across the strings, not expecting much. The sound hit him, a tiny wave of pure music, and he shivered, surprised to realize how much he'd missed it. He looked at the others. "Sounds like it's pretty much in tune."

They didn't answer, just watched him. Dulcie looked mildly interested. Raleigh looked avid.

West lifted the guitar out of the case and settled the strap around his shoulder. It felt good, but subtly wrong, and he missed Jessica with a sharp pang of longing. *Has it come to this? You're excited by this piece of crap? It's second-hand and second-rate. It's ...*

It's a guitar. What are you going to do, put it back and go back to bitching about how you lost yours?

Raleigh said, "What's the matter?"

There were no words to explain the tangle of emotions in his chest, so he let his fingers talk instead, through the guitar string. He did it without thought, his fingers finding the positions without any help from his brain, his thumb starting to strum. At first it was just random notes, little jagged pulses of emotion, each one disconnected from the rest. Then he noticed he was playing a song. *Mountain Blues*, from Mars, a melancholy tune about pioneers who know they can never go home. He played, and it felt good, so he started to sing. It was soft at first, but he felt his voice rise higher and higher with every verse.

Earth was far away. He'd seen death, he'd met eager fans on Freedom and they hadn't made it to the lifeboat. Death had come for them at a time when they were supposed to be at his show.

Gone. Cold and dead and gone, and there wasn't a single damned thing you could do for them. At first he'd been busy being scared and relieved he was still alive, but it had rattled him, more than he knew. A big part of him wanted to take that guitar and hurl it across the bay. What right did he have to play music when so many people had died, and so many more were stranded in this floating steel box with a pitiless enemy hunting them?

Music felt like a sick joke. It was the only thing he was good at, the only thing he had ever cared about, and now it felt like a travesty. Every note felt like a mockery of the people who had died.

Dark emotions had been festering in the back of his skull for days, and now the guitar brought them swirling up. It was bleak and awful, and he took all that horrible energy and poured it into the song. The cheap guitar seems to come to life in his hands in a way that even Jessica never had. He sang, holding nothing back, and heard his own voice echoing from the bulkheads. He sang of pain and loss and danger and the hopeless yearning to go home. He sang until his fingertips ached and his throat was raw. It was just one song, but he felt like he'd done a two-hour show.

Finally the last note trailed away, and he lifted the guitar from around his neck. He felt drained, but at peace. He set the guitar in the case and turned around.

Dozens of people filled the bay. He saw civilians and cadets, sailors and officers. They stared at him, some of them smiling, some of them blank-faced. Some of them wore a raw, shocked expression that matched the way West felt. He stared back at them.

And then someone started to clap. In an instant the bay rang with applause, and the closest people surged forward. Someone shook his hand, someone else clapped him on the shoulder, and a big man in a pyjama shirt and blue jeans put himself in charge of crowd control and started holding people back.

West could hear people asking who he was, and others telling them, "That's Mathew West." A dozen people filed past, meek under the stern eye of the man in the pyjama shirt. They shook his hand. A young woman beamed and told him he was awesome. A man shook his hand and said "Thank you," his voice strangely hoarse. A matronly woman didn't speak, just threw her arms around him and squeezed him hard.

At last the crowd began to break up. People streamed out, smiling and chattering. A familiar figure at the back gave West an ironic salute and said, "What did I tell you? National treasure."

Dulcie said, "You know Dalton Hornbeck?"

"He's a fan," West admitted.

"Wow."

Raleigh grinned. "So, I'm going to tell Mick you'll be hanging onto his guitar."

West nodded. "I guess I will be."

The grin deepened into a smile. "And now I'm going to hit my rack." He headed for the corridor.

"And I'm going to work on some boxes," Dulcie said. She wagged a finger under West's nose. "You're not allowed to do another show without telling me first."

"It's a deal."

He watched her work for a couple of minutes. Then he carried the guitar to a bench along one bulkhead where it would be out of the way and safe from damage. He set it down and went back to work.

CHAPTER 30 – JANICE

Janice slipped quietly into the starboard lounge. There was a single cadet on duty, a bored-looking young man slouched deep in a padded chair. He sat up and looked around, saw who it was, and gave her a wave. Then he sank back into the seat and resumed staring at the stars.

It had to be the most boring assignment on the ship, she supposed. Still, she didn't think she'd mind it. Crisp, bright stars unhindered by atmosphere made a view that still took her breath away. Even after nineteen long days in the gulf between the stars the view from the windows entranced her.

The next wormhole jump was imminent, and she meant to see it happen. It had been a goal since the ship left Deirdre, and she hadn't managed it yet. New Avalon was only a few jumps away, which meant this was nearly her last chance.

If she was perfectly honest, she had another reason to be in the almost-empty lounge. She was shirking her duties. The lounge was a place she could avoid the crew and passengers without actually looking as if she was hiding.

"Janice! There you are. I've been scouring the ship for you."

Janice grimaced through the window, then noticed that she could see the other woman's reflection in the steelglass. She hastily smoothed her features and turned. "Ms. Barnard. What can I do for you?"

Hammett had made up the title of "passenger liaison", but in the aftermath of the battle it had become true. With so many automatic systems fried, the *Alexander* had become a very labor-intensive ship. Many of the cadets had died, leaving her short-handed, while more than a hundred passengers found themselves crammed into tiny staterooms and bunk rooms with time weighing heavy on them.

Janice had suggested putting the passengers to work, and after some initial resistance on both sides, everyone had embraced the idea. How she had ended up in charge of all those passengers Janice wasn't sure, but the role of passenger liaison had become her aegis and her albatross.

"We have a laundry crisis," Barnard announced. "It's the misfits, of course." The misfits were that subset of passengers who had escaped Freedom Station with only the clothes they wore, and were the wrong size to borrow anything from the crew or the workmen from Kukulcan. "They've been doing the best they can, but they drop off laundry and it doesn't get back to them for a day and a half." Barnard shook her head. "That's fine for the rest of the ship's company, but for the misfits it causes a real problem. They need preferential laundry treatment. Just once every couple of days, mind you. I'm sure you understand."

Janice nodded. "I see what you mean. Maybe I can go down to – no. I want you to go. I want you to go into the laundry compartment and take charge of things."

Barnard's eyebrows rose in distressed arcs. "But no one's going to listen to me!"

"I'm deputizing you," Janice announced. "I'm giving you complete authority to act in my name where matters of laundry are concerned." She gave the other woman a sharp look. "It's a lot of responsibility, and I'm trusting you not to abuse it."

Barnard nodded, looking impressed.

"Tell whoever's there that I've given you this authority. Don't take any attitude from them, either. And be warned." She held up a finger. "Every time someone brings me a laundry-related problem, I'm going to refer them to you."

Alarm showed in Barnard's eyes, but to her credit she simply nodded. "You can count on me."

Janice smiled and sent her on her way.

The moment the woman's back was turned, Janice whirled. "Did we jump yet?" she demanded.

"Hmmm?" The cadet gave her a startled look. "No, I don't think so."

"Good." Janice chose a couple of the brightest constellations and tried to fix them in her mind. Each jump only took the ship a short distance, but for a very close star it might be enough. She wanted to see a star move. She wanted to *know* the ship had jumped, to actually see the evidence and not just understand it in an intellectual way.

A dark shape moved in the reflection on the steelglass. Someone was coming into the lounge. Janice ignored whoever it was, staring fixedly at the stars, hoping they would take the hint.

"Liaison Ling."

She turned in spite of herself, and a cadet in a pressed uniform snapped a crisp salute. "Cadet Thorpe reporting."

He was young and earnest and terribly serious, and she smiled, trying to hide both her annoyance and her amusement. "You don't have to salute me, Cadet Thorpe. I don't have a rank in the Spacecom armed forces."

Thorpe stared at her, looking flustered.

"What's your name, Cadet?"

His eyebrows rose. "Thorpe?"

"Your first name."

He flushed. "Rory, Ma'am."

"Rory, you must never call me Ma'am again. It makes me feel old. My name is Janice. All right?"

"Yes, M— That is, all right, Janice." He relaxed his rigid posture, letting his shoulders slump. It was a big improvement.

"Thank you, Rory. Now, what can I do for you?"

"We could use some backup message runners during General Quarters. We have enough cadets if there aren't too many messages, but if the phones go down and things get busy, there won't be enough. It has to be people with vac suits, though. They'll be running messages in corridors and compartments that are close to the skin of the ship."

Janice nodded her understanding. "I'll add the people from Baffin. They're the only ones with suits. If I move—"

Rory glanced past her shoulder and said, "Neat! We just jumped."

"Damn it!" Janice turned, trying to find one of her bright stars before she could forget their positions. There was a change, though, in the constellation she had dubbed the Duck. The stars hadn't moved, not that she could see. But there was a new feature, a blue-white line just beyond the tip of the Duck's bill. She stared, then pointed. "Is that …?"

"It's a comet," Rory confirmed. "It looks like we've reached New Avalon." A metallic clang echoed through the corridor behind them, and both of them stood silent, counting. Six clangs rang out in total, followed by a moment of silence. Then they heard the patter of rushing feet.

"General Quarters," Rory said. "I guess we're here, all right."

CHAPTER 31 – HAMMETT

"The next jump will take us into the system," Hammett said. "We'll still be a good hundred million kilometers from the Gate, so if the enemy is there, the odds of being spotted before we have time to bug out is infinitesimal. Nevertheless, we shall be ready."

He looked around the bridge. It was a much different place than it had been three weeks before. The telephones had proper handsets now, banana-shaped plastic handles with an earpiece on one end and a mouthpiece on the other, and they hung from the bulkheads on clips, or sat in cradles at bridge stations. The deck was clear of cables. The wires now ran under deck plates or made tidy patterns across bulkheads.

The system had built-in redundancies now. Breckenridge and his Baffin technicians had installed two relay stations, compartments with dozens of telephones and a patch panel, with a handful of crew standing by. Every key location on the ship was connected to the bridge by at least two routes. If a wire was cut, the relay crews could create a secondary connection in moments.

"Get me the shuttle bay," Hammett said. "I want to talk to Lieutenant Kasim."

Along the bulkhead a cadet named Sadiq nodded and lifted a phone to her ear. He was getting much better with names, mostly because he'd instituted a change to uniforms. There were too many cadets, and too many civilians working alongside them, for anyone to keep track, and he didn't want communication slowed by people stumbling over names. Now everyone, including himself, wore a strip of tape on their chest with their name in block letters.

"I've got him, Sir," Sadiq said, and he crossed the bridge to take her phone.

"Lieutenant Kasim. I want you to take the *Falcon* out for a test flight." The *Falcon* was the runabout from Baffin, now gutted and refitted with entirely manual controls. Breckenridge had made it his pet project, working day and night for a week and a half. Kasim and a handful of technicians, some from Baffin and some from the *Alexander*, had worked with him. Now they were stripping a shuttle and giving it the same modifications, but so far only the *Falcon* was spaceworthy.

Probably. As the ship jumped again and again they hadn't taken the time for a test flight.

"We'll be doing practice maneuvers," Hammett

told him. "Make sure you signal the ship before you come back in." There wasn't a single working radio on the *Alexander*, so they had fitted the *Falcon* with signal lights. There were more signal lights in the shuttle bay to let him know it was safe to land.

"Aye aye, Sir," Kasim said, sounding cheerful. "I'll put her through her paces."

For the next hour the *Alexander* played tag with a comet. They swept in close to the flying snowball, matched velocities, then flew away. They raced past, almost close enough to touch the comet, then drifted in slowly, seeing how close they could come. Finally they parked a hundred kilometers off and tore the thing up with rail gun rounds.

"The new slugs are working fine," DiMarco reported. They had brought a small fabricator up from Baffin before abandoning the station. The machine had nowhere near the versatility of the big Level III replicator they'd left on Kukulcan, but it was adequate for making simple things like telephone handsets and control equipment for the *Falcon*. Solid rail gun slugs were no problem at all.

"The *Falcon* is coming in for a landing," Sadiq said. "Lieutenant Dixon requests that we maintain our position."

Hammett glanced at Cartwright, who nodded.

"Sound General Quarters again," Hammett ordered. Technically there were still at General Quarters, but the crew would have relaxed their vigilance somewhat. This would warn them that the *Alexander* was about to make its final jump.

"Spotters report no activity in the system," Cartwright said. "For what that's worth." They were a good light month from New Avalon. They would see nothing unless the aliens had been in the system for a long time.

"I guess we'll know shortly if they're waiting for us," Hammett said. He looked at Sadiq.

"The *Falcon*'s back on board," she reported.

"Bring us about, if you please, Ms. Cartwright." Hammett waited as she spoke into three different telephones. "Ask Lieutenant Rani to jump us as soon as we're lined up."

Cartwright spent a minute or so getting the ship aligned with the nearby star, then announced, "We've jumped."

Cadets began chiming in with reports from the telescopes in various lounges and windowed compartments. The Gate was visible and looked intact. No other shipping was in sight.

Then the report he'd been dreading came through. A cadet named Murphy looked at Hammett with wide, alarmed eyes and said, "Several ships spotted near the Gate."

Aw, hell. He didn't speak, just waited.

"At least five craft," Murphy said. "She says it's hard to count them at this range. They're stationary. No indication we've been spotted." There was a long, tense silence. "She can't be certain," Murphy said at last, "but it looks like the enemy."

For a moment Hammett clung to the idea that it could be Navy ships keeping watch on the Gate.

The *Alexander* had no way to pick up transponders, after all. But every Spacecom vessel had a distinct profile. If the *Alexander* was close enough for the spotters to see the Gate, they were close enough to recognize military craft.

He sighed. "Lieutenant DiMarco."

The weapons officer looked up from his console.

"I'll need you to go to the missile bay and prepare me a nuke. It'll have to explode on impact. Where are you at with the guidance system?"

DiMarco had spent much of the last two weeks taking apart a missile guidance system, testing the components one at a time, and using the fabricator to replace what couldn't be salvaged. "I'm pretty confident," DiMarco said. "All the essential code is burned in. I'll have to be close when I launch it, though."

"Works for me," Hammett said. "How close do you need to be?"

"The closer the better. A couple of hundred kilometers would be great, but I know you're not taking us that close. Anything less than a hundred thousand should be fine." He considered. "The thing is, I know pretty much what the orbit of the Gate is. I could hit it from anywhere close to the planet, if we were in an equatorial orbit at a similar altitude."

Hammett nodded. "We should be able to manage that." He turned to Cartwright. "Bring us around, Ms. Cartwright. I want you to jump us pretty close to the planet."

She gave him a dubious look. "How close, Sir?

Our range is pretty much an educated guess right now."

"We won't jump straight at the planet," he said. "I want to pop out on the far side of the planet from the Gate."

She nodded. "Okay, no collision risk, then."

"I want the planet between us and the Gate," Hammett told her. "That's the only place we've seen the enemy so far."

Cartwright closed her eyes, her lips moving as she did calculations in her head. When she opened her eyes there was a worried line between her eyebrows. "I can't guarantee anything, Sir. You would think an entire planet would be a big enough target, but at this range ..."

"I understand. Just do the best you can."

She nodded and reached for a telephone.

The star known as New Avalon had extensive bands of asteroids and just one planet. The planet, an airless ball of rock orbiting far outside the Goldilocks zone, was unfortunately also known as New Avalon. It had been a source of endless confusion for decades. Gate Eight orbited New Avalon (the planet).

For many years the planet had been home to a vast mining operation, with a steady flow of cargo ships and personnel carriers going back and forth through the Gate. The mines had been abandoned long since, and there was no longer a human presence in the system. Hammett was grateful for that much. He wouldn't have to worry about any more civilians.

"Do you think it's happenstance?" said

Carruthers.

Hammett raised an eyebrow.

"The aliens being here, I mean. It proves they don't need the Gates, doesn't it?" He grimaced. "Unless it means they've already conquered the Earth, and they came through the other way."

Hammett decided to ignore that idea. "It could be coincidence. Maybe they're spreading through the whole galaxy. Popping up everywhere." It was an unpleasant thought.

"Maybe they're following us." Carruthers rubbed his jaw. "Maybe they can track wormholes."

Cartwright set down a telephone. "They wouldn't need to. We were in view of alien ships when we jumped out of Deirdre. We were pointing straight at New Avalon when we jumped." She made a face. "I should know. I handled the maneuvers."

"New policy," Hammett told her. "When we leave here, we jump in a random direction. Then we turn and aim for Earth."

Cartwright nodded. "We're lined up for the next jump."

"You're getting faster," Hammett said, and she smiled. Now there was nothing to do but wait for the wormhole generator to cycle. Somewhere just ahead of the ship a ball of energy was forming, contained within a perfect sphere generated by force fields. The sphere would grow smaller and smaller, condensing that ball of energy into a point smaller than an atom. Eventually it would reach a critical threshold and a wormhole would open, sucking the *Alexander* through in the blink of an eye.

Hammett had cornered Rani and demanded to know why a process as complex as wormhole generation could still function when even simple timepieces no longer worked. She had shrugged and said, "Redundancy." The wormhole generator had the capacity to go utterly, disastrously wrong. Forward-thinking engineers had built endless layers of redundancy into the system. He didn't know what labors she'd gone through in the immediate aftermath of the first battle, but against all reasonable expectations the wormhole generator was working again.

The unmistakable sound of stomping feet came echoing in from the corridor beyond the bridge. Hammett looked up as Dalton Hornbeck came storming in. He was a small man, slender and not especially tall, but he seemed much bigger, transformed by outrage until he seemed to almost fill the bridge. He swept the compartment with a frosty eye, then fixed his gaze on Hammett. "Captain. I've been hearing wild rumors that you're planning to destroy yet another Gate."

Hammett sighed. "Yes, it's true. Now, this is my bridge, and—"

"You can't do it!" The administrator's arms came up in an agitated flapping motion. "It was the wrong choice back at Deirdre, and it's the wrong choice now. How many alien ships have you detected?"

The urge to simply throw him off the bridge was strong, but Hammett decided to be diplomatic. "Half a dozen."

"This ship has faced more of these aliens and survived!"

"It's not open for debate, Mr. Hornbeck."

"The Gate is right there!" Hornbeck pointed at the forward bulkhead. "We need to rush past these alien craft and jump through to Paradiso. From there we can be home in no time."

"It's too risky."

"Risky?" The man's voice was very nearly a screech. "And stranding us in deep space with hostile aliens isn't risky?"

"This isn't your station, Mr. Hornbeck." Hammett could feel his irritation rising. "It's the bridge of a warship. I'll need you to—"

"This is why the military need civilian oversight!" Hornbeck advanced on Hammett, one accusing finger raised like a weapon. "You're a lunatic, Hammett. You've been displaying criminally bad judgment ever since your arrival in Deirdre."

Hammett stood. "Now, look. I—"

Hornbeck stepped in close. "You can't keep making high-handed decisions that put everyone around you at risk. I won't stand for it, do you hear me? If you think you—" His finger jabbed toward Hammett's chest – and a hand closed around the administrator's wrist.

Hornbeck let out an indignant squawk and turned. Crabtree stood beside him, a dangerous glitter in his eyes. A twist of his elbow had Hornbeck's finger pointing at the ceiling. "Let's you and me have a chat in the corridor, shall we?"

"Let go of me, you oaf!"

Crabtree released him.

Hornbeck turned back to Hammett. "You can't be trusted to run this ship, you irresponsible—"

His tirade ended in a grunt of pain as Crabtree planted a fist in his stomach. Crabtree hardly seemed to move, but the punch had a devastating effect. Hornbeck sagged forward, his mouth hanging open. He would have dropped to his knees if Crabtree hadn't put a supporting arm around his shoulders. Crabtree marched him briskly to the hatch, then said, "Now, don't you come back until you're invited." A hard shove sent Hornbeck stumbling out of sight down the corridor.

Crabtree turned to face Hammett, planting his hands on his hips. He looked pleased with himself. "I beg your pardon for coming onto the bridge without permission, Sir. It seemed ... expedient." He glanced over his shoulder in the direction of the departed administrator. "Captains didn't have to put up with that sort of foolishness before the Corps was disbanded."

Hammett looked him over. "I had you pegged as ex-military, Mr. Crabtree."

Crabtree nodded. "Twenty years in uniform," he said proudly.

"Were you by any chance a marine?"

Crabtree grinned. "Not every Navy man is as quick on the uptake as you, Sir. I started out as a jar, and then ten years as a sergeant. My last two years I was a master sergeant."

"I've known some marines in my time,"

Hammett said. "They were tough men, every one of them. They lived in fear of their master sergeants, though."

Crabtree nodded, accepting the compliment as his due. "Begging your pardon, Captain, but I was hoping to talk to Lieutenant DiMarco about the laser batteries. I've had some experience with manual aiming on personnel carriers."

"You'll find him in the missile bay," Hammett said. "In the meantime, how would you like to be my Chief of Marines?"

Crabtree's eyebrows rose.

"You will also be my only marine, until you do some recruiting. We won't be taking a Gate home. That means about another four weeks in deep space. It may be necessary to put a guard on the food supplies."

"I'll put together a plan straightaway, Sir." Crabtree saluted and hurried out.

"I like him," said Carruthers.

Hammett grunted. "I'm certainly glad he's on our side."

Carruthers chuckled. Then his expression grew serious. "I didn't like that Hornbeck fellow so much." He shrugged. "Still, do you think he might be right? Maybe we should rush the Gate. Fight our way through, and get home. If there's only a handful of ships ..."

"And maybe there's a whole fleet tucked in behind the Gate, or sitting on the surface of the planet." Hammett shook his head. "No, a nuke gives us our highest probability of stopping them. It makes for a long flight home, but we can't take a chance on leaving them a Gate."

Carruthers nodded.

"We can get into firing range," Hammett said. "I'm pretty sure we can take out the Gate. After that, the only trick will be getting away."

CHAPTER 32 – HORNBECK

Pain.

For a time it was all Dalton Hornbeck knew. It was centered in his stomach, but it seemed to fill his whole body. Every breath was an agonized labor. He knelt in the corridor, the top of his head touching a bulkhead, wondering with each breath if he would be able to inhale again. It grew easier, but it still hurt.

As the worst of the pain passed a hot fury rose to take its place. It wasn't just the pain that stung him. It was the humiliation, and his utter impotence. He was nothing aboard the *Alexander*. Him, Dalton Hornbeck, the most powerful man in Deirdre. He had less authority than a cadet on this miserable tub.

He heaved himself to his feet and leaned against the bulkhead, holding his stomach. The casual, uncaring brutality of Crabtree's attack had rattled him deeply. *This*, he thought, fighting the agony in his midsection as he forced himself to stand upright. *This is why military forces need civilian oversight.*

He set off down the corridor, moving at a slow shuffle. *I'm a civilized man surrounded by barbarians. I'm the voice of reason – which they desperately need – and they won't listen.*

He would go back to his quarters, he decided. There he would be surrounded by his people, the survivors from Freedom Station. He grimaced. He was responsible for them, and he'd just failed them.

There were almost a hundred of them, and he was their leader. He felt his responsibility keenly. They were what mattered. The people, the innocent civilians who hadn't asked for an interstellar war. Why couldn't Hammett see that?

The man was a barbarian. He was like a little boy with a pellet gun, determined to shoot something just because he could. He was so keen on fighting the aliens, playing soldier, that he blinded himself to the whole reason that a military even existed.

"It's the people who matter," Hornbeck muttered. He thought of his staff back on Freedom Station. Most of them were dead. He remembered a man named Jerry, a retired spice farmer from a colony called Apricot. Jerry and Hornbeck had played squash twice a week for years. He'd become Hornbeck's best friend. Hornbeck had scoured the *Alexander*, hoping to find him, but Jerry wasn't there. He was gone.

So many people were gone. He saw their faces every night when he closed his eyes. It was costing him sleep. His friends, his colleagues, and casual acquaintances who had lived on his station. So many dead, and the rest in desperate danger. They were all his people, and he needed to get them home.

Which meant he needed to stop Hammett.

Hornbeck slowed his pace. He no longer wanted to rush to the comforting privacy of his little cabin. He hadn't risen to the top position on Freedom Station by being timid. By being afraid to make the tough choices. No, he'd always been willing to step up, take responsibility, and face the consequences of his actions.

He stopped. The idea that had taken root in the back of his mind frightened him. If he followed through, the consequences would be dire indeed.

But what were the consequences of doing nothing?

He whispered, "I can't let him destroy the Gate."

I can't do it on my own. But I'm a leader. And I know I'm not the only one who wants to get home. We could storm the bridge, take control. Put Hammett in the brig, along with anyone who insists on following him.

And then what?

Another officer would take command, and nothing would change. Hornbeck scowled. The civilians couldn't fly the ship; they didn't have the skills. He needed the cadets and the regular sailors, and yes, even the officers on his side. But there was no way he could convince them all. They were brainwashed. The military did that to a person. They were rigorously trained to follow a chain of command. To follow it blindly, even when the man at the top of the chain was an obvious lunatic.

If Hammett's in the brig, who takes charge? Probably that dolt Carruthers. He'll just do whatever he thinks Hammett wants. Hornbeck scowled, then hesitated. He remembered the meeting in the Baffin boardroom. Carruthers hadn't been there. Hammett had brought some woman. What was her name?

Velasco. Commander Velasco.

Wasn't Carruthers a lieutenant? Hornbeck didn't keep up to date on military ranks, but he was pretty sure a commander outranked a lieutenant. He thought back to that long-ago meeting and the three or four brief times he'd met Velasco since. He'd sensed something from her, especially when she and Hammett were together. She wasn't his puppet. In fact, if Hornbeck was any judge, she saw right through Hammett. She recognized him for a dangerous fool.

Would she see her greater duty?

Would she support a mutiny?

Hornbeck straightened up. The pain in his stomach wasn't so bad now. It was a dull ache, just enough to remind him of the consequences of settling for the status quo. He knew what he had to do. Now it was time to assemble his team.

He squared his shoulders and headed aft. Ben Wyatt would be his first recruit. He'd always struck Hornbeck is a sensible, reasonable man. Once he was on board, the Baffin team would follow. That would mean the effective support of every civilian on the ship, except that reporter woman. It was probably best to leave her out of it. She seemed pro-military.

Deep in thought, he rounded a corner and almost collided with a brawny young man with flaming red hair that showed dull brown at the roots. Two more young men flanked him. All three of them were rough-looking and uncouth. Hornbeck tried to move around them, but a beefy arm blocked his way.

"Well, well, well. Look what we have here. Dingleballs Hornbeck, in the flesh."

Hornbeck gave him a stern look. "I'm in a hurry. I'll need you to get out of my way."

"You're not going anywhere." The man stepped close, looming over Hornbeck, and his companions circled around, blocking every escape.

Hornbeck found himself perversely wishing Crabtree would show up. The thought annoyed him, driving the rising fear from his mind. He snapped, "What do you want?"

The red-haired man blinked, taken aback. Then he scowled. "We want proper food." He grimaced. "We're tired of this muck they're handing out. But a fancy man like you? I bet you're getting the good stuff."

For a long moment Hornbeck stared up at the man, weighing his options. He was deeply irritated, but he made himself bite back a sharp retort. These were desperate times, and the men confronting him could be valuable. He needed every tool he could get his hands on, and someone, after all, would have to face Crabtree.

He smiled.

Red Hair gave him a suspicious look.

"The food is about to get worse," Hornbeck told him. "After all, it has to last another four or five weeks."

The man's brow furrowed. "What do you mean? We're supposed to be back on Earth in a couple of days."

Hornbeck nodded. "Yes, that was the original plan. But the captain has spotted some more aliens, and his response to just about any stimulus is to blow something up." He let them see his disgust. "His current plan is to destroy Gate Eight."

The man looked horrified, as well he might.

"I don't plan to let him," Hornbeck said. "We can still be home in two days. I just have to put someone else in charge. But I can't do it on my own. I need your help."

The three imbeciles exchanged glances.

"I need you to do what you do best," Hornbeck said. "Intimidate some people, and make sure you get your fair share." He rubbed his stomach. "And act as my personal bodyguards."

"What do you mean, get our share?"

Hornbeck smiled. "Help me effect a change in leadership, and I'll see to it that you eat the captain's personal meals for the rest of the voyage. He won't object. He'll be in the brig."

CHAPTER 33 – VELASCO

I'm going to be an admiral.

Velasco repeated the phrase under her breath, over and over, like a mantra. It was the only thing keeping her going. *I'm going to be an admiral. It won't always be like this. I'll be one of a tiny handful of officers with actual field experience against the aliens. This will catapult my career.*

I'm going to be an admiral.

In the meantime, her life was a nightmare of cloying trivialities. Her years at Spacecom headquarters seemed like a sparkling golden dream. She'd been walking the same corridors as the most powerful people in the Navy. Building a power base. Building relationships. Building a career.

And now she was drowning in the minutia of keeping a battered starship running.

Her current task was mapping telephone lines.

Most of the installation had been done by technicians from Baffin. They had done a credible job, but they hadn't documented a single thing. Now Velasco, armed with a couple of notebooks and a pencil, was working her way through the ship from stem to stern, tracing every wire. The idea was to create a master document that would make it faster to diagnose and fix problems.

It was beneath her, but Hammett insisted. He said she needed to know the ship, and this was certainly one way to learn it.

We're two or three days from Earth, she fumed. *I should be preparing my reports for the Admiralty. I should be preparing my strategy. I need to think about who to talk to, in what order. What information to give out, and what to hold back. Not tramping through a lot of corridors following wires.*

The problem with Hammett was that he had no political sense. It was why he faced retirement with the lowly rank of captain. He didn't value what she did, didn't understand why it was vital to her. He honestly thought that mapping out wires and learning the ship was more important.

The Navy isn't about ships, you fool. It's about people. And the people who matter are back on Earth.

A sailor with a pistol on his hip stood in front of an armor-plated door a dozen paces away, staring at the bulkhead across from him. She wished he would go away. It embarrassed her to have a witness as she did such menial work. He was guarding the *Alexander*'s weapons locker, which was locked and unlocked by the ship's computer. That meant it was permanently unlocked until the ship could get a refit, so there was a sentry around the clock. He wasn't paying any attention to her, but she could imagine what he was thinking. Her cheeks burned as she worked her way along, one slow pace at a time, trailing her fingers along an insulated wire held by brackets glued to the bulkhead.

Wires would run along side by side, then veer off in different directions. Sometimes they crossed each other. There was no pattern to it that she could detect. The only way she could be sure which wire was which was to trace every miserable centimeter as she worked her way from one handset to another.

At last she came to a junction in the corridor and followed the wire around the corner, out of sight of the sentry. That made it easier to pretend she wasn't humiliated.

Feet rustled on the deck plates behind her, and she turned, irritated, to glare at a timid-looking cadet. "Well? What is it?"

"Message for you, Ma'am." The cadet thrust a scrap of paper at her, then scurried away.

Velasco sighed, pushed the hair back from her forehead, and looked at the paper. It was a page torn from one of the countless notebooks that everyone seemed to carry now. She recognized Hammett's blocky printing. His penmanship was improving, she decided. Instead of awful it was merely quite bad.

I need you to take charge of food supplies. We

will be four more weeks in space. Plan accordingly. Hammett.

She stared at the note, disbelief warring with fury inside her. Four more weeks? It was unthinkable! Meals were already close to intolerable. The last of the fresh food was long gone. They had some flour, which meant several slices of bread every few days. There were canned supplies, but they were nearly gone.

The staple of every meal was a gruel made up of powdered protein mixed with a carbohydrate paste. There were machines back on Freedom Station that would reconstitute those raw ingredients into something almost indistinguishable from fried chicken, or mashed potatoes, or corn flakes.

Those wonderful food processing machines, though, had been left behind. The kitchen staff of the *Alexander* could do nothing more than mix it with water and dump it into bowls. The taste wasn't really so bad, not for the first meal or two. By now she was long past the point of being merely sick of it, and she wasn't the only one.

Well, there wasn't enough to feed everyone for four more weeks anyway. Missing a meal here and there would give everyone a whole new appreciation for the gruel.

"Oh, my God. Four more weeks? Why the hell aren't we going home?" What was that idiot Hammett doing?

She sighed, put her notebook and pencil away, and started toward the galley. She passed a civilian going the other way, a middle-aged woman in an expensive dress that should have been sonically cleaned only. The dress had obviously gone through the ship's industrial laundry facilities a few times. Fabric that should have billowed and flowed around her now hung limp and lifeless. She looked ridiculous, and Velasco felt a mix of sympathy and irritation. Civilians could be so impractical!

The woman glanced at Velasco as she passed. Her eyes widened, and she picked up her pace. Velasco could hear the woman's heels clicking on the deck plates in a rapid-fire drumbeat behind her. She heard the woman call out, "I found her!"

Velasco stopped. Muffled voices echoed through the corridor behind her, and she heard more hurrying feet. After a moment the bedraggled woman returned. "Commander Velasco? Could you come with me, please? It's very important. Some people really need to talk to you."

Velasco felt her pulse increase. She didn't know what was going on, but she knew political maneuvering when she saw it. She smiled for the first time that day. At last she had a role to play in a game she understood. "Lead the way."

Six men and two women waited in a tool room just outside the shuttle bay. They were all civilians, she noted, and they all had the tense posture of conspirators. She recognized Hornbeck, the administrator of Freedom Station, and Wyatt, the man with the barbaric accent who ran things on Baffin. There was a fiery light in Hornbeck's eyes. The buttoned-down little bureaucrat was gone, replaced by a zealot with a mission.

She looked at Wyatt and saw doubt. He looked troubled, like a man reluctantly going along with something distasteful but necessary. He would be vulnerable if she needed a lever to use against Hornbeck. The rest of them were followers, and she ignored them, turning her attention to the administrator.

"Thank you for coming," said Hornbeck. His eyes flicked over her uniform, and she caught a hint of a grimace at the corners of his mouth. He didn't approve of her, but he thought he needed her. *Well, I can work with that.*

"We want to speak to you on behalf of the civilians aboard the *Alexander*." His diffident tone was at odds with the gleam in his eye. *He's hedging his bets. He won't lay his cards on the table until he has a sense of which way I'll jump.*

She said, "I take it you have some concerns?"

He nodded. "This plan to destroy the Gate and spend another four weeks in deep space. It's unacceptable."

Destroy the Gate? That was news to her, and it shocked her. She was good at hiding her reactions, but she could see in Hornbeck's eyes that he saw. They were two of a kind, probably the two most accomplished politicians on the ship.

What was he up to? What did these people want? There was one obvious way to get them to show their cards, at least a little. She said, "I don't know if that's an entirely wise decision."

The tension level in the room, almost painfully

high, dropped perceptibly. Plenty remained, though.

Hornbeck gave her a searching look. Finally he spoke, choosing his words with obvious care. "Some people have been wondering if it's possible to stop Captain Hammett from doing something rash and irreparable."

Aha! Now we get to the crux of the matter. Speaking with equal care, she said, "Stop the captain? How, exactly?"

Hornbeck's eyes narrowed. *He wants to see my cards before he shows me everything. I can understand that.* "We have a window of opportunity," he said. "A window that's rapidly closing. Once the ship jumps again, Hammett will fire a nuclear missile at the Gate. Then it won't matter how determined we are, or how right we are. We'll be trapped here. This ship has survived two battles with the alien fleet, at a terrible cost in human lives. Will we survive a third battle?"

A cold hand seemed to squeeze Velasco's stomach. *Christ, he's right. The clock is counting down. How long has it been since the last jump? How much time do we have left?*

"You don't want to do anything hasty," Hornbeck said softly. "I understand that. People in a leadership position have to consider their options carefully. After all, it's the innocent people who follow them who pay the price for blunders."

She stared into his eyes. He was a very persuasive speaker, and she sensed that, though he was perfectly capable of playing people with consummate skill, in this instance he was utterly sincere. She gulped.

"There is no time, however, for meticulous decision-making. If we are to act, we must act quickly." He held his hand up between them and made a fist. "We have an opportunity, and we must seize it. It will not be available to us for much longer."

"I ..." She felt a precipice yawning before her feet. It terrified her, and she stared at Hornbeck, unable to speak.

He gave her a searching look. Then he said, "You need time to think on what we've said. When the time comes to take action, I'm sure you'll make the right decision." It was a perfectly innocent statement, but loaded with deadly layers of meaning. "We don't want you to do anything your conscience wouldn't allow," he told her. "We just want you to know that there are concerned civilians who would rather we hurried back to Earth."

She nodded and turned toward the door. A pair of goons stood just outside, big knuckle-draggers who gave her suspicious looks and glanced at Hornbeck before letting her pass. She moved between them, gained the corridor beyond, and started to walk. As soon as she turned the first corner she broke into a trot. Before long she was almost running.

What the hell just happened? Was I in danger? If I'd threatened to turn them in for fomenting mutiny, would they have let me leave?

Mutiny.

The word, cold and ugly, confronted her, and she slowed. Finally she stopped, leaning against a bulkhead as she caught her breath. A cadet approached, started to speak, and she glared at him. He blanched and hurried past.

Mutiny. They hang people for that, don't they? Or they would, if it ever happened. I don't think it's happened in a hundred years. Because no one would cross that line.

I should report them. Go to Hammett, give him names, let him round them all up before they ...

Before they what? Remove him from power? Put me in command instead?

I could countermand the order to nuke the Gate. I could fly us through instead. We could be home in no time. Hornbeck said we're one jump from the Gate. We could charge through, not stop. We could be in Earth orbit in a day.

They could hang me.

She imagined military policemen marching her to a gallows, her hands manacled behind her, utterly disgraced. But another vision intruded. Throughout history the truly exceptional leaders – the ones whose careers had really taken off, the ones who had left their mark – had been those who rose to meet the challenge of exceptional circumstances. She would never distinguish herself by following every order issued by a bad captain. But if she was the one officer with the courage, the vision, to step in and take decisive action to avert disaster ...

I could be the hero of New Avalon. My career wouldn't have to stop at the admiralty. There would be no limit to the possibilities. No limit at all.

She took a deep breath and headed up a staircase, following in reverse the path she'd taken to the clandestine meeting. *I bet they've all scattered by now. Just in case I turn them in.*

At last she rounded a corner and reached the weapons locker. The same bored sailor stood there, giving her a brief incurious glance before resuming his examination of the opposite bulkhead. He would be the first casualty in the coming conflict.

I should warn him. I should tell him he's in danger. He's done nothing wrong. He doesn't deserve the fate that's in store. She stopped in front of him. He met her eyes, and she took a deep breath, not sure what she was going to say until the words came out.

"I need into the weapons locker."

He lifted an eyebrow, then stepped aside and pulled on the armored door. "Light's not working," he said. "Sensor's fried."

She walked inside. The locker was small, maybe three paces wide by five deep, with racks of weapons and bins of ammunition. Would laser weapons still function? Well, old-school chemical guns were a safe bet. They didn't have a single electronic component. Velasco selected a pistol, loaded it, and pocketed a spare clip and a handful of cartridges. The gun belts tempted her, but she needed to be discreet. She put the gun in the back of her waistband and tugged her jacket down to cover it.

There was no good way to tell the sailor to keep

his mouth shut. She nodded to him instead, and he closed the door behind her as she walked away.

I haven't made a decision. I'm just being proactive. Preparing myself for whatever might happen. I haven't done a single thing wrong. I haven't crossed any lines.

The gun seemed unnaturally heavy as she squared her shoulders and headed for the bridge.

CHAPTER 34 – DIMARCO

"Why are we blowing up the Gate, Chief? Don't we want to go home?"

Lieutenant Tony DiMarco shot an irritated glance at the cadet who knelt across from him on the other side of the missile. Higgins was an earnest young man who tended to ask interesting, challenging questions about missiles and how they were targeted. He had a knack for looking at things in bizarre ways, and he'd already provided DiMarco with some real insights. DiMarco wasn't sure he could have fixed the targeting system in his hands without the kid's endless, unexpected questions.

However, not every question was insightful or relevant. "That's not our decision, Higgins. The captain makes the tough calls. We just carry out his orders."

"But what if he's wrong?" the cadet persisted.

DiMarco sighed. "First of all, he has access to far more information than we do." He patted the casing on the missile. "Any time there's a disagreement about missile function, we're probably right. When it's a disagreement about big-picture stuff, my money's on the captain." Higgins opened his mouth, but DiMarco spoke over him. "Second, I've served under Captain Hammett for ten years, and I've heard a few stories about his record during the war. He makes good decisions. If he says to nuke the Gate, then the Gate damned well needs nuking."

Higgins looked at the third member of their little team. "What do you think, Shira?"

Shira Mbeki had been a computer consultant on Freedom Station. Her specialty was helping clients recover from disastrous hardware and software failures, and DiMarco found her completely indispensable. She grinned at Higgins. "Setting aside the fact that my opinion is irrelevant, I would have to say that I don't have enough information to contradict the captain."

Higgins said, "But what if he—"

"Help me with this," DiMarco interrupted, lifting the targeting assembly into the nose of the missile. Higgins immediately stopped arguing, leaning forward and moving connecting rods into place while DiMarco held the assembly still.

They were done in a minute or two, and DiMarco stood, knuckling his lower back as Higgins put the outside cover in place. DiMarco walked over to the telephone station on the wall and lifted the handset. "Missile bay to bridge." He listened for a moment, then frowned. "The phone is dead."

Higgins looked up, his face alight with interest. No technical problem was too big or too small to fascinate him. DiMarco thought the destruction of so many ship's systems by the enemy's mystery weapon might have been the high point of the young man's life.

"Forget it," DiMarco said with a grin. "You don't get to fix the telephone. You get to run up to the bridge with a report." The cadet's face fell, and DiMarco chuckled.

A distant boom echoed through the corridor, and DiMarco looked around, puzzled. "That sounded almost like an explosion." He looked at Shira. She was staring at the hatch, her body strangely tense. He said, "What is it, Shira?"

Metal clicked against metal and the hatch popped open, the panel sliding back several centimeters. A couple of hands grabbed the edge of the hatch, sliding it farther open.

Shira cursed and lunged forward. Her hand slapped down on the fat red emergency button beside the hatch. The door started sliding shut, and a man shoved a burly forearm in the way. The hatch pinched his arm against the frame, and he cursed. Then he tugged his arm free, grabbed the edge of the hatch with both hands, and heaved.

Shira pried at his fingers, and one hand popped free. She grabbed at the other hand, and the first hand returned. DiMarco could hear the man grunting with effort, and he started toward the hatch.

A woman's face appeared in the gap. She had wild blonde hair, and the single eye that peered into the compartment looked feverish, almost demented. She snaked a hand through the opening and aimed a pistol blindly at Shira. Shira had her head down as she struggled with the man's fingers, and the pistol lined up unerringly with the top of her skull.

Time seemed to slow down. DiMarco was running in slow motion, knowing he would be far too late. He could see the skin over the woman's knuckle moving, turning white as she squeezed.

At the last possible instant Shira looked up, then flinched aside. The gun fired, the noise like a hammer blow against DiMarco's ears, and blood sprayed red from the side of Shira's head. Bone gleamed white for just an instant, and then she collapsed.

The man heaved, the hatch slid open a hand span or more, and then DiMarco's foot slammed into the back of the woman's hand. He distinctly heard the crackle of small bones breaking, before all sound was drowned out by her scream. The force of his kick drove her hand into the side of her face, and he felt a satisfying impact that jarred him all the way up to his hip. The barrel of the pistol hit the hatch, and the gun went clattering across the deck plates.

DiMarco had a quick glimpse of the corridor. It was jammed with people. He pulled his foot back and stood. The hatch was a lost cause. He whirled, scanning the missile room.

Higgins stood beside the missile, eyes wide, his

jaw hanging slack. DiMarco reached him in four running steps. "Come on!" He grabbed a handful of the cadet's uniform and hauled him across the bay.

Behind him he heard grunts of effort and a low mechanical hiss as the invaders shoved the hatch open. Then came excited voices and the thump of feet as people poured into the missile bay.

He didn't look back.

Higgins, recovered now from his momentary paralysis, ran beside him. He was young and terrified, and he was a couple of paces ahead of DiMarco by the time they reached their only possible destination: a low hatchway at the far end of the room. Higgins smacked the access panel and the hatch slid open.

"Stop them!" The excited slap of feet told DiMarco that pursuit was coming. Someone shouted, "Get out of the way! You're blocking my shot."

Higgins ducked through the hatch, and DiMarco threw himself after the cadet. He landed hard on one shoulder, grunted as his skull banged against the deck plates, and rolled up onto his knees.

Higgins, though, was already in action. He hit a button, the hatch slid shut, and he pried open the emergency panel beside the hatch controls. The panel popped open, Higgins shoved a hand into the cavity behind it, and the hatch started to open.

The hatch froze, open no more than the width of a man's fist. The muscles of Higgins's back moved as he twisted on an invisible handle, and the hatch began to slide shut.

Someone grabbed the edge of the hatch from outside, a man with thick, muscular fingers. DiMarco rose to his feet, thinking of Shira. Fury and terror filled him, and he screamed as he lifted his foot and drove his heel with all of his strength at those fingers.

His boot hit the hatch, the fingers vanished, and a scream echoed through the compartment. There was a moment of silence as the man took a breath, then another scream that was suddenly muted as Higgins finished closing the hatch.

"It's locked," said Higgins. "Or as good as. The automatic controls don't work once you've started turning the manual control." He was resting on one knee, and he drew his hands out of the little opening, flexing his fingers and rotating his shoulders. "They could open the hatch from their side, though, and turn the same handle. We could try to hold it from our side, but ... They have guns."

"Maybe they'll think of it," DiMarco said. "Maybe they won't." He was panting from exertion and adrenalin. He made himself take a couple of slow, deep breaths, and then he looked around.

They were in the auxiliary storage room, used for extra guidance chips or other useful parts. The room also contained several toolkits, left there by DiMarco himself. He hated having to run to Engineering for a wrench or a laser cutter. He found the biggest tool box, opened the lid, and started to rummage.

"What are we going to do, Chief?"

DiMarco straightened up, a large hammer in his hand. He wished he'd had it when those fingers had grabbed the edge of the hatch. "First, we sound General Quarters." He stepped forward and swung at the hatch, and Higgins flinched back. Six times the hammer crashed against the steel panel, and by the end of it Higgins had both hands pressed to his ears.

"Next," DiMarco said, then paused. He couldn't hear his own voice. He set the hammer down and waited for a moment. When the worst of the ringing was gone from his ears he said, "Next, we find another way out of here."

"Another way?" Higgins looked around the rather small chamber. "There *is* no other way out."

DiMarco favoured him with a grim smile. "We're engineers. We don't let other people's design mistakes stand in our way." He shoved a toolkit toward Higgins and gestured at the back bulkhead. "Let's get to work. We're going to make a new hatch."

CHAPTER 35 – HAMMETT

The *Alexander* popped out of a temporary wormhole into normal space less than a hundred thousand kilometers from the night side of the planet New Avalon. As reports came in from various observation stations Hammett felt some of his tension ease. It was a nearly perfect jump, putting the bulk of the planet between the *Alexander* and the enemy ships that surrounded the Gate. "Good work," he told Cartwright. "Ease us into a nice slow orbit around the planet. I want the engines cold by the time we have line of sight on the target."

Cartwright nodded and lifted a handset. She spoke, frowned, and shook the handset. She wiggled the wires where they connected to the bottom, then held the handset to her ear and said "Hello?"

A voice said, "Um." Hammett looked at the line

of cadets manning telephones along the starboard bulkhead. Cadet Wilkins met his gaze and said, "My phone just died."

The cadet beside him picked up her handset and listened. "Mine's dead too."

"I think it's all of us," said the cadet at the end of the line.

Beside him Cadet Nakatomi spoke into her handset." Bridge to port lounge. Do you copy?" She listened for a moment. "Thank you." She lowered the phone. "My phone is fine." She frowned and looked down, then lifted the handset. "Port lounge? Are you still there?" She looked up and shook her head.

"Runner," Hammett said. There were only two, a cadet and a civilian girl who couldn't have been more than twelve. She stepped forward, looking nervous and excited. The strip of tape on the front of her shirt said "Smith".

Hammett said, "I need you to find Peter Breckenridge and tell him the bridge telephones are down."

She bobbed her head. "Yes, Sir. Where is he?"

"I have no idea. Go to the forward telephone hub first. See if the phones there are working. Don't come back and tell me. I don't care. Tell Breckenridge."

Smith looked alarmed, but she gave him a crisp salute, then whirled and ran from the bridge.

Carruthers said softly, "This is not a good time for technical problems."

"No. Maybe—"

A distant metallic clang interrupted him. He

went silent, counting. Six clangs in total rang out, and he stared at Carruthers. "Who the hell is sounding General Quarters?" Before the man could answer he said, "Never mind. Who has a working phone? Anybody?" The sailor at the weapons station raised her hand, and Hammett hurried over to her. He grabbed the phone from her and barked, "Who's this?"

"Janice Ling," said a wary voice.

There was no time for pleasantries, not if the half-formed worm of fear squirming in his guts had any basis in fact. "I need you to get to the shuttle bay. Don't let anyone stop you, either. Find al Faisal and tell him to launch the *Falcon*. He has to destroy the Gate. Then find yourself a quiet closet and lock yourself in."

She was silent for several long seconds. Then she said, "Got it," and he heard a thud as she set the handset down. He heard the distant thump of her feet, receding with distance. By the sound of it she was running.

Then silence.

Hammett handed his phone to the sailor and pointed to the line of cadets along the wall. "All of you are runners now. Get to the engine room, the missile bay, and the weapons locker. Tell them we may be under attack."

Carruthers said, "Under attack? By who?"

"Either we've been boarded by the enemy, or it's mutiny." *Or it's a mechanical failure and someone dropped six wrenches, in which case I'll be quite embarrassed shortly.* He gestured at the cadets. "Go!"

Five of them surged forward, moving as one.

Wilkins, in the lead, was a couple of paces from the bridge hatchway when a crowd came surging in. Cadets stumbled to a halt, Wilkins staggering into a slim figure in dark pinstripes at the head of the arriving mob. There was a burst of light, a smell of ozone, and Wilkins flew back, his arms and legs spasming. He landed on his back on the deckplates, his limbs twitching, froth coating his lips.

Hornbeck stood in the entrance, a stunner in his hand. He looked down at Wilkins, then lifted his gaze and locked eyes with Hammett. The stunner zeroed in on the center of Hammett's chest, the barrel never wavering as Hornbeck stepped onto the bridge. Men and women crowded in behind him, seven of them in total, civilians armed with kitchen knives and improvised clubs.

Hammett said, "How many times do I need to throw you off my bridge?"

"I regret the necessity of violence," Hornbeck said, his voice cold and steady. "But it's indeed necessary. All that's left to be seen is just how much violence will be required." He came to a stop in front of Hammett. "That part is up to you." He raised his voice. "There's no point in resisting! All of you need to understand that. Wyatt's team has taken the weapons locker and missile bay by now. You can't destroy the Gate, and you can't retake the ship. Do as I tell you and we'll all be home in a couple of days."

"Are you in such a hurry to hang?" Hammett

murmured.

Hornbeck didn't answer, just stared at him, chin thrust out. They stood face to face, Hornbeck just out of arm's reach. Hammett thought of going for the stunner, and estimated his chances at about fifty percent. Hornbeck's followers were moving around the bridge, spreading themselves out. Hammett counted three knives. If he made his move, there would be a bloodbath. Still, nine trained Navy personnel would prevail against eight civilians, weapons or no weapons. He took a deep breath and bent his legs, ever so slightly.

There was movement over Hornbeck's shoulder, and Hammett felt a surge of hope. Velasco walked onto the bridge, stepping lightly, her feet silent on the deck plates. She held a gun in her hand.

"Now!" The cry came from Carruthers, and he sprang as he shouted, tackling a burly man with a knife and knocking him sprawling. Hornbeck's head turned, and Hammett stepped forward. His left hand slapped the stunner aside as his right fist slammed into the side of Hornbeck's face. The little administrator flew back, landing on the deck beside the captain's chair. The stunner bounced once and came to a stop at Velasco's feet.

Something moved in the corner of Hammett's eye, he started to duck, and a club made from a table leg grazed the back of his skull. He saw stars, and hurled himself at his attacker before the man could swing again. His shoulder hit a man's chest, strong arms wrapped themselves around him, and he strained against the man, looking over his shoulder at Velasco.

She stooped, picked up the stunner, and straightened. For a moment she stood there with a gun in each hand. Then she took careful aim with the stunner and fired.

Hammett didn't see where the shot hit, but he heard Carruthers cry out.

Velasco turned. Just inside the hatchway a pair of cadets had a civilian woman by both arms. A cadet lifted his knee, striking the woman's wrist, and a knife dropped from her fingers. Velasco fired twice, and both cadets fell, leaving the woman standing there, arms out, with a look of comical astonishment on her face.

Struggling figures went still all over the bridge. Velasco, her face expressionless, scanned the room. Nakatomi knelt by the weapons station, a deep slash on her forearm dripping blood. She glared up at Velasco, then lowered a thick-bladed carving knife and set it on the deck beside the curled-up body of a fat man in a white suit. The suit was liberally splashed with blood, hers and his own. He had both hands pressed to his face, and blood welled between his fingers and pooled under his head.

Hornbeck rose unsteadily, holding a hand to the side of his face. Velasco handed him the stunner, then extended the pistol and took it in a two-handed grip. She pointed the gun at the center of Hammett's body and said, "That's enough."

Hammett looked at the man he was struggling with. "I think she means you."

The man snorted and let go of Hammett, stepping back quickly. Hammett turned to face Velasco. He felt no fear, just a weary frustration. The other mutineers drew back from the crew, edging in closer to their leaders. Velasco said, "All of you. In that corner. Move!"

A sailor named Vincenzo was on his knees beside Nakatomi. He stood, his hands completely covered in blood, and said, "I'm getting the med kit."

He started walking across the bridge, and a mutineer stepped into his path, knife in hand. "She said—"

"Don't make me shove that knife up your ass." Vincenzo didn't wait for the man to reply, just stepped around him and opened a wall panel marked with a red cross. He lifted out a plastic case and carried it to Nakatomi.

As he knelt beside her, the mutineer tried again. "Treat Hutchins first." He gestured at the man in the white suit.

Vincenzo didn't even look up. He took several items from the med kit, then shoved the kit in the direction of the bleeding man. The mutineer with the knife took a step forward, and Velasco said, "Leave it. The rest of you, in the corner." She looked at Hammett. "You too, Hammett."

Hammett said softly, "What are you doing, Velasco?"

"It's simple. I'm taking command."

CHAPTER 36 – WEST

Mathew West sat on his bunk with his guitar on his lap, listening to the fast, frightened thumping of his heart. He had no idea what all the banging and clanging outside meant. That had been bad enough, but then had come gunfire and screams. He felt as if he'd been transported back to the ballroom on Freedom, before he'd lost Jessica and almost his life. He wished Hornbeck and his stunner would show up to rescue him one more time.

The sound of a fist banging on a hatch made him jump. It wasn't even his hatch. By the sound of it, it was one room over. A muffled voice shouted, the tone angry, the words indistinguishable. Someone else yelped.

West tightened his grip on the guitar.

More banging, even louder. That last time must have been two rooms away, then. Now it was next door. He heard thumping from the next cabin. Then, inevitably, the hammering of something solid on the hatch in front of him.

He stood, and the hatch swung open. *Why didn't I lock it? But that would just have made them angry. Whoever they are. What's going on?*

The man who leaned in looked wild-eyed and angry. He wasn't military, not with that flying hair and unkempt beard. He held a length of pipe in one fist, and he said, "Get out here. Now."

West, too terrified to ask what was happening, stooped through the hatch and stepped into the corridor. Frightened-looking people lined one wall, seven or eight men and women with the same cowed look he remembered from Freedom Station. The bearded man and two companions stomped back and forth, their victims cringing back as they passed. There was a man with no weapon but his fists, and a woman who held a pistol as if she thought it might bite her. West had the distinct impression that if anything startled her – even a loud noise from another deck – she was going to shut her eyes and just start shooting.

"All right, get moving," the bearded man said. When nobody moved his face turned red and he bellowed, "Now!"

West, with no idea where the man wanted him to go, took a couple of steps down the corridor. A thick arm barred his way. "What are you doing?" The man screamed the words, and flecks of spittle hit West's cheek and lips. "Go the other way!"

West pivoted and followed the miserable line of prisoners as they shuffled along. There was a cadet in front of him, a boy with a hanging head, a long red welt that matched the pipe decorating the side of his face. He was the only military prisoner. The rest were ordinary folks like West, probably survivors from Freedom Station, the same as him. *Did we get through that nightmare just to die here today? Killed by imbeciles who don't even know what they want?*

A staircase appeared on the right, and the woman with the gun used her free hand to shove the first prisoner sideways. It was a thin teenage girl, and she stumbled, clutching the railing to keep from falling down the steps. The others took the hint and followed. West, still clutching his borrowed guitar to his chest, brought up the rear, the bearded man's hand between his shoulder blades.

There was more shouting when they reached the next landing. It seemed no one except Beardy actually knew where they were heading. The prisoners stood in a wretched knot while their tormenters screamed conflicting orders. West, terrified by their twisted faces, turned his head away.

He found himself staring through the railings into a shadowy space under the stairs. In that dark cave he saw another face staring back at him. It was a cadet, looking very young and frightened, holding himself motionless, gazing at West with wide, unblinking eyes. It took a moment for West to notice the others. There were at least three cadets under the steps, their dark uniforms blending into the shadows.

A hand closed on West's collar and yanked. "Get moving, you. I'll break your fucking skull."

He stumbled to the bottom of the steps, then followed the others down a short corridor and into the shuttle bay. More prisoners waited there, dozens of them, crowded together in one corner, pressed up against stacks of plastic boxes. Half a dozen men and women stalked back and forth in front of the prisoners, guns in hand.

West let them herd him toward the corner. His hands were sweaty on the guitar. The teenage girl was beside him, and she shied suddenly sideways, bumping into him. He let go of the guitar neck long enough to catch her shoulder and keep her from falling, then felt his fingers tighten as he saw what had startled her.

A corpse lay on the deck. It was a fat woman in her forties, and she lay on her back with three gaping holes in her chest and stomach. West could see raw flesh, but no sign of blood coming from the terrible wounds. She was dead.

"Ouch, you're hurting me. Ow!"

The girl twisted from his grip, rubbing her shoulder, and he muttered "Sorry" without taking his eyes from the dead woman.

Just beyond the corpse a sailor lay on his back in a pool of blood. West couldn't see if it was a man or a woman. Three people knelt around the body, an older man in a medical officer's uniform and a pair of cadets. As West shuffled past, the officer looked up and said, "You have to let me take this woman to Medical!"

"Forget it," said the nearest gunman. His voice

sounded high and frightened, and he levelled a pistol on the doctor, as if he thought the man would leap up and attack him. The doctor turned his attention back to the injured sailor and West joined the rest of the prisoners in the corner.

He sensed fright from everyone around him, but the mood of the crowd was changing. A woman was bleeding to death not more than six paces away, and West heard frustrated muttering, turning quickly to anger.

The bearded man with the pipe led his two followers back out to the corridor, leaving six guards alone with thirty or more surly, restless prisoners. The injured sailor moaned, and West felt the tension in the bay rise sharply. In a moment there was going to be violence. How many shots could six people get off before the mob overwhelmed them?

It didn't bear thinking about it.

His ankle bumped into one of Dulcie's plastic boxes, and he sat on it. The plastic sides groaned but held, and he told himself he would just sit there quietly and do nothing to draw attention to himself. From a sitting position it would be quicker to hit the deck when the shooting started. He could see people discreetly grabbing rail gun rounds, one in each hand. They made a nice solid handful. They would make excellent missiles. It was, after all, what they were made for. He imagined the guards going down under a hail of hand-thrown cylinders. Would it be enough?

Not likely. Some of these people were going to die.

His fingers slid along the neck of the guitar, seeking comfort in the familiar touch of smooth wood and taut strings. He didn't even realize he was playing until people near him turned to gape. He played a simple melody, a lullaby he'd learned more years ago than he cared to count. The notes, low and soothing, flowed out from the guitar and one prisoner after another turned to stare.

"What are you doing?" The speaker was a wild-eyed young man, advancing on West with his arm stretched out straight, the gun trained on West as if he thought the lullaby was an attack. *He's scared,* West realized. *He's much more frightened than I am, and I'm terrified. He's in over his head and he knows it. He just doesn't know what to do. The gun's all he has. Shooting someone is the only trick he knows.*

He kept playing, not speaking, not making eye contact. He could see the gun in his peripheral vision, levelled at his head, then swinging left and right to cover the other prisoners. "Stay back! Don't move! Back up! Don't move!"

Idiot. And some other idiot gave him a gun. God help us. The kid didn't want to shoot anyone, though. He was just out of his mind with fear.

"I'm going to play a song," West said. He kept his voice soft and conversational. "It won't do any harm, and it'll help keep everyone calm." He strummed the guitar. "Is that all right?" More strumming. The kid didn't speak, just stared at him with the whites showing all around his irises. West said, "Well, shoot me if it bothers you," and started to play in earnest.

He couldn't have said what song he was going to pick, but his fingers knew what they were doing. It was a song he hadn't played since he was a teenager, and he heard himself bungling a few chords. *Well, I don't see any music critics in the room.* It was an old ballad, something from his parents' generation, the kind of sappy, sentimental thing he'd rebelled against when he decided to dedicate himself to smoky blues.

He sang, trying to keep his voice soft, but gaining power with every verse in spite of himself. He sang about kids going off to war, afraid to go, afraid to stay home, hoping desperately they were doing the right thing.

And when I cross that ocean wide, and I reach that distant shore,

And I walk those long green fields, and I hear the cannon roar,

With a musket in my hands, and my comrades by my side,

Will I do my duty then? Will I keep my honor bright?

Will I be brave? Will I do right? Will I keep my honour bright?

Will I be strong, through the long night? Will I keep my honour bright?

The song had struck the teenaged West as preachy nonsense, but it felt different in that feverish room under the barrels of guns. He squeezed his eyes shut and poured his heart into the song, and when the last note trailed away he looked up just in time to see the doctor vanishing through the main hatchway. The injured sailor lay on an improvised stretcher made from a bedsheet, with a prisoner at each corner. They followed the doctor into the corridor, and a woman with a gun brought up the rear.

Now there's only five guns in here. The odds just improved.

CHAPTER 37 – KASIM

It was his first combat flight, and it was going to be his last.

Kasim flew through the void, his mouth as dry as moon dust, wishing desperately for a drink of water. He was going to die. It was an absolute certainty, and he was afraid.

It would be a good scrap, though. A handful of enemy ships against the bulky, lumbering *Falcon*. The ship was armed now, with a single laser on the top hull, pointing directly forward. The only way to aim it was to aim the entire ship.

Just above the laser, a crude-looking metal rack held one of the *Alexander's* nuclear missiles. He would be able to fire the missile with perfect precision. He would use the laser as a pointer. When he saw a red dot on the Gate, he would launch.

And then that handful of alien ships would

come after him. He would fight as best he could, with the laser and with skill and raw talent. However, he knew perfectly well he would lose.

He would die beside the remains of Gate Eight.

"That's right, you bastards," he muttered. "It's me again. The guy who keeps blowing up your Gates." Brave words, but he could taste sour bile on the back of his tongue. Only a stubborn bravado kept him from moaning out loud with fear.

That, and the thought of Sally MacKinnon. Every time he thought of her, and he thought of her often, a fresh wave of grief and rage would crash over him. He wanted to avenge her. He wanted to strike a blow in her name, and if it killed him, well, that was all right with Kasim.

The worst part was that he had nothing to do, nothing to distract himself with. The *Falcon* was on a ballistic trajectory, hurtling through space at a fantastic velocity with the engines off. It was a long fall around the planet to the target, and nothing for him to do but fret.

The fingers of his right hand ached. He ignored the pain. He'd gotten good at ignoring it over the last two weeks. The burns were pretty bad. His hand was pink and delicate with brand-new skin, some of it deadened by nerve damage, some of it excruciatingly sensitive. When he wasn't dropping things or bumping things he was cringing back from the gentlest contact. And underlying all of it was a bone-deep ache that felt as if it would never go away.

Well, it won't be bothering you for much longer.

The stars were crisp and lovely all around him, and he decided he would spend his last hours taking in the view instead of imagining his own death. The glittering arm of the Milky Way shone to his left, and he traced that glorious river of stars with his eyes.

And blinked.

One of those sparkling points of light was moving. He wasn't quite alone after all.

Something else was orbiting the planet. Had the miners put a satellite up, or some kind of space station? Or was it aliens?

All the delicate scanners on the *Falcon* were long since fried. He stared through the cockpit window, then took out the telescope someone had left for him in the luggage net behind the seat. It had the look of something whipped up on that fabricating machine he'd seen in the shuttle bay. It was a tapered cylinder of dark plastic longer than his arm, and he had to unstrap himself from his seat to use it.

He removed his helmet, clipped it to the mount beside the pilot's seat, then let himself float at the back of the cockpit. With the gravity off the telescope was easy to line up. It hovered in place, and he nudged it into line, then peered through the eyepiece.

The ship leaped into view, hovering like a gray plum in the void. It was oval in shape, and not quite as bizarre as the alien craft he had seen. He wondered if it might be a Navy ship sent to investigate the spreading alien threat. He had a brief fantasy of reinforcements, his life spared as dozens of corvettes swarmed through to seize New Avalon.

They would have food. Actual foods that wasn't gruel.

A pattern of shadow caught his eye, and he squinted through the eyepiece. An indentation marred the hull of the other ship. It was triangular in shape, and the more he examined it, the sicker he felt. That indentation would perfectly match the hulls of the smallest alien craft. One of those little ships could dock perfectly with the big vessel.

That put things in perspective. He could estimate the size of the ship now. It would be fifty or sixty meters long, and half as wide. He was frighteningly close, well under fifty kilometers. What if it spotted him? What if it broke into a swarm of smaller ships and—

No. That smooth, seamless hull told him it would not break apart. This was not a collection of smaller ships, but one larger craft. Maybe a supply ship, a fuel tanker of some sort. Or a repair ship, or ... It could be anything, he realized. Anything at all.

I could blow that thing up. The thought was seductive. He could strike a meaningful blow against the enemy, then turn and retreat to the *Alexander*.

He could live.

He went as far as resting a hand on the engine ignition switch that jutted from the dash. Then he let go of the switch and leaned back. *Forget it, Kasim. You have to blow the Gate. Do it for everyone back home. Do it for Sally. You want to make the bastards suffer, and the Gate is the best way to do it.*

The *Falcon* continued in its orbit, and Kasim returned to his morbid thoughts. He glanced back one last time before the ship vanished over the horizon. *You don't know how lucky you are. Killer Kasim spotted you, but he chooses to let you live.*

The alien ship vanished behind the curve of the planet, and Kasim continued his lonely journey toward his destiny.

CHAPTER 38 – WYATT

"Tell me how the bloody engines work." Peter Wyatt loomed over Susan Rani, doing his best to intimidate her. She had confronted him, bristling with indignation, when he had stormed into the engine room with a dozen mutineers on his heels. One of Wyatt's men had backhanded her across the face. Her lip was puffed out to twice its normal thickness, and she had a trickle of blood on her chin. Just looking at her made Wyatt feel ill.

Now he was trying to frighten her, which was much worse. Even worse than that, it wasn't working.

"Shoot me," she said.

He looked at the gun that dangled in his right hand, carefully pointed at the deck plates. He knew he could never use it. He couldn't even bring himself to threaten her with it. Instead he gestured at the four cadets and two sailors who knelt along the aft bulkhead. "Maybe I'll start shooting cadets," he said.

Her eyes drilled into him, and he squirmed at the contempt he saw there. "Go ahead," she said. "Bloody cadets. I never liked them." She glanced at the line of prisoners. "Do me a favor and start with the gangly kid with the big ears."

There were two cadets that might have fit the description, and they looked at one another, alarmed.

"I'm trying to take the ship home," Wyatt said. "Why can't you see that?"

"We'll go home when our job is done. That's how it works." She looked him up and down. "You don't like it, I'm sure we can drop you off back at your station on Kukulcan."

Wyatt scowled, not liking the reminder that these people he was terrorizing had rescued him. He stuffed the gun in the back of his waistband, afraid he would clench his fists and shoot himself in the foot. He hated the bloody pistol. It was a disaster waiting to happen.

"Give me five minutes with her." The speaker was Digby, a burly man with an unhealthy smile and hair the color of a safety poster. Most of the mutineers were alarmed by the enormity of what they were doing, but bleakly determined to do what they must. Digby seemed to be loving every minute of it. He had a pistol, and when he wasn't pointing it at someone he would fondle it and stroke it. He looked at Susan Rani now, and his eyes glittered.

"Forget it." Digby frowned, and Wyatt said, "Take a couple of men and scout the corridor. There'll be a counterattack sooner or later. I want to know about it before they storm in here." When the man gave him a stubborn look, Wyatt said, "Go on. Maybe you'll get to shoot somebody."

Or maybe somebody will shoot you, and all of us will be better off.

Digby gestured to a couple of other men, bullies cut from the same cloth, and the three of them headed into the corridor. The tension level in the engine room dropped perceptibly.

"I could start pulling handles and twisting knobs," Wyatt said to Rani. "Maybe get us all killed. Is that what you want?"

Rani didn't deign to answer.

Fear and adrenalin and frustration churned together in his stomach, making it difficult to think straight. He was well into middle age, with years of experience at leadership and dealing with crises, and he was a mess. How much worse would it be for the younger mutineers? How long before someone got hurt?

That was assuming no one had died already. The young woman at the weapons locker had a concussion at the very least. What was happening on the rest of the ship? Wyatt felt his stomach heave. *It wasn't supposed to be like this.*

A sound came echoing in from the corridor, a sound Wyatt wouldn't have recognized an hour earlier. But he'd seen Digby smash a length of pipe into the skull of the sailor guarding the weapons locker. There was nothing quite like the sickening thump you got when a human skull hit metal. That was the sound he heard now, and his head came whipping around.

A man screamed. He thought it was Digby, but he couldn't be sure. There was another fleshy thump, and the scream stopped abruptly.

Mutineers began to cluster in the doorway, looking at one another and fingering their guns. Some of the prisoners were giving Wyatt speculative looks, and he said, "Don't even think about it."

"Hello in the engine room!" It was a man's voice, almost obscenely cheerful. It was that man from Freedom Station, Wyatt realized. The old guy with the cold eyes. Crabtree.

"We've got guns now," Crabtree called. "Three of them. Thanks very much."

Wyatt opened his mouth to tell his people to get back out of the doorway, but he never got the chance. A shot rang out, and Hank Laycraft seemed to spring backward. He landed flat on his back, his head a bloody mess. The rest of the mutineers scrambled backward, retreating deeper into the engine room.

Not all of them. A man lay on his stomach, arms splayed out. As Wyatt watched, he rose to his knees and shuffled forward, his left hand clutching his right shoulder. Blood soaked his shirt. When he had put the bulk of a cooling array between himself and the doorway he collapsed on his chest, still clutching the wound.

I didn't even hear the second shot. He killed a man and critically injured another, and he did it in, what? A second? Everybody is staring at me. I'm supposed to tell them what to do. I don't know what to do! I'm a technician, not a bloody commando. He looked around at the shocked, frightened faces of his followers, then looked past them at the corpse sprawled in the doorway. *Hank's dead. Good God. He's bloody dead. He's been my friend for fifteen years. He wouldn't even be here if I hadn't recommended him for the Baffin job.*

"What should we do? Peter?"

Wyatt didn't know who had spoken. All he could see was Hank, a smart, funny man who would never crack another joke. *Oh, God. He has a daughter. Oh, God, I can't believe he's dead.*

A scream snapped him out of it. A woman was on her knees beside the injured man, trying to peel his shirt back from the wound. He moaned, and she looked up, meeting Wyatt's gaze. "He's hurt bad."

"I hear screaming." Crabtree's voice was low and mocking. "Would anyone like to surrender? No? I can promise you, the screaming isn't over."

Wyatt reached back and touched the butt of his pistol. *We need to get to Medical. We could storm the corridor. There's only three of them with guns, right?*

Yes. One crack shot, and a couple of friends who will probably just stand back and watch him work. Because he won't need their help. He'll kill every last one of us, and we won't even manage to mess up his hair.

So how can we reach Medical?

We could retreat. We could climb the ladders in

the emergency access tunnels at the back. Can we lug that poor bastard up a ladder?

"Let's go," he said. He gestured at the aft wall. "We're abandoning the engine room. We'll go two decks up and join up with the team in the missile bay."

A woman said, "We can't abandon the engine room!"

Wyatt shrugged. "Were we achieving something here?"

Will we achieve something in the missile bay? He pushed the thought aside. "Come on. Let's go. And for God's sake, put those guns away before one goes off."

The woman who knelt beside the injured man said, "What about Thomas?"

"Once we're out of the way they can take him straight to Medical. But the longer we stay, the longer he lies there bleeding. Let's go!"

A couple of mutineers unlocked the panels that covered the access tube, then checked inside. A moment later, Wyatt gave the engine room a last, sour glance. Then he stepped into the tube and started to climb.

CHAPTER 39 – HAMMETT

There were two guns on the bridge, and four mutineers. Hornbeck had bustled out several minutes before, taking most of the mob with him. Now Velasco was trying to get the ship lined up to make a run for Gate Eight.

Hammett sat with his back to the port bulkhead, cadets pressed in close on either side. A fat man stood before them, his knuckles white on a long chunk of pipe. It was an adequate weapon under the circumstances. Hammett kept a wary eye on the man, thinking of the ceremonial sword back in his quarters. It would have made a good equalizer.

Carruthers, Wilkins, and a couple other cadets lay stretched out on the deck beside the prisoners. Wilkins was in a bad way, twitching and moaning. Stunners were dangerous at point-blank range. The other two cadets seemed to be fine, if unconscious. Hammett had a strong suspicion that Carruthers was awake and faking it.

Another mutineer stood at the entrance to the bridge, a stocky man with tattoos covering his thickly-muscled arms. He held a crowbar, but he held it gingerly, like he was afraid of what it might do. He looked scared and a bit sick, like a man who desperately wished he was somewhere else.

Katie was his opposite in many ways. She was the only mutineer whose name Hammett knew, mostly because Velasco kept speaking to her, reining her in. She was, as far as Hammett could tell, completely insane. He could see the outline of a gun in the thigh pocket of her jumpsuit, but she hadn't touched it. She was far too enamored of her knife.

The knife was an ornate thing with an engraved blade as long as her hand. Hammett had the impression that if the mutiny ended before she had a chance to cut someone, she would be keenly disappointed. Right now she was standing over Cartwright, alternately testing the edge of the blade with her thumb and touching the point to the side of the woman's neck.

"That's enough, Katie." Velasco sounded weary. "Katie! Back off."

Katie pouted, then retreated a couple of steps. She held the knife in front of her stomach, tilting the blade back and forth and watching light play across the engravings.

"Take us home, Cartwright." Velasco spoke like the parent of a cranky toddler who wouldn't eat. "That's all I ask. What any sane person would ask." She gave Hammett an accusing glare. "Get us through the Gate. Take us back to Earth." She touched the pocket where she'd put her pistol, then seemed to think better of it.

"Sure," said Cartwright sarcastically. "I'll get right on that. I'll grab one of these phones that stopped working when your new friends cut the wires. I'll start calling all the cadets who are dead, or locked up wherever you maniacs put them. I'll get them working on those maneuvering thrusters." She made a show of lifting a handset. "Hello? Starboard lounge? Hello? Hello, can anyone hear me? No? How about now?"

Velasco clenched her fists, and Hammett smiled. "Quit being a smartass," she grated, "and find a way to make it work."

"Sure," said Cartwright. "I'll try this phone instead." She lifted a different handset and said, "Hello? Port lounge?"

"I'll make her cooperate." Katie stepped forward, the knife stretching toward Cartwright's face. Cartwright had to lean back, the blade almost touching her left eye.

That, Hammett decided, was bloody well enough. He stood. The fat man took a step back, raising the pipe. Carruthers chose that moment to sit up, and the fat man turned, lifting the pipe over his head. Nakatomi shifted, and Vincenzo rose to one knee. The fat man retreated another step, almost bumping into Velasco.

She drew her pistol and levelled it at Hammett's chest. "Sit down."

Katie turned to gawk, and Cartwright knocked

her arm aside. She sprang out of her chair and the two women grappled, struggling for control of the knife.

Hammett took another step.

Velasco took careful aim at his heart. "I'll shoot you, Richard."

"That's Captain Hammett to you." He took another step.

"I'll kill you. I swear. I'll do it."

He looked past her to where Cartwright fought for her life. "Well, get on with it, then." He took another step.

"Captain …" Velasco's voice was desperate and afraid.

Hammett took one more step, she started to back away, and for just an instant her head turned as she glanced behind her. In that instant Hammett moved, his left hand catching the barrel of the pistol and twisting it up, his right hand lashing out in a punch that caught her in the center of the face. She fell back, hit the captain's chair, and sprawled across the seat.

She left the pistol in Hammett's hand.

Cartwright and Katie faced each other, both of Cartwright's hands wrapped around the other woman's right wrist. Katie was trying to punch with her free hand, but Cartwright had her elbows out to protect herself. Katie changed tactics, hooking a foot behind Cartwright's heel and then shoving with her arms. Cartwright fell back, losing her grip on Katie's wrist. Cartwright landed on her back, and Katie, crowing with triumph, lifted the knife high.

Hammett shot her three times in the chest.

There was a metallic clatter as the mutineer at the door dropped his crowbar and raised his hands. Hammett turned in time to see Carruthers take the length of pipe from the fat man, who didn't resist.

Hammett sighed, pocketed the gun, and turned to face Velasco. She had both hands pressed to her nose. Blood covered her mouth and chin and dripped onto her blouse. She stared up at him, her eyes wide, and he said, "Get out of my chair."

CHAPTER 40 – WEST

When the first armed sailor took a quick peek into the shuttle bay, the mutineers didn't even see it.

West sighed. A man's head and part of one shoulder appeared for just an instant, then pulled back. A moment later the head returned, and he saw the outline of a rifle in the man's hand. A group of sailors and cadets crossed the open doorway, all of them armed, and West knew the carnage was about to start.

He looked at the remaining mutineers, five men and women who thought they were doing the right thing, and now found themselves in over their heads. They were scared and desperate, and he found he didn't want to watch their bodies being ripped apart by a hail of bullets. He laid his hand across the guitar strings, silencing them, and shouted, "Wait! Hang on. Don't come in yet."

Every head in the shuttle bay turned to stare at him.

Now you've done it. You spoiled the element of surprise. Now the body count will be much higher. This better work, or you'll have a lot of blood on your hands. "Sailors outside the shuttle bay doors," he boomed. "Please wait for just a moment. I'm negotiating a peaceful surrender."

Most of the mutineers were facing the entrance now. A couple of them even had the sense to take cover. One young man stood over West, shoving the barrel of a pistol in his face. "What are you talking about, man?"

West stared down the gun barrel, suddenly sick of this circus of idiocy. "Take the gun out of my face. Then we'll talk."

The man responded by jabbing him on the forehead. "Who are you talking to?"

"Oh, for fuck's sake." West looked past the gun at the man's pale, sweaty face. "Shoot me or don't shoot me. Just get on with it."

A tendon stood out in the man's neck. "I'll kill you!"

West shifted on his plastic crate, turning slightly so he was staring at the side wall. He strummed the guitar, pointedly ignoring the man. The other mutineers were all behind cover now, and most of the prisoners were lying flat. Someone in the corridor was using a mirror to scan the inside of the bay. The gun wobbled in the corner of West's eye, and the man said, "I'll shoot you."

West strummed the guitar.

Slowly, a painful degree at a time, the pistol descended. When it was pointing at the deck, West turned and looked the man in the eye. "You were saying?"

Instead of an armed desperado, the man suddenly looked like a frightened kid. "What's going on?"

"I think the mutiny is over. There's armed men just outside. They've got long guns, too. That means they have a huge advantage." He looked past the man at the entrance to the bay. "The doors are, what, forty meters away?" It was barely more than half that distance, but West chose to exaggerate. "It's pretty hard to hit anything at that range with a pistol. A trained man with a rifle, though?" He shook his head solemnly.

The pistol started to rise. West gave the man a hard look, and the pistol descended again. The man's voice was barely above a whisper as he said, "What am I going to do?"

"Surrender, of course." West tried to make it sound obvious, inevitable. "Or take a bullet in the head." He gestured around the bay. "And get a lot of other people killed, too."

The man touched his tongue to his lips, looking around, seeking inspiration. "We could—"

"Don't be an idiot! I don't care if you get yourself killed, but I'm not dying in a crossfire. Put that stupid gun away before you make things even worse." He glared at the man, letting all his frustration show. Then he spoke again, enunciating each word carefully. He made sure his voice carried to all the mutineers, and to the sailors in the corridor outside. "It's over. No one else needs to die. There's only five of you, armed with handguns. You're up against trained military personnel. You don't have a chance. Lay down your arms, and two minutes from now you'll still be alive."

A long, tense moment stretched out. The man seemed to be paralyzed with indecision, so West reached out a hand, ever so slowly. He closed his fingers around the barrel of the pistol and tugged it gently from the man's hand.

"You made the right choice." He spoke for the benefit of the sailors outside, and the other mutineers who had their eyes glued on the doorway. "I'm going to set the gun down on the deck. The rest of you need to do the same thing. It's okay. Just lay down the guns, and raise your hands." He set the pistol on the deck, put his foot on top of it, and laced his hands behind his head. The sailors when they came in wouldn't know who was a mutineer and who was a prisoner. West was a pretty big target, and he didn't want anyone making a mistake.

He heard faint metallic clicks as mutineers set guns on the deck plates. A pair of hands rose, then another, and another. When he was sure every gun was on the floor, West took a deep breath and called, "All the mutineers have surrendered. You can come in now. No one is armed."

Sailors and cadets poured in at a rush, a dozen of them, rifles and pistols levelled. West felt tension drain from his body, until it was a struggle to remain seated upright.

It was over.

CHAPTER 41 – WYATT

Peter Wyatt sat with his back to the inside bulkhead of the missile bay, heartily wishing that Dalton Hornbeck had died on Freedom Station. Wyatt's ears rang from the concussion of gunfire at close range. He smelled smoke and fear and blood, and it sickened him.

The hatch was to his right. They had jammed the hatch from the inside, but not before the crew outside had slid the door open a good five centimeters. It was more than enough room for a gun barrel, and from time to time someone outside would take a shot.

Fourteen mutineers lined the bulkhead on either side of him. It was the only place the guns outside couldn't reach. There was a fifteenth mutineer in the room. It was Breckenridge, and he was dead. He'd tried to fight back, stepping up to the gap in the hatch and trying to fire into the corridor. Someone out there had fired first, and now Breckenridge lay on the deck plates with a hole in his forehead.

He'd been a good man, and a very good engineer. Everyone's odds of survival had gone down when that bullet struck. Wyatt stared at the body and thought about the waste of it all, and fumed. *Why did I listen to that bloody idiot? How much more harm will he do before somebody finally shoots him?*

What am I still doing at his side?

He knew the answer to that last question, at least. Wyatt couldn't leave. He was trapped with the rest of the mutineers, like a rat in a bucket. The only question was how long his torment would continue before a bullet finally found him.

Hornbeck sat beside Wyatt, looking remarkably unruffled. His lips moved, and Wyatt shook his head. "I'm half deaf from the gunshots, Hornbeck. You'll have to speak up."

Hornbeck leaned closer. "We need to launch a counterattack. We have to mop up the last of this resistance."

"Tell it to Breckenridge," Wyatt said sourly, and Hornbeck frowned.

"That's no attitude to take, Peter. We are winning. It's inevitable. After all, we have reason on our side."

I thought we did, but now I'm not so sure.

"So long as we don't weaken, the rest of them will see reason." Hornbeck gestured toward the corridor. "They'll see that it's hopeless, and they'll lay down their arms. After all, all we want to do is take them home. They've lost Hammett. Without him goading them, it won't take the rest of them very long to give up."

"I wouldn't be so sure of that," said a voice from the corridor.

Hornbeck's head jerked around. "Hammett? What happened to Velasco?"

"I had to relieve her of her duties. Listen, Hornbeck. I'm coming in. Open the hatch so we can talk face-to-face."

As Wyatt watched, a variety of emotions played across Hornbeck's face. Indignation, suspicion, and then an ugly, malicious cunning. Hornbeck stood, then made urgent gestures to the mutineers along the wall. He mimed holding a pistol, lining it up on the hatchway, and squeezing the trigger.

Then he walked to the hatch. It took him a moment to pull out the wrench that jammed the hatch in place. He laid his stunner on the deck in front of the hatch and said, "It's unlocked. Go ahead and pull it open. But don't try any tricks." He stepped back, an expression of malicious anticipation on his face. His foot came down on Breckenridge's leg, and he grimaced, edging to one side.

Metal scuffed against plastic and the hatch slid open. Hornbeck pasted a welcoming smile on his face, spreading his hands to show they were empty. Hammett appeared in the hatchway, also empty-handed. Hornbeck took another step back and said, "Please, come in. We need to find a peaceful resolution before someone else gets hurt." He glanced sideways at Wyatt, looked at the pistol in Wyatt's hand, and gave a tiny, imperceptible nod.

Beyond Wyatt, several mutineers lifted their pistols, taking aim.

Hammett stepped into the room.

Wyatt brought his gun up and shot Hornbeck in the chest.

Hammett sprang back into the corridor, and Wyatt heard a babble of excited voices. He set the pistol down beside his leg and vowed he would never touch another gun for the rest of his life. Hornbeck was still on his feet, staring at Wyatt with a look of baffled astonishment on his face. He coughed once, and a froth of blood coated his lips. Then he toppled backward to land sprawled across Breckenridge's corpse.

"What the hell?"

Wyatt didn't know which mutineer had spoken, and he didn't care. "Put 'em down," he said. "The mutiny is over."

CHAPTER 42 – KASIM

Kasim was trying to line up his telescope on the distant speck that was the Gate when a missile flashed past. He spent a moment staring at the blazing tail of the missile, wondering how close it had come to hitting him, then started analyzing the probabilities. He could continue flying forward, getting close enough to see if the missile hit, close enough to take his own shot if the Gate survived.

Or he could turn back. He could live. It wouldn't be an entirely selfish choice, either. He could save the only small craft with manual controls and weapons, and the only qualified combat pilot on the *Alexander*.

A stubborn pride made him want to continue, to do his duty no matter what the cost. But if that missile failed to destroy the Gate, it would certainly attract the attention of the aliens. By the time he showed up they would be waiting for him, watching for another attack. He would sacrifice himself, and the *Falcon*, and very nearly the last nuke in the arsenal, for nothing.

He stowed the telescope so it wouldn't fly around the cockpit during maneuvers, and strapped himself into his seat. He started the engine, then grabbed the handle that controlled the ventral nose thruster. Pulling back made the thruster fire, and the nose of the ship whipped around. He gave it a second of burn, then grabbed the handle for the dorsal thruster and gave it a second as well.

It took a couple more tiny adjustments to even things out, but shortly he had the *Falcon* pointed back the way he'd come. He hit the main engine and felt the seat press against him. He was still hurtling toward the Gate at a pretty good clip, but he was slowing, and before long he'd be racing back toward the *Alexander*.

"Sorry, Sally," he murmured. "I wanted to avenge you. At least someone is giving them a black eye. It just isn't me. Not this time."

By gradual degrees the *Falcon* lost its backward velocity. He could see the planet beneath him, see craters sliding past, moving slower and slower. Finally the planet appeared to be stationary under the *Falcon*. Then, ever so slowly, the pocked landscape crept toward him as the ship reversed its course.

Somewhere behind him the Gate would be blasted apart in a nuclear explosion, or it wouldn't. It was out of his hands now. All he could do was wait as the *Falcon* gained speed, heading back around the planet, back toward the *Alexander*.

Back toward that alien supply ship, or whatever it was.

"Forget it," he said aloud. "Don't push your luck."

Still. He had a nuclear bomb, and the ship made such a fat, lovely target. It would never see him coming.

Probably.

"What should I do, Sally? Would you want me to avenge you?" Probably not. She would want him to live, to keep himself safe. Caring and decency had been such an integral part of her nature.

"You bastards should have killed me and let her live," he said, and pulled his lips back from his teeth in an atavistic snarl. "You made a mistake, and now you're going to pay for it. I'm sorry, Sally, but you're going to be avenged."

He disengaged the engine. After all, it wouldn't do to go whipping past the enemy ship at too high a speed. He wouldn't have time to shoot.

Kasim took out the telescope and started searching the skies above New Avalon.

It was about twenty minutes before he spotted his prey. The alien ship showed as a glittering point of light on the horizon, and Kasim altered course, steering straight for it. He misread the alien's orbital path and had to spend several minutes making course corrections, but at last he had the *Falcon* lined up, her nose pointed straight at the enemy ship.

By this time he could see the outline of the ship as a shining oval several degrees above the disc of the planet. He lined up the telescope, and the ship seemed to leap toward him. He was much closer than on his last pass, and he could see a lot more detail. There were antennas, and nozzles that could have been thrusters or weapons. He got the telescope hovering perfectly still in front of the cockpit window, then peered through the eyepiece. He could see the ship drifting, which told him he was slightly off target. He made a tiny adjustment and looked again.

Still drifting. He reached for the controls, then hesitated. He wasn't firing at a stationary target. Nor was he moving in a straight line. He was orbiting the planet, and so was the alien craft. The other ship had a lateral motion relative to the *Falcon*, and both ships were curving around the planet as they flew. The missile wouldn't fly straight when he fired it, either. The planet's gravity would pull at it. The missile's path would curve as well.

Kasim frowned. He supposed there was a way to calculate all the vectors and forces involved, but the math was entirely beyond a seat-of-the-pants flier like him. No, there was only one solution he could think of that would work.

He would fire the missile at extremely close range.

For a moment he sat frozen, a cold lump of fear in his stomach, asking himself if he was making the right choice. Then he sneered at his own cowardice, stowed the telescope, strapped in, and ignited the main engines.

A giant hand pressed him backward, and he laughed despite the gravity of the situation. Now *this* was flying. With the engine blasting at close to full power, every touch of the maneuvering thrusters would have immediate, drastic effects. A blunder of half a second would send him tumbling hopelessly out of control. It was high-stakes, high-velocity flying, in a clunky runabout that was never designed for manual control. He should have been frozen with terror. It should have been the most harrowing, awful experience of his life.

It was glorious.

The alien ship seemed to rush toward him. He activated the laser, nudged the nose of the *Falcon* down ever so slightly, watched with horror as the planet filled his view, and over-corrected. For three sickening seconds the nose of the ship whipped up and down as he fought for just the right vector.

Then all he could see in front of him was metal, and a red glow that terrified him until he realized it wasn't an enemy weapon, it was the *Falcon*'s laser, burning into the alien hull. He reached up and grabbed the handle that released the missile, hauling down with all his might. The *Falcon* wobbled as her center of gravity changed, he glimpsed the crimson flame of the missile's rocket burning, and he put the *Falcon* into a dive.

The runabout shook, he felt the seat vibrate

against him, and a storm of metal fragments sailed past the window. He heard the hiss of air escaping, and his ears popped. He cut the engine, made sure he wasn't plunging toward the planet, then grabbed his helmet and snapped it in place.

Without a computer it was difficult to do a damage assessment. The *Falcon* was losing air, but he couldn't see any visible damage. He tested the maneuvering thrusters one by one, and they all worked. Finally he restarted the engine, and it worked as well.

He shrugged. He'd let the shuttle bay crew back on the *Alexander* sort out the details.

A touch of power to the port thruster brought the *Falcon* drifting around in a stately pirouette, and he looked back at the alien ship.

It was gone.

One large chunk of wreckage tumbled slowly toward the surface of New Avalon. Nothing else remained.

"That's for you, Sally," he said. Then he turned the *Falcon* toward the *Alexander* and started the long flight back.

CHAPTER 43 – HAMMETT

"Jump's complete. We're in the Oort Cloud."

Hammett nodded. "Pity we haven't got any working scanners. We could do some useful mapping while we're here." His stomach rumbled, and he thought of going to the galley and helping himself to some of that repulsive gruel. He was almost hungry enough to enjoy it.

Almost.

The last of the canned food was a distant memory. No one had eaten anything but protein and carbohydrate paste in a week, and not very much of it. They could reach Earth within a day. Earth, planet of a thousand cuisines. Steak, and carrots, and fresh fruit, and green vegetables …

He suppressed the thought with an effort. "Tell the spotters to look sharp. We're in a crowded neighborhood. After all we've been through I'd hate to get creamed by a comet." Odds were the ship could float around the Oort Cloud for a decade and never even see another object, much less hit one. Still, it would be stupid to be careless.

"Aye aye," said Cartwright, and murmured into a telephone. She was able to juggle eight telephones without any apparent effort, and Hammett told himself for the hundredth time that he'd made the right choice when he shot the knife-wielding Katie. Cartwright was indispensable.

Katie's death still haunted him, though.

Wilkins and Nakatomi were back on duty, fully recovered. There were still a couple of patients in Medical, making a slow recovery, and half a dozen injured civilians and crew who spent most of their time in their bunks.

Most of the mutineers still walked the corridors. The brig wouldn't hold them all, and the spirit was gone out of them. They were no further threat. Many of them seemed remorseful, and had become some of the most enthusiastic workers in Janice Ling's corps of volunteers.

Velasco was in the brig, along with the worst of the conspirators. The ship only had four tiny cells, and for a time there had been two prisoners per cell, with half a dozen more locked in a bunkroom. Crabtree spent a couple of days interviewing witnesses, and put together a pretty clear picture of who had done what. The very worst offenders were dead, and he identified a couple of real thugs who had used the mutiny as an excuse to go on a rampage.

On the third day after the mutiny Hammett decided to release the other prisoners, keeping only Velasco and a couple of apparent sociopaths. He'd hesitated over Wyatt. The man was a ringleader, after all. He seemed to be a good man, though. Hammett had a long talk with him, and ultimately decided that Wyatt, released from his cell, would be a calming influence on the other civilians from Baffin.

Over the last three weeks Wyatt had more than justified Hammett's faith in him, and Hammett found himself regretting the fact that the man might still hang once they got back to Earth.

One crisis at a time, he reminded himself. *For all we know, the aliens beat us here. The Earth might be a cratered ruin by now.*

"Shuttle bay reports fighters launching," Wilkins reported.

"What's the status of the fighter squadron?" Hammett asked.

Carruthers smiled. "The drones are working better than I ever would have believed. I tell you, that Kasim's some sort of genius."

Nakatomi looked up and snorted. "Please. All he did was make a suggestion. I did most of the work." She looked at Hammett. "The last test flight was brilliant. The runabout and both shuttles are, to quote Lieutenant al Faisal, lean, mean fighting machines."

Hammett had visited the shuttle bay when the shuttles were still being modified. They didn't look particularly lean. They'd been blocky and angular before. Now they looked scabrous, covered in bulbous lumps.

Nakatomi and a crew of technicians had

welded half a dozen drone fighters to the hull of each shuttle and the runabout. The computer controls in the drones were irreparably fried, but they had lasers and engines that could be activated with the touch of a newly-installed button inside the cockpit. Four drones pointed forward and provided firepower. Two drones pointed aft and provided thrust for hard braking. According to Kasim the ships were much more nimble now, able to stop on a dime, whatever that meant.

Six pilots took turns flying the three fighters between wormhole jumps. Kasim was the only one who showed real aptitude, but the others were becoming at least competent. This would be the last training flight, Hammett decided. After the next jump he wanted the fighters on active patrol.

The next jump would put them almost half a light-year from Earth. The odds of seeing another ship were laughably small. Still, it would be stupid not to be ready.

It was the jump after that when things would get interesting. Spacecom had to know by now that humanity was under attack. They'd had weeks to investigate the Gate failures. They would be braced for trouble, expecting the worst, when a wormhole would open practically on Earth's doorstep. The *Alexander* would pop through, without a transponder, and ignoring hails.

Hammett walked over to the communication station, which had been abandoned for weeks. A cadet named Dixon sat there now. His job was to monitor the radio. They had a radio of sorts, with a telephone handset connected to it. Hammett reached past the cadet and lifted the radio, examining it dubiously.

A plastic cylinder tightly wound with copper wire formed the bulk of the contraption. The cadet was apparently supposed to move a piece of wire back and forth along the coil to listen at various frequencies. It looked ridiculous to Hammett, but Rani had insisted it would work when she presented it to him. There was no way to transmit, but they would at least be able to hear broadcasts at close range.

"Nothing so far, Sir," Dixon said. "Of course, at this range ..."

At this range, any transmissions from Earth would be several months old. Hammett nodded and set the radio down. "Everyone into vac suits." He turned to the line of cadets at the telephones along the bulkhead. "Spread the word. I want everyone suited up before the next jump." He took his own suit from a locker and pulled it on over his uniform, then put his helmet in the rack on the back of his seat where he could grab it in an instant.

After that there was nothing more he could do to prepare. They could only jump and hope for the best.

CHAPTER 44 – KASIM

Kasim boarded the *Falcon*, trying to quiet the fluttering of his stomach. They were still a jump away from Earth, after all. A short jump, granted, but they had to be several light-weeks out. What were the odds of encountering anything but vacuum?

Still, it was the first time he'd been ordered to patrol, rather than practice. In all likelihood nothing would happen, not until the next jump. But you never knew ….

He ran through his pre-flight check, which was minimal. There was no real way to know if the *Falcon* was spaceworthy except to launch it and see what happened. He put on his helmet and retracted the faceplate. Finally he started the engine and waited for the improvised "launch" light to turn green. The shuttle bay crew had rigged a lamp near the end of the bay to tell pilots when they were clear to launch.

Kasim waited, and the lamp remained stubbornly dark. He started to fidget, wishing heartily for a working radio. He'd adjusted to so many things, from manual flight controls to telephones, but it was the little things that drove him absolutely crazy. There was no way to know what was going on ten whole meters away except by opening the hatch and walking out to ask somebody.

The launch light would probably come on as soon as he finished unbuckling his harness. He waited, staring stubbornly at the lamp, as the minutes crawled past. At least his irritation took his mind off his fear.

Finally a cadet walked out in front of the *Falcon* and waved. Kasim held his hands out in an I-don't-understand gesture, and the cadet flapped an arm in a disgusted, dismissive way.

Either he's got a really bad attitude or I'm not launching. Kasim climbed out of the pilot's seat, headed aft, and opened the hatch. The cadet met him at the bottom of the ramp. "We're standing by," the young man reported. "Reason unknown, of course. Why would anyone tell us anything?"

"You've been hanging around cynical pilots too long." Kasim clapped him on the shoulder, then headed down the ramp. He could see a cluster of sailors and cadets grouped around the telephone on the back wall, and he headed in that direction.

A sailor named Chupik, the senior crewman present, left the group and came to meet him. "Back in your ship, please, Sir. We need you to be ready to launch at a moment's notice."

Kasim stopped. "What's going on?"

"Distress call, apparently. The *Alexander*'s going to investigate. You'll launch as soon as we get there, but nobody actually knows where "there" is. We're just flying in a straight line and looking for trouble. As soon as we spot it, you launch."

"Right," said Kasim, and spun on his heel. He hurried back onto the *Falcon*, shut the hatch, and dropped back into his seat. He was back to waiting, but it was much worse now. *Distress call? What's that about?*

And how in space did anyone pick up a distress call?

The launch light turned green, and he started the engine, lifted off the deckplates, and headed out into vacuum.

He saw nothing but stars at first. He turned the *Falcon*, hugging the hull of the *Alexander*, scanning for threats. He'd learned to ignore the countless patches and welds that marred the skin of the ship, but he noticed them now. *Those bastards are dangerous. Look what they did to the Alexander. They'll split this little tin can in half like a—*

Suppressing that unproductive line of thought, he massaged the maneuvering controls and swept along the *Alexander's* ventral hull. Marco and Sharina would be launching the modified shuttles behind him. There was no way for the three of them to compare notes. He would find out what was going on, then wait for the other two to join him before he headed out to deal with ... whatever it was.

He reached the starboard side of the *Alexander* and looked around, mystified. There was nothing to see but the blank expanse of the stars. What was he supposed to be doing?

Then he spotted motion directly ahead of the *Alexander*. He did one last visual scan for other threats, then brought the nose of the *Falcon* around. He moved out ahead of the *Alexander*, dropping low to stay out of line with her rail guns, and watched as the shuttles formed up on either side.

A ship hung in the void before him, tiny as a pebble in the distance. He raced toward it, adrenalin surging through his veins, and the shuttles kept pace. He started firing lasers when he was much too far away to hit anything. There was always a chance he'd get lucky, and the *Falcon* had plenty of power.

Then he swore and stopped firing, leaning forward to peer through the cockpit window. The ship ahead of him looked almost like a Navy corvette. It was only when a dark shape moved across the pale hull that he saw the second ship.

Both ships grew as he raced closer. It was a corvette, all right, and it was locked in a death battle with a bulky alien craft. The alien ship – five or ten of the smallest ships joined together, Kasim estimated – was maybe a quarter the size of the corvette. As he watched, the alien darted in and a point of red light appeared on the corvette's hull.

The corvette darted sideways, and laser light

splashed across the hull of the alien ship. The alien jerked out of the way, then started a dogged pursuit.

Kasim blinked, trying to make sense of what he'd just seen. Had that been a plume of vapor? He shook his head in disbelief. The corvette, its electronics undoubtedly fried, was maneuvering the only way they could.

They were venting air to create thrust.

"Crazy bastards," he muttered. It was an insane tactic. How much air could the little corvette possibly hold?

Still, it was keeping them alive for the moment.

"I want to meet that lunatic captain," Kasim muttered. "I guess I better keep him alive, or I'll never get the chance." He raced toward the battle, the two ships loomed suddenly huge before him, and he fired his lasers and braking thrusters simultaneously. The alien craft filled his view, and four laser beams drilled into it. A moment later four more lasers joined the barrage from the shuttle to his left, then four more as the third shuttle joined in.

He could make out the shapes of individual alien craft within the cluster, lit up in a red glow. The lasers seemed to be doing no damage, diffusing across some sort of shield. Then, as he watched, the shield failed and a dozen powerful lasers burned into the massed hulls.

One of the component ships vented a plume of vapor and seemed to collapse inward, and then the cluster broke apart. Two more small craft died, sliced up by that lethal convergence of laser fire, before the rest of the cluster spun away, fleeing in half a dozen directions at once.

Kasim whooped, soared through the space where the alien ship had been, and heard debris rattle from the *Falcon*'s hull. He chose a fleeing alien and pursued it, lasers blazing. The enemy craft jerked and twisted, trying to avoid him, and he singed it several times. Finally it went spiralling off to his left, and he brought the *Falcon* around, searching.

The alien was gone.

He looked around, disoriented, then brought the *Falcon* around in a slow loop, trying to spot the corvette. He saw it at last. The *Alexander* had arrived, and if any alien ships had survived, they were long gone. Kasim was relieved to spot both shuttles, still intact, hovering between the two warships. He flew back, taking station just below the *Alexander*'s hull.

A man in a vac suit left the *Alexander* through an airlock just above Kasim's position. A cord of some sort trailed behind the man, and Kasim chuckled as he realized what was happening. Someone was taking a phone across to the corvette.

Soon after that, he saw the flashing light of a recall signal coming from just inside the shuttle bay. He was the only pilot in a position to see it, so he flew out and waggled the *Falcon*'s body in front of one shuttle and then the other. It was a ridiculous way to communicate, but it worked. Both shuttles followed him back to the *Alexander*.

"Good shooting, Lieutenant," Chupik said. "I

couldn't see a thing, of course, but third-hand scuttlebutt says you three were awesome."

"Every word of it is true," Kasim assured him. "We were incredible. Especially me."

"You get five or ten minutes while we top up your fuel and check for damage," Chupik said. "Then the ship jumps and you go right back out again."

"Naturally. What's the story with the corvette?"

Chupik spread his hands. "The bridge didn't tell me a thing even before we had our systems fried. You think they tell me anything now?" He made a disgusted face. "Nobody respects a deck dog."

"You should have become a pilot," Kasim said. "They treat us like gods."

Chupik snorted and headed for the *Falcon*.

Sharina came up beside him. She was a lowly cadet, but she'd flown atmosphere craft on Earth before she joined up, so she was a fighter pilot now. As far as he was concerned, they were equals. She gave him a frazzled grin and said, "I got one, after they broke up. They didn't even put up a fight. All they wanted to do was run away."

He nodded. "They panicked. Which makes sense, considering how awesome we are."

She smirked. Then the smirk faded and she said, "That was the easy fight, wasn't it? The main enemy fleet went on to attack Earth. They just left this little handful behind to finish off a stray corvette."

Kasim nodded. "That's how I read it. I wonder

how long the corvette was holding them off. A few hours at the most, I'd say."

"I guess we're going to jump to Earth now," she said. "God only knows what we're going to find."

"We've had a nice warm-up," Kasim said. "Now the real flying begins."

"All right," said Chupik, backing away from the three fighters. "Back in the saddle, kids. We're about to jump."

Kasim punched Sharina on the shoulder, she punched him back, and they ran to their ships.

CHAPTER 45 – HAMMETT

"Jump complete."

Hammett nodded to Cadet Jessop and waited, managing not to drum his fingers, for reports from the ship's various observers. After five seconds that felt like five years Wilkins looked around and said, "We came in about four hundred thousand K from Earth."

Someone whistled, and Hammett shook his head. For a planet with the kind of traffic Earth got, a million kilometers was generally considered the minimum safe distance.

Well, we didn't hit anything. The rest is details. He nodded to Jessop and waited for the next report.

"Holy crap!" It was Wilkins who had spoken, and he flushed as Hammett stared at him. "Sir, the aliens are here!" He listened, said "Hang on," and lowered the handset. "The fleet's in a tight orbit around Earth. At least two dozen ships. The aliens are holding off for the moment. He can see four big ships. We're too far away to see any of the little ships." Wilkins lifted the handset. "Okay, go ahead." He listened some more, then lowered the phone. "There are missiles coming up from the surface. They just go past the enemy without detonating. There's no fire coming from the fleet."

Hammett took a deep breath. Every eye on the bridge was on him, and he could see fear on more than a few faces. That was understandable. By the sound of it, the aliens were here in overwhelming force, and Earth and the rest of the Navy were going to be no help at all. The *Alexander* was about to fight its last battle, and everyone on the bridge knew it.

He smiled. It wasn't easy, but he did it. "Great. We've won every single engagement we've ever had with these invaders, and now they've gathered together in a nice, fat, target-rich environment. They've walked all over everything Spacecom could send against them, from Calypso to Deirdre, and now Earth. But they only have one trick. They fry electronic systems. It's all they know how to do." Well, they also had some remarkably versatile ships, and weapons that had cut through the hull of the *Alexander* with terrifying ease. But this was no time to quibble over technicalities.

"We have a ship they can't touch. We have a seasoned crew with direct manual control over every thruster and weapon and system on the ship. Which means they can't touch us. But we've got three rail guns, a dozen laser batteries, three fighters, and a magazine full of missiles, including one last nuke. We can certainly touch them, and by God that's what we're going to do!"

A low cheer went up, surprising him, and for a moment his phony smile became real. He turned to Cartwright. "Ms. Cartwright. Take us in. Point us at the biggest cluster of alien ships you can find and give us plenty of thrust."

She nodded and grabbed a phone, and Hammett sat down, doing his best to look confident and calm. He felt less afraid than he would have expected. *We're going to die today, but it's going to be a hell of a scrap.*

Reports trickled in, fragments of the battle reported by distracted cadets at observation windows. "Dozens of little enemy ships. Dozens and dozens!" "Forward rail guns firing." "Missiles launched." "Enemy moving, coming toward us." "Taking fire, evade, evade!"

A missile detonated at close range and Hammett felt a hint of vibration through the soles of his boots as debris rattled against the hull. Several cadets spoke at once, describing the action on every side of the ship. None of it mattered, really. He'd put the *Alexander* in the thick of the fight, and it was all he could do. His crew would fight a hundred small battles now, at the laser batteries, in the missile bay, at the triggers of the rail guns and the controls of the maneuvering thrusters, and in the fighters outside. Hammett could only sit on the bridge, frustrated, a spectator who couldn't even watch the action directly.

Wilkins said, "A cluster of five ships just came in for a hull attack. The front rail guns blew them apart."

"Sounds like we're giving them quite a beating," Hammett said, not because he believed it but to boost morale. Carruthers gave him a sardonic look, but wisely kept silent.

Then a terrible sound filled the bridge, a metallic scream, the sound of steel plates bending and tearing. The deck shuddered, and Hammett grabbed the arms of his chair. Someone gasped, and Hammett felt a breeze past his nose. He got his helmet on an instant before the entire bridge went dark.

CHAPTER 46 – KASIM

Chaos filled the sky above Earth.

Kasim, light-headed from an endless string of high-speed maneuvers, darted the *Falcon* back and forth through the crowd of enemy ships that swarmed around the *Alexander*. Lasers from the ship's batteries flashed all around him. He was sure they'd hit him by accident at least once, but he hadn't taken serious damage.

Not from friendly fire, at any rate. The *Falcon* was soaking up its share of abuse. All the air was gone, and he could see a twinkle of starlight through two different hull breaches. One of the drones welded to the outside of the ship was down, leaving him only three lasers. He still had all his thrusters, though. The aliens had him outnumbered, but he could out-fly them.

The Earth was a beautiful blue and white disc the size of his hand at arm's length. The Spacecom fleet, such as it was, was scattered through the void between the *Alexander* and Earth. It looked like a floating scrapyard, a vast collection of lifeless ships slowly drifting away from one another. At least they seemed to be disabled, not destroyed. He imagined their helpless crews, staring out the windows, able to do nothing but watch as the *Alexander* fought for their lives.

The fight was going badly. There had to be more than a hundred of the little alien ships, constantly regrouping and breaking apart. From time to time a cluster would race in and try to burn through the hull of the *Alexander*. Kasim had tried firing on one such cluster. His lasers had made no impact, dispersing against some sort of energy shield.

Once he saw the *Alexander* spin on her axis and fire a missile which obliterated a cluster of at least a dozen ships. Another cluster was blown apart by rail gun rounds. The *Falcon* and the shuttles had destroyed several of the smallest craft, and more had been demolished by laser fire from the *Alexander*.

A hopeless number of ships remained, though.

A gleam of pale silver caught his eye, and he turned the *Falcon* toward it. It was a shuttle, he didn't know which one, and it was in trouble. The entire back end was a twisted, burning mess. The main engines were gone, and the shuttle was flying backward, relying on the reverse thrusters in the drones. Half a dozen enemy craft harassed the shuttle, diving in to scorch the hull and then zipping away.

Kasim charged into the fray, aware that he was leading his own entourage of enemy ships. Still, he had to do something. Before he could reach the scene of the dogfight, however, the shuttle accelerated hard and raced away. It flew backward, edging slightly to port as the pilot gave a gentle squirt on a maneuvering thruster in the nose. Kasim saw what was going to happen and gave a shout, a wordless cry of fury and horror.

Eight or nine enemy ships had come together in a cluster, and they were sweeping toward the hull of the *Alexander*. The shuttle, steering with a skill that would have been hard enough to believe had it been undamaged and moving forward, smashed directly into the cluster.

Kasim arrived a moment later, lasers blasting, cutting into the component ships as they broke away. It was too late for the shuttle, though. He watched the remains of the brave little ship tumble sideways, scrape against the hull of the *Alexander*, and then spin away into the void.

An instant later Kasim was past the site of the battle and involved in a fresh fight for his life with several more of the small craft. There wasn't time to wonder which of his friends had died. There wasn't time to wonder if any hope remained, with yet another weapon gone from the pitifully small arsenal that remained to the *Alexander*.

To humanity.

An unfamiliar lump on the hull of the *Alexander* caught his eye. It was an alien craft the size of a shuttle, and it was pressed to a jagged tear in the hull plates just aft of the shuttle bay. He didn't know what the alien ship was doing, but it couldn't possibly be good. He brought the *Falcon* around in a dizzying turn and raced in, firing.

Holes appeared in the enemy craft, and chunks of metal came loose and spun away. As he raced past he saw the ship break loose from the *Alexander*, nearly hitting the *Falcon* as it fell away. Kasim flew in a twisting path around the *Alexander*, wondering what that alien ship had been doing. What was happening aboard the *Alexander*?

CHAPTER 47 – VELASCO

Metal clicked against metal, and the door to Velasco's cell swung open. She lifted a hand to shield her eyes as she waited for them to adjust, then swung her legs to the floor and sat up. "Exercise time already?"

There was no response. Her doorway stood empty. She stood, stretched, and stepped out of the tiny cell. Her two fellow prisoners, a pair of irredeemable thugs if ever she'd seen one, stood in their own doorways, squinting.

A petite Asian woman stood at the entrance to the brig. She wore a vac suit with the faceplate retracted, exposing only a narrow slice of her face. "We're in battle," she said. "I gather it's not going well. The officers are ordering everyone into vac suits, but I think they forgot about you. I thought I'd better let you out, give you some kind of a chance if we get a hull breach." She stepped out of the doorway, vanishing from sight.

Velasco looked at the two goons, got blank stares in reply, and strode to a locker with a vac helmet logo stencilled on it. She grabbed herself a suit and pulled it on, relieved to see it had no markings to identify her as a prisoner. When she pulled the helmet on she felt an immediate sense of relief. She was largely anonymous now. She could move through the corridors without the crew recognizing her shame.

When she moved toward the exit one of the goons put a hand on her shoulder, grabbing the fabric of her suit. He started to speak, some kind of threat or demand she supposed. He never quite got an entire word out. Velasco's martial arts training was years behind her, but she found she still remembered a few things. She locked her left hand around the man's wrist, leaned back to pull his arm straight, and slammed her right hand against the outside of his elbow. He let out a howl of pain and she stepped around him and left the brig.

She realized she had no destination. She walked briskly away from the brig, wanting to be as far as possible from that awful little cell. The ship had to be at Earth, she supposed. She'd be back in a cell soon enough. For a few minutes, though, she was going to enjoy being free.

When she came to a staircase she started to climb. Some instinct was drawing her to the bridge, she realized. *To hell with that.* Nothing good would come from showing up there. She would head for her cabin, she decided. Someone else probably had the room now. Well, no matter. Whoever it was, they'd be on duty. She'd wash her face, stretch out on the bunk, enjoy a bit of privacy in a room so big she couldn't touch all four walls at once.

In truth, her cabin wasn't all that much bigger than her cell in the brig. The door didn't lock from the inside, though, and that made all the difference.

She reached the next deck, moved down a corridor, and rounded a corner. Three people were coming down the corridor toward her. The suits made them anonymous. There were no rank markings. Even civilians wore Navy suits aboard the *Alexander*.

Even prisoners did.

Still, something in the way they carried themselves told her they were military, and the youthful look on what she could see of their faces said they had to be cadets. Their posture as they saw her reinforced that impression. They hesitated, wondering if she was an officer or a crewman. Everyone but the civilians outranked the cadets.

I'll hurry past them before they recognize me, Velasco decided. *I'll pretend I'm in a hurry.* She quickened her pace.

She was three meters from the nearest cadet when the deck lurched and she stumbled to her knees.

She had her faceplate down before she even knew she was thinking about it. She got to her feet, panicked tugging at her brain. She was hyperventilating, and she wondered if the oxygen in her suit was flowing. It should have come on automatically when the visor came down, but ...

Another face stared into her own, a cadet, wide-eyed and terrified. For a moment the cadet's fear fed on her own, and Velasco felt panic like a dark void looming in front of her, threatening to pull her in. She had a brief image of herself in a screaming fit on the deck plates in front of three cadets.

It would be career suicide.

It was a ridiculous thought – she might very well be executed for mutiny, after all – but it jerked her out of her spiral of growing panic. Clear thought returned, and she stretched out a fingertip, tapping the cadet's faceplate to be sure it was down.

A second cadet was screaming, hands clenched in the air in front of her, and Velasco took her by the shoulders and gave her a hard shake. It was a girl, impossibly young, with a fringe of blonde hair showing above wide blue eyes. She stared at Velasco, her lips moving silently. She seemed to be unhurt, and Velasco let go of her, turning to the third cadet.

It was a young woman, with the look of someone who'd been in the grip of panic a moment before, but had been startled out of it by the sight of someone shaking her friend. She gave Velasco a sheepish look that changed to startlement.

So you recognize me. Well, I'll be embarrassed later. Right now I'm busy. She stepped around the cadet.

A hand clutched her arm.

Velasco turned to see three earnest young faces gazing at her. With the suit radios fried it was impossible to communicate, but she could read those expressions easily enough. They were terrified. They didn't know what to do.

Velasco sighed. "I'm not the kind of officer you're looking for." She gestured around her, and the cadets looked where she pointed, as if they could understand. "I don't know how ships function! I can't tell you what to do. What do I know about space battles?"

The cadets continued to stare at her.

On the other hand, I know about things like laser batteries. I was helping with the crew schedules before the mutiny, after all. I wonder if those batteries are being manned. We should have backup people, just in case. No one can use the telephones if the ship has lost air.

"Come with me," she said. They couldn't hear her, of course, but she made a beckoning gesture. She headed back toward the staircase, and the cadets trouped along behind her.

She was almost to the staircase when the bulkhead beside her bulged inward and the metal began to tear. Velasco scrambled backward, and a couple of metal spikes, each one as long as her arm, burst through the bulkhead at chest height. Two more spikes came through at knee height. Then the spikes spread apart, and ripped a hole in the bulkhead.

A moment later, something came through.

Velasco didn't see any details. She whirled and ran, the three cadets in front of her. They reached a corner, and Velasco glanced back.

The creature behind her had the volume of a large human being, but it was utterly inhuman. There were six limbs, each ending in a meter-long metal spike. It skittered down the corridor, making good time, the limbs moving so quickly it was hard to make out details. There was no head, just a compact metallic torso where those awful limbs came together.

It galloped down the corridor toward her, using all six limbs for propulsion.

Velasco shrieked and raced after the cadets.

They ran into four more crew. For a moment the corridor was a jumble of bodies, people pushing each other away, Velasco and the cadets trying to force their way through while the other crew tried to look past them to see what they were running from. Then all of them were in flight, Velasco trying to run with the others pressed close on either side. Her foot hit someone's ankle and both of them fell, and when she rose to her knees there was a man with a gun in front of her.

His faceplate was down, but something in his posture made her sure it was Crabtree. He stood with his legs apart, relaxed and confident, a pistol in a two-handed grip. The others pressed past him on both sides and he waited for them to get out of the way. Velasco stayed on her knees, skidding sideways and putting her back against a bulkhead.

Crabtree fired several times, the pistol eerily silent. Velasco turned and saw the creature, maybe a dozen steps behind her, bring its limbs up to protect itself. Sparks flew as bullets ricocheted from the steel arms, and a hole appeared in the bulkhead beside the creature. Crabtree lowered the pistol, grabbed Velasco by the hand, and hauled her to her feet.

And they ran.

Ahead of them the crowd of running crew parted to flow around an imposing figure standing in the center of the corridor. It was Hammett, in a vac suit decorated with shoulder stripes and his name stenciled across the chest. She couldn't think of a single thing he could do – he was just one man, after all, and not even armed – but she felt a surge of completely unjustified confidence. She darted around him and paused.

For a moment Hammett and Crabtree stood there, shoulder to shoulder, looking indomitable, indestructible. Crabtree brought the gun up and fired several times, slowing the invader for a moment as it brought its arms up to shield itself. Then both men turned, pushing her, and she wheeled and ran.

The corridor ahead was jammed with bodies now. Someone had fallen, and she almost stepped over the sprawled legs and kept going. She felt a strange sense of responsibility for her three cadets, though she had no idea if this was one of them. She grabbed the figure by both wrists and heaved the person upright. Crabtree was there beside her, helping, and the three of them started to run.

That was when she noticed that Hammett was gone. Her stomach lurched. That rotten bastard!

Ahead of her the corridor turned, and she saw crew coming back around the corner, then milling uncertainly. This was the corridor that ran past her cabin, and she suddenly knew what had happened. There was an emergency pressure door just around that corner. It must have slammed shut when the hull was breached.

They were trapped.

The creature advanced, slowing when it saw they were no longer retreating. *It's worried*, Velasco realized. Not that it needed to be. She remembered how those steel arms had torn open a bulkhead. They would do the same things to vac suits, and the bodies inside.

A hatch slid open just behind the creature, and Hammett stepped out. In his hand he held a glittering silver sword with a jewel set in the hilt. It was just about the most unexpected sight Velasco could have imagined, and she shook her head, wondering if she was getting enough oxygen.

Hammett charged the creature. It didn't turn, just shifted its limbs, but the change in posture made it seem as if it was facing the other way. It stood on four limbs and brought two more limbs up to meet Hammett's charge.

Hammett slashed, the creature blocked with a steel arm, and Velasco saw sparks fly. Then he lunged, the sword stretched out, and a steel spike stretched for his wrist. Hammett seemed to stumble, his hand dropping away from the hilt of the sword. He felt to one knee and clutched the back of his hand.

The sword, though, was jammed in the creature's body.

Crabtree moved forward. He hadn't fired yet; Hammett would have been in his line of fire. Now he stepped in close, looming over the creature and aiming downward. Hammett scrambled back out of the way, and Crabtree fired twice.

This time, the creature made no attempt to block the shots. It drew in all six limbs and lifted its torso high. The sword rose with it, the hilt wobbling like a baton in the hands of a parade leader. Then the creature went slack and limp.

Hammett stood, hesitated a moment, then stepped in close. He planted a foot against the creature's body, grabbed the sword in both hands, and pulled it free. Blood darkened the blade, and he made a whipping motion with the sword. Red-brown blood, so dark it was almost black, splashed against the bulkhead and deck.

A dark shape moved behind him, and Velasco pointed, shouting a warning he couldn't hear. Hammett turned as another creature came skittering down the corridor toward him. Hammett and Crabtree advanced together, and the creature charged. It wasn't fast, no quicker than a brisk jog for a human, and Hammett lunged to meet it. Crabtree had his gun levelled, but he didn't fire. Hammett's sword hit the alien's steel arms once, twice, three times. He skipped sideways as a steel spike stabbed for his shin.

Then he lunged, feinted, waited for a limb to come across in a block, and he struck.

The creature's limbs flailed, sweeping Hammett's legs out from under him. He rose, unhurt, and pulled his sword free. The creature seemed to be dead, but he stabbed it one more time. Then he and Crabtree continued down the corridor, weapons at the ready. They reached the corner, peeked around, then turned and vanished from sight.

Velasco put her hands on her hips. "Well, what the hell do I do now?"

Crewmen hurried past, busy on errands of their own. In a moment she found herself alone with her three cadets. "I wish I could just talk to you guys."

They stared at her, waiting.

"All right, come on. Let's see if we can make ourselves useful."

They descended three decks, and she led the cadets forward. A figure in a vac suit sat at the controls of the center laser battery, firing almost continuously as the gun tracked back and forth. Velasco touched a cadet on the arm and held up a hand, palm out. *Stay*. The cadet nodded her understanding and Velasco led the others away.

She couldn't reach the portside laser battery. A pressure door blocked the way. Some compartments still had air, then. She turned back, the cadets tagging along behind her like ducklings.

There was a corpse at the controls of the starboard gun.

For a long moment Velasco stood frozen, taking it all in. The alien weapon had burned the gun station. The paint on the deck and bulkhead was blackened and bubbled, and the body in the gunner's seat was burned all across the chest and the front of the helmet. Velasco knew that the gun itself was remarkably sturdy, though. An attack powerful enough to damage the laser battery itself would have left nothing of the gunner but a pair of boots.

She took a deep breath, willing her stomach to remain calm. To vomit inside a vac suit would be disastrous. Then, fighting revulsion and an unreasoning fear, she stepped forward and dragged the gunner's body from the chair.

By the time she had the corpse stretched out in a corner out of the way, one of her cadets was in the seat and firing. The other cadet looked at Velasco, who gestured aft. The cadet nodded and led the way back into the corridor.

They hadn't gone more than half a dozen steps when the deck vibrated and Velasco stumbled. She steadied herself, then looked at the cadet, who had paused and glanced back. Some instinct made Velasco gesture her forward. The cadet continued on her way, and Velasco returned to the starboard gun.

The cadet who'd taken the controls just moments before was dead. A terrible energy blast had taken away the side of her helmet and much of her left shoulder. Velasco stared, horrified and sickened. *I brought her here. She took that seat because of me.*

Her instincts screamed at her to flee, to run inward, to get as close as possible to the center of the ship. She could return to her cell in the brig. She could lock the door and hope for the best.

Instead, she took the cadet by her good arm and tugged. It would have been nice to be gentle, but a human body in a vac suit was a lot of mass to move, and there was no time to be delicate. She dragged the cadet out of the way and sat down in the gunner's seat.

She was immediately startled by how much she could see. The barrel of the laser was huge, thicker than her body, longer than she was tall. It was below her, only blocking a bit of the view. The hull was cut away from her on every side, angled outward, giving her almost a hundred and fifty degrees of vision. The stars were bright and sharp, beautiful enough for a person's last sight.

Then an alien ship appeared on her right, flashed past at high speed and close range, and vanished. Another ship raced past in pursuit. It was gone before she recognized the runabout.

She reached for the controls, a pair of handles with a trigger on the right-hand side. She twisted the handles and her seat moved along with the gun barrel. She was always above the barrel, looking where the gun would fire. She swivelled the barrel left and right, then up and down. It was physically difficult, requiring a couple of kilos of force at least. It was surprisingly easy, though, considering her own mass and the mass of the gun barrel. The chair and the gun had a remarkably precise balance.

Motion to one side caught her eye. Several alien ships were coming together, joining up to form a larger vessel. She hesitated, wondering if they were in range. But the range of a laser in vacuum was effectively infinite. She remembered that from her Academy days. Atmosphere reduced the effectiveness of laser weapons quite rapidly, but in space, you were only restricted by your ability to aim.

Velasco swivelled the gun around, aimed as best she could, and started shooting.

A couple of shots hit the larger ship, and she saw a red glow as her shots spread across an energy shield. Then she caught a little ship in the last instant before it connected. She blew a sizeable hole right through the little ship, and it collided with the larger craft, then bounced away without linking up. She whooped, then poured more fire into the larger ship. It jerked to the side, and she tracked it, trying to hit it again.

Suddenly a single small ship loomed in front of her, blocking most of her view. She hauled on the handles, swivelling the gun, and mashed the trigger. A dark nozzle on the near side of the alien ship glowed red, heat washed over her, and then her laser burned a long, ragged line right through the hull of the little ship. She sliced the thing in half, and it spun away in two pieces.

"Oh, my god." That was how the cadet had died, she realized. And the cadet before her. It might have even been the same ship. *If I'd been an instant slower ...*

Another ship loomed, she fired, and it twisted

away. She thought she'd burned it at least a bit. She screamed and swore, swivelling the gun back and forth, and sent a few shots after a distant ship. Then another little ship loomed close, and she brought the gun sweeping over. She went too far, the alien weapon glowed, and she brought the gun swinging back. In a distant corner of her mind she told herself to memorize every detail. She had just one chance of coming through the aftermath of the mutiny looking good.

She had to fight like a hero.

The laser burned a hole in the alien ship. A red glow engulfed her, and she sawed the gun frantically back and forth, trying to disable the weapon. The ship jerked to one side and disappeared, but the red glow persisted. Too late she realized there was another alien firing on her. She screamed from a mix of agony and battle fever, feeling her fingers burn inside her gloves as she twisted the handles and brought the laser swinging left. A fat beam of amplified light burned into the side of the alien ship, an instant too late.

Velasco's last thought was a blend of rage and frustration as she realized she would never get to see the alien ship destroyed. Her body jerked back in the seat, her hands releasing the gun controls as the universe turned to fire around her and faded into merciful blackness.

CHAPTER 48 – KASIM

The *Falcon*'s cockpit windows glowed red, and the fabric of Kasim's vac suit was suddenly hot against his skin. His hands moved across the control panel, frantically activating thrusters, and the *Falcon* whipped forward and to one side. He nearly hit the *Alexander*, correcting at the last instant and whipping along so close to the hull that just rotating the *Falcon* would have caused a collision. He hadn't had much room to maneuver in this entire battle. Staying close to the *Alexander* and her guns was the only thing that gave him a chance.

Half the steelglass window in front of him was warped now and bubbled from the heat of the alien weapon. It distorted his view, and he leaned to one side to look through the undamaged part of the window. He saw a red glow on the skin of the

Alexander straight ahead, which told him he had enemy craft on his tail, firing. He twisted the *Falcon* on her axis, flying close along the hull of the *Alexander*, following the curve of the larger ship as he cut underneath her and raced up along the starboard side.

A trio of enemy ships made a lucky guess and came around the *Alexander* to pop out directly in front of him. He swore, braking and firing, and discovered that the last skirmish had cost him a couple more drones. He was down to two lasers, and he was missing one of the drones he'd used for reverse thrust. Instead of slowing the *Falcon* slewed sideways, and he felt a jar of impact as he struck the *Alexander* a glancing blow.

Then he was racing along the spine of the starship, little alien craft surrounding him in a cloud. He jerked and twisted, but he could feel the *Falcon* growing hot around him as alien weapons played across her hull.

The destruction of the *Falcon* was seconds away, and he reached for the maneuvering controls, thinking to bring the ship sharply up and crash it into one of his tormentors. As his hand closed over a thruster control, though, another ship suddenly loomed directly ahead. It was the remaining shuttle, three lasers blazing as it raced toward him. It flashed past above him, so close that he ducked, and he brought the *Falcon* sweeping up in a curve that took him fifty meters from the *Alexander*.

The shuttle twisted and dove in a swarm of enemy craft. The glow of enemy weapons caught the shuttle, then lost it as the shuttle made frantic evasions. A barrage of laser fire took down an alien ship, and a shot from the *Alexander* took down another. Then a drone on the side of the shuttle exploded, and the shuttle spun sideways, out of control.

Kasim snarled and headed into the thick of the fight. The shuttle pilot was back in control, fleeing Earthward, a couple of dozen enemy ships in pursuit. Kasim brought up the rear, cursing as his two lasers seemed to take forever to disable one enemy ship, then another.

Another drone failed on the shuttle, and smoke billowed out from several holes in the hull. The shuttle seemed to lose control, spiraling toward the distant Earth, and the aliens broke off pursuit.

They turned on the *Falcon* instead.

Kasim craned his neck, peering through the ruined window, trying to orient himself. His pursuit of the beleaguered shuttle had taken him far from the *Alexander*. He looped around, trying to spot the ship. The glitter of sunlight reflecting on hulls and the flash of weapons fire caught his eye. He turned toward the battle, but it wasn't the *Alexander* he saw before him. It was a corvette.

He cursed, looking around for the *Alexander*, then hesitated. Alien ships swarmed around the corvette, at least a dozen of them. Why were they bothering?

If the enemy saw this corvette as a threat, then perhaps he should interfere. He remembered a mangled quote from *The Art of War*, which had been popular during his days at the Academy.

Don't attack your enemy's forces. Attack your enemy's strategy.

At the very least the corvette might distract some of the horde that swarmed around the *Falcon*.

As he closed in on the corvette he saw an alien craft break apart. The corvette had its laser batteries working, then. Kasim brought the *Falcon* in close, taking a small ship by surprise and crippling it with a barrage of laser fire. He looped around the corvette again and again, adding his fire to that of the warship.

What had been a coordinated attack on the corvette quickly deteriorated into chaos. Ships wheeled and spun in every direction, and he saw a couple of enemy craft collide with each other. He was firing almost constantly, rarely destroying a ship but doing bits of damage here and there and adding to the general confusion.

Lines of fire played across the hull of the *Falcon*, and he watched scorch marks appear on the nose of the ship. He screamed his fury and defiance at the enemy horde, then screamed at the corvette. "I'm giving you a bloody breather. You'd better be doing something with it!"

As if in response, the corvette's main thrusters fired. It raced away, and Kasim cursed. "You're abandoning me, you rotten bastards?"

As he watched, though, the corvette turned in a graceful arc and flew toward the *Alexander*. Kasim whooped and followed.

The corvette looked magnificent as it charged in to the rescue, but the crew had only minimal control. They couldn't aim the lasers, Kasim realized. They could only shoot and hope for the best. The ship could barely maneuver, and it couldn't brake. It was closing on the *Alexander* at high velocity, and it was going to go flying on past.

Well, I can still maneuver. He raced after the corvette, then overtook it, and a persistent cloud of alien ships swarmed around the *Falcon*. He was taking damage with every passing second. How long before he lost his last thruster, or lost his life? He sensed that, for him, the battle would be over in moments, and he scanned the battlefield for a good way to end it.

Ships were starting to coalesce into a lethal cluster just below the nose of the *Alexander*. The forward laser batteries were no longer firing, and the aliens were gathering to exploit that weakness. Kasim aimed the *Falcon* at the cluster and accelerated hard. He screamed, knowing he was about to die, and fought the urge to squeeze his eyes shut. He wanted to see that last, glorious moment of impact.

He was seconds away from the cluster when it started to break up. He just had time to scream, "No!" before a missile flashed past him. One side of the cluster exploded, shrapnel tore into the other ships, and he rammed one of the small ships straight-on. He slammed into the underside of the *Alexander*, crushing the little alien ship like an acorn between a hammer and an anvil.

The impact slammed him against his seat straps. He saw starbursts, and when they cleared he saw the hull of the *Alexander* a few meters away. He hit the braking thrusters to back away, and nothing happened.

The *Alexander* rotated, and for a moment he was looking down the barrel of a rail gun. Then the nose of the ship loomed in front of him. He could see a steelglass window, and the shape of a figure in a vac suit staring out at him. The crewman swung a heavy wrench, hammering out some sort of signal on the bulkhead beside him.

The *Falcon* continued to drift backward, turning as it drifted, and he saw alien ships flying to pieces around him. The *Alexander* was firing its rail guns into the swarm that had hounded him.

Then, beyond the swarm, the corvette arrived at last.

If the aliens had kept their nerve for an instant longer, Kasim was sure the ploy would have failed. For an instant the corvette seemed to fill the sky, powerful lasers firing in every direction, and in that instant the attack broke. Alien ships fled in every direction.

The corvette was past in moments, its velocity taking it beyond the battle and into empty space. The ship began to rotate, the tail swinging around so it could begin the laborious process of returning.

It vanished from sight as the *Falcon*, completely crippled, continued to turn. Kasim watched the stars sweep past through the bubbled and blackened cockpit window. Then he saw the *Alexander* again. The warship was a mess, nearly as badly shot up as the *Falcon*. Great tears showed in the skin of the ship, and he saw nothing but smoke through the port lounge windows. Still, the ship lived.

Bright points of light shone from enemy ships as they hurried away. At first they fled blindly, but he saw them joining together into clusters before continuing their retreat.

Closer in, he saw debris and burned wreckage. No other trace of the alien fleet remained.

The last of the fleeing alien ships faded into the distance and disappeared. The battle was over. Earth was saved.

CHAPTER 49 – HAMMETT

Hammett wore his sword to his meeting with the admiralty. He sat in a plush waiting room in Spacecom headquarters, fighting to stay awake. It was two days since the final battle, and he was exhausted. The *Alexander* was a hulk, drifting in a high orbit above the Earth, the only life on board the science crews analysing the remains of the boarding party and studying the damage the ship had taken.

He had no regrets. His ship was gone, but she'd died gloriously. There would be no ignominious decommissioning for the *Alexander*. She was legendary now. She would never truly be gone.

For himself, he had a pretty good idea what the future held. There would be endless debriefings, like the gruelling sessions he and every member of the crew had been through ever since the aliens broke and ran. He would spend the last few months of his Navy career in meetings and sitting in front of committees while they picked his brain for every scrap of insight he might have.

It would be ignominious, and vexing, and unbecoming to a warrior. But he would do his duty, and he wouldn't complain.

A low chuckle escaped him. "Like hell I won't complain." It was all right, though. His time in the Navy was ending, but he was the man who had fought the alien horde to a standstill. He was a legend too. He would never truly be gone.

As he waited he scanned a news feed projected from the arm of his chair. His implants were still not repaired, and he was feeling badly out of touch. The big news was the alien invasion, followed by the fall of Earth's planetary government. A terrified populace was blaming the old leadership for being soft, complacent, and trusting.

A minor parliamentarian named Acton was poised to sweep into power on a platform of unflinching strength and the wielding of an iron fist. Hammett found a still pic of the guy. He had the fiery, soulless eyes of a fanatic, and his speeches were full of vitriol. He was promising to punish anyone who failed to support the war effort, and Hammett felt a stirring of unease in the pit of his stomach. Not all the harm that the invaders had done was direct damage to ships and stations. They were damaging the foundation of an entire society, making cracks that would take a long time to heal.

"Captain Hammett?" The lieutenant who stood

in front of his chair looked barely older than his brave cadets. But then, his cadets looked like battle-hardened veterans now. Which they were. He closed the feed, glad to be distracted from politics. *Give me a nice simple war any time.*

"This way, please," she said. "Can I get you anything? A beverage, perhaps?"

Two days of meetings and interrogations had taught him the value of managing his fluid levels. Admirals didn't like it much when captains excused themselves to use the bathroom. "I'm fine," he told her, and followed her through the tallest set of doors he'd ever seen in an office space. The boardroom beyond gleamed with understated elegance. It was an opulent cave of thick carpets and polished oak, with a conference table you could have landed the *Falcon* on, and a double row of stern admirals seated in plush chairs.

"Sit down, Captain." The speaker was Admiral Castille, a sharp-featured man with hard, shrewd eyes. Hammett saw an unexpected hint of compassion, though, as Castille said, "You've been through a tremendous amount over the past several weeks, and I understand we've been running you ragged ever since. Please, sit down." To the lieutenant he said, "Bring a snack tray. The captain has been on restricted rations for quite some time."

Hammett smiled his thanks and lowered himself into a chair. Quiet electric motors hummed as the chair reshaped itself to fit his body, and he sighed quietly. He was as comfortable as a man could be while facing almost all of the senior admiralty in Spacecom.

"I assume you know you've performed brilliantly and done your planet a great service," Castille said, and smiled. "However, you might want to know that we've noticed. You have our gratitude and our congratulations."

"Thank you, Sir." They were kind words, but they had the feel of a spoonful of sugar designed to prepare him for a dose of bitter medicine.

The smile disappeared. *Here it comes*, Hammett thought.

"I hope you've had a chance to rest a bit," Castille said, "because I'm afraid your work is not done." He made a gesture and a star map appeared above the table. "The alien invaders – the media are calling them 'The Hive' for reasons I haven't been able to figure out – have been driven away for the moment, but they most certainly have not been defeated."

Hammett nodded. He was pretty sure Castille was right.

"We have learned from them," Castille said, "but they have also had the opportunity to learn from us. You and your crew have reported instances where they modified their tactics in response to an earlier encounter."

"Yes, Sir. They learn and adjust."

"When we face them again, it will be a very different sort of fight. We are going to find out who can learn and adapt more quickly."

It was a sobering thought. Hammett didn't speak, just waited for the admiral to tell him which science facility he was going to be consigned to.

"You're the only captain in the fleet with direct, successful experience against these creatures," Castille said. "You've also demonstrated that you can learn and adjust and think on your feet. Therefore, we think you'd be wasted here on Earth. You'll be going back into space, just as soon as we can complete an emergency refit on the corvette Tomahawk."

Hammett felt his jaw drop open, and quickly closed it.

"The ship has its own wormhole generator, and it's being fitted with extra weapons. You'll be leaving within forty-eight hours," she continued. "It isn't prudent, but we're under tremendous pressure to get a ship to Naxos and protect the colonists there. Your assignment will be to fly immediately to Naxos and assess the situation, then remain on station until a support fleet can reach you."

The Naxos system lit up on the holo-map, and Hammett stared at it, trying to figure out if he was horrified or delighted. *You're going to get me killed. But I'll die in space. I'll die fighting those things.*

Castille said, "When the fleet reaches you, you will continue with the next phase of your mission. It won't be a very large fleet, I should warn you. It will be the ships we will be able to refit within a week or so."

"Not all the ships we'll be able to refit," another admiral interrupted. "Somebody has to protect the Earth."

Castille nodded impatiently. "A small fleet," he repeated. "With that fleet you will repair Gates Four and Five, and travel through Gate Five if it functions."

Hammett felt his pulse increase as Deirdre lit up on the map.

"You will retrace the path the invaders took on their way to Earth. You will engage and destroy whatever enemy forces you encounter. You will work your way from system to system until you reach Calypso, and then you will look for clues to the original source of these attacks. By this time I hope that the Gate system will once again be online, and we will be able to directly supply and reinforce you. You will carry on regardless. You will not stop, and you will not return, until you have tracked the enemy back to their hive and destroyed them."

FROM THE AUTHOR

Thanks for reading. I'd love to hear your comments.

Go to http://steampunch.com/elwood/ to leave me a note or to learn about other stories, or sign up for my newsletter to hear about new releases. I can be reached by email at brentn@aim.com.

The Hive Invasion continues in *Starship Tomahawk*.

Manufactured by Amazon.ca
Bolton, ON